Divine Moves

By Ellyn Oaksmith

Hope you enjoy the
book as much as
I enjoyed writing it.

Ellyn Oaksmith

<u>Also by Ellyn Oaksmith</u>

Adventures with Max and Louise

For my best friend and sister,
who happens to be the same person.
Thank you.

Author's note:
To my friends and neighbors on the hill and in the 'hood: these characters are not based on real people. What is borrowed from reality is a sense of belonging to a supportive community.

ISBN: 9781494375133
Printed in the United States of America
First Printing, March 2014
http://www.EllynOaksmith.com

1.

"All men make mistakes, but married men find out about them sooner."
-Red Skelton

In the soft light of the single bedside lamp, Meryl could see the woman's back: long, white and slender, her high pony tail bobbing. Beneath her was Meryl's husband. Instead of exploding in anger and pain, Meryl found herself taking in odd details: the lamp was from her days of shopping at Target, now mostly over. White and simple, it still looked good against the dark wood of the bed. It needed dusting. Later she'd think it odd that in the midst of seeing her husband screw another woman, she'd still notice the dust. What did that say about her?

The night had gone so well. There was the bottle of champagne, heavy and cold in her hand, waiting to be shared. The evening had been a huge success. They'd exceeded their goal. After tossing her coat on the couch, ignoring the urge to neatly stow it in the coat closet, she'd tiptoed upstairs, trying to decide how to wake up Ethan. But the light was on; he was reading.

Ethan was vaguely aware that someone had entered the bedroom. His brain was lost in a pungent cloud of post-orgasmic bliss. Leslie, God Leslie, what she was doing to him drove everything away, even the guilt, his constant companion, an evil little gremlin drilling burning hot needles into his brain. Leslie, a sexual gymnast, had a Teflon conscience (and buns of steel) but Ethan always worried until the moment he climaxed. He had a twenty second reprieve before resuming his tormented existence. Those twenty seconds were spellbinding and exquisite. He lived for those twenty seconds of forgetting, for a moment; that his life was an avalanche of bad decisions.

A gasp, coming from somewhere in the room, poked its way through Ethan's sex-addled brain. It took a second for him to focus; he was so close. So close. The gasp didn't come from Leslie, whose eyes and mouth were shut. It came from near the door.

"Meryl?" Although he said her name, he didn't really believe he'd been caught until he leaned over the side of the bed. Only one thing could distract him from Leslie's nubile body.

The second he saw Meryl's face, reality hit him like a cinematic slow motion car accident. It was surreal, as though glass and bodies were flying slowly through the air.

Leslie, ever aware of *her* orgasm, *her* pleasure, looked down angrily at Ethan's face as she felt his muscles constrict. To Leslie, having sex with her neighbor's husband was like going to the gym: what's the point if you don't work up a good sweat?

"What the fuck Ethan? Let's-" She followed his shocked gaze, twisting around.

She saw Meryl. With a frantic squeal, she hopped off Ethan, sprinting through the nearest door: Meryl's walk in closet. The door slammed, echoing in bedroom. The remaining spouses were equally lost, way outside the boundaries of norms and expectation. This was something that happened to other people. This was something they'd shake their heads over, whisper about at a party.

"Can you believe it?"

"I heard…."

Meryl's mind, for a split second, went utterly blank. It was hard to reconcile what she had just witnessed, with what she'd expected to see. On the drive, following the misty fall roads she'd imagined kissing Ethan awake, stashing the book he'd been reading on the bedside table, explaining she'd forgone the girls' night out in favor of spending some much needed couple time. The auction was over. It was time to work on their relationship. She'd even thought of the cheesy title of her sister's book: Marriage Maintenance. Yes, it was long overdue.

The world had shifted on its axis. She had no script to follow in this scenario. Ethan had been having sex with someone else. The idea was absurd but here was the evidence, boxed into her closet: shivering and nude.

She stared at the wall of children's photos in black and white intermixed with her children's artwork above the bed. Could there really be a naked woman in her closet? Was that really her neighbor? She'd had a good look at her face but what exactly was happening here? People's lives didn't fall apart the moment they decided to fix them.

Her brain flapped around, looking for something real. She tightened her grip on the champagne bottle just to have something to hold onto, to brace herself. A mere two hours ago she'd laughed with Melinda Gates. They'd had the same coat, complimenting each other on their great taste. What was she doing thinking about Melinda Gates' coat?

In Vegas as a teen, she'd smoked pot and felt as if she'd slipped into a parallel universe. While she was high, nothing bothered her. The tethers of everyday life had been unbound. Of course one of her mom's friends had given it to her. *It'll help you relax. You two girls worry so much. Here, just a little toke or two. You're young.* She felt like that now. Slipping. Nauseous. Out of control.

"Mer, honey, this isn't what it looks like." Ethan tugged the sheets up to his chest as if their flimsy coverage would offer some protection.

His words woke her up. She wasn't stoned. She wasn't that sad kid in Vegas. She was Meryl Howe. She'd just raised a boatload of money for sick kids. She tried to concentrate on feeling anger but she nearly laughed. "Well you're not doing the hokey pokey, that's for damn sure."

"I thought you were spending the night at the Hilton." He was using a diversion tactic. Sometimes it worked in business.

"Yeah. Very inconvenient when your wife comes home at these awkward moments. Who is it?" She knew but didn't want to say her name. Not until he did. That would make it real.

Ethan groaned. "Shit." He really, really didn't want to say her name. "Uhhhh, it's Leslie."

"Leslie? Leslie from next door?"

Ethan shook his head. "I'm so sorry. I don't know what the hell I'm doing."

A burning, black rage flooded Meryl. "You know exactly what you are doing. Leslie? Leslie the flight attendant with the yappy dogs? The Leslie who borrowed my Kitchen Aid last Christmas and broke it?" Her voice was shrill, quavering. She turned toward the closet wall, screaming, "You broke it. I was too nice to say anything but it cost me seventy-five dollars to get it fixed."

One glance at Ethan, naked and miserable, and her fury renewed itself. She screamed at the adjacent wall. "Get out of my fucking closet!"

Ethan covered his eyes, wishing he could rewind time. Go back to that first moment when Leslie smiled at him. He'd been mowing the lawn. Meryl was at another meeting. He needed someone to talk to.

"I want you out of my fucking closet and my house!" Meryl's fists clenched so hard she dug angry marks in her palms. She sounded like her mother. If she could just get Leslie out of the closet, out of her house, then she could think. It took courage but she opened her eyes, staring directly at Ethan.

"Where are the kids?" Tears welled in her eyes.

Ethan felt a sledgehammer coming down on his head; once for Nathalie, another hit for Henry. His mouth was dry and cottony, not an unfamiliar state lately. The moments between anxiety attacks had gotten very small. "Sleepovers."

"How handy." Meryl pounded on the exterior wall of her closet. Leslie amid her clothes, her shoes; the things she wore on her body. "Get out!"

Leslie emerged from the closet wrapped in Meryl's white Egyptian cotton bathrobe, a Christmas gift from Ethan. The final insult: the robe looked better on Leslie.

"Take off my robe!" Meryl snarled.

Leslie wasn't the slightest bit flustered. "Look, Meryl. I can't walk home naked." She could have been gathering her coat after a party.

"Did you walk over here naked?" Leslie contemplated pushing past Meryl, down the stairs and out the door. Meryl blocked her way, clutching, white-knuckled, the champagne bottle.

"Look, I know this is awkward but you don't have to be such a bitch."

"Yes I do. Wait 'till your husband screws the tramp next door. See how you feel."

Leslie rolled her eyes. "It was only sex."

Meryl lifted her left hand, pointed at her wedding ring. "Do you know what this means you whore?"

Leslie looked at her nails, blasé. "Yes. It means you're boring."

Ethan clamped a hand over his eyes. "Leslie, shut the fuck up. Meryl, let her take the robe," Ethan ordered. It was what Meryl thought of as his CEO voice, the one that had coaxed millions from Silicon Valley venture capital firms.

"I'll bring it back. It's too big for me anyway." Leslie smirked.

But Meryl had drawn the line and somehow, it came down to the bathrobe. "You are not taking my bathrobe. You can have my husband. In fact, take him with you but you are not taking my bathrobe or my coat. The only fibers you're taking out of here are the ones stuck to your sweaty butt."

"Why don't you just let me go and you two can work things out."

"Work things out? Is that how it happens in flight attendant land? You screw someone's husband and then everyone just works it out? I want to know how it is you managed to get from your house to my house without a stitch of clothing on."

Ethan was shaking his head. "Leslie, go back in the closet. I'll talk to her."

Ethan was helping Leslie. That sunk the whole ship.

Leslie smoothed and refastened her pony tail; something Meryl had seen her daughter Nathalie does when reasoning something out. She was, Meryl thought, probably closer in age to Nathalie.

"Oh for God's sake, Ethan. Really? In the closet?" Leslie pulled the robe tightly around her, hardening her face as she spoke. "He left his trench coat at my house last week so I wore it over here. It's downstairs. There. Are you fucking happy?"

Leslie un-wrapped the bathrobe, stepped out of it like a queen. Theatrically, she raised the robe, dropping it to the ground. Her body was perfect.

Ethan watched Leslie's white form skip nimbly down the stairs, flooded by an innate sense of relief that both women were no longer in the same room. When the front door slammed, he met Meryl's eyes for the first time.

"We need to talk," he said.

For the first time in decades, Meryl acted instinctively. In that moment, there wasn't a single thought in her brain, just a hot flash of adrenaline and fury. She lifted the green bottle high. The gold foil glinted in the dull lamplight. It happened so quickly. She flexed her gym toned muscles, throwing the bottle as hard a she could at Ethan.

He ducked. The bottle shattered against the teak headboard. Champagne soaked the cream quilted bedspread. His arm hurt, the smell of champagne filled his nostrils but Ethan stared at his wife, mesmerized. Never in his life had he witnessed Meryl lose control or act with any sort of violence. One of the things he'd most admired about her was her complete and utter composure in the face of his formidable parents. Hell, he was afraid of his own parents, wasn't he? It was Meryl that slid into every situation, perfectly poised.

Now look at her, he thought. She was on fire. Although he felt buried in a sinking, pervasive doom, Ethan felt a strange sort of admiration. Maybe he'd been wrong. Maybe she had more of her mother's nature inside her than she'd ever admit. And maybe that wasn't such a bad thing. It was perverse. At the exact moment she wanted to strangle him with her bare hands, he felt a tiny blister of hope. He needed her so desperately and never more than at that moment.

"You're bleeding." Her voice was flat. A thick green piece of glass stuck up from a jagged cut in the crook of his elbow. Bright red blood trailed down to the sheet, horror movie bright.

She went into the hallway, reappearing with a clean white towel. "Keep the glass in. It might be an artery. Have Leslie take you to the hospital," she said in a detached monotone. Although Ethan was bleeding, Meryl was the one in shock. He was happy for the pain. He deserved it.

There was an awful lot of blood. Ethan listened to her, wrapping the towel around his arm, pulling on his jeans with one hand. He couldn't get the zipper without lowering his hand. He tried once but could feel the blood pumping out, soaking the towel. He looked up to see Meryl watching him, curiously detached. He fumbled again with the zipper before deciding to lie down on the bed.

"We raised nearly $72,000." She paused, frowning. "You should have been there."

"I think it's a little weird that you're telling me this right now." The towel was getting soaked.

"It's what I came home to tell you." She plopped down the on the leather couch by the door, amazed at how little her success now mattered, or the blood or anything, really.

Ethan stomped into his closet, slipped on his loafers, managing to zip himself halfway into a fleece jacket by holding the bottom of the jacket with his elbow. His hurt arm he re-wrapped, leaving a dangling sleeve.

He emerged from his closet, finally responding. "I wanted to be there. I really did. I've been trying to tell you for weeks. You've been so busy with this auction and I've been working all the time. The reason I didn't go tonight is because…" Weaving a little, he came closer to her. He was dizzy. How much blood had he lost? He had trouble focusing his eyes.

She held up her hand, blocking his face. "Go over to Leslie's, Ethan. I don't care anymore." She dropped her arm, her be-numbed mind turning to the kids.

"No, no." He looked at the ground, his arm, the ceiling, trying to summon the courage. "I have to tell you. It's no excuse for what happened here tonight but I really need to tell you."

"Just leave. Please? Your arm looks really bad." She couldn't handle any more details. It was enough that he'd left his trench coat at Leslie's. The Burberry she'd bought him, when they couldn't afford it, so he could fly down to Silicon Valley looking like a CEO.

"I have to tell you Mer. It's not what you think. I'm falling apart." His voice cracked. His eyes shone with fatigue and tears.

How could this be happening to her? It was like watching a movie, not quite believing that it was herself on the screen. This was one of her mother's scenes: the tears, broken glass; a lover running barefoot and guilty into the night. If he shared one more ugly detail she'd scream. He needed medical attention. She needed him out of here.

She held up her hand again. "It's exactly what I think," she whispered. "Just leave."

She stared at her hands. They were shaking. He'd stopped pleading. It could have been loss of blood or common sense. He walked to the door of their bedroom and turned around to face her, fly undone, hair messed.

"Mer, I'm really, really sorry."

She couldn't look at him. "You've ruined everything."

As he walked out of the bedroom he muttered. "You don't know the half of it."

2.

"Sometimes I wonder if men and women really suit each other. Perhaps they should live next door and just visit now and then."

-Katherine Hepburn

It was a slow Saturday night in downtown Kirkland. Lake Washington lapped at the shoreline, home of the six figure income, Seahawks headquarters and a quaint, thriving Lake Street shopping area. The upscale restaurants were closing down, ushering out the last diners. Officer Sam Richer waited in his cruiser, facing Hector's Restaurant. He was keeping tabs on a stumbling middle-aged couple, waiting for them to find their car. Probably a Mercedes, Sam guessed. They'd likely gotten all gussied up after the Seahawks win, decided to join friends for dinner. After dinner drinks turned into more drinks.

Yawning, he checked his watch: 12:34 am. He'd pulled this shift thousands of times in his 20's. When did it get so freakin' hard?

Eyeing the tipsy couple, he waited to fire off a DUI and call them a cab. His radio crackled to life. "Officer needed at Evergreen ER for domestic abuse report. Stabbing victim. Male." Normally he wouldn't have taken a DA report at Evergreen Hospital but when he saw the couple flagging a taxi, he picked up his radio. He was bored, cold and fed up with sitting in his car. His middle-aged muscles needed a good stretch.

There was a cute nurse at Evergreen who flirted a little, a decent cafeteria. Maybe a cup of coffee and a piece of fruit, or preferably pie, would make this night a little shorter.

A pie eating cop. I'm a cliché. At least it's not donuts.

Pulling his cruiser into the ER U-turn, he thought of his father. Every overtime shift kept his dad at Merrill Gardens, and his son Kevin, at Washington State University; worth it but exhausting.

As he signed in at the hospital, asking the triage nurse about the location of the DA couple, a medic stopped by to brag, told him he was engaged to the cute nurse. A day late and dollar short, thought Sam as he pushed through the ER doors. The story of his life.

Ethan was bandaged, waiting impatiently for his release papers from the doctor when he saw the tall, gangly policeman. Expecting him to pass by, he was surprised when Leslie flagged him. She'd fixed herself up a little, put on some snug jeans, a black t-shirt and leather jacket. It had annoyed Ethan, the lipstick application while he bled. Waiting for her he had stood outside on his front walk, wondering if there was one other person in the neighborhood who would take him to the ER. Leslie wasn't exactly what you'd call empathetic. Then it hit him: she owned the only house in the cul-de-sac where he was welcome.

The cop's face perked up when he saw Leslie. He sucked in his slight gut, stood up a little taller.

"Hi, are you Ms. Keller?"

Ethan was confused. "You called the cops?" He frowned at her.

Sam smiled easily, raised a finger. "One. Singular. It doesn't really matter who called…"

Leslie introduced herself politely, making a point of calling him Officer Richer before turning to Ethan, hissing,

"You just had seventeen stitches. I think you should report it."

Ethan was firm. "No. No way. Sorry for wasting your time."

Sam thought for a second, hesitated to get out his notebook. "The problem here sir, is that in cases like this, once the call gets made, I have to follow through."

"I understand that but I didn't call you. She did." He turned to Leslie. "I'm totally fine."

"I don't call that wound on your arm fine," Leslie snapped.

Sam took out his notebook, facing her. "And you are?"

She inhaled, stretched her long neck and, without looking at Ethan, offered, "Leslie Keller. K-E-double L-E-R." Her gold earrings glinted in the bright ER light.

Sam hated this next question. It always led to more trouble. "And you are... the spouse?"

Before Leslie could open her mouth, Ethan interjected, "No. She's not the spouse. The spouse had nothing to do with this."

Sam lowered his notebook, appraising them both slowly and evenly. "That glass didn't just jump into your arm on its own."

A nurse with squeaky shoes passed, wheeling a cart. Leslie just wanted the hell out of here. "Oh, for crying out loud Ethan." She turned to Sam. "His wife did it. She lobbed a champagne bottle at him. It hit the bed and shattered."

"Not true," Ethan snapped.

"Okay, then California sparkling wine. Whatever. She was aiming to kill. When he came into my house he was bleeding like a stuck-"

Ethan shot her a terrifying look.

Sam raised his hands, the notebook flapped open. "Okay, okay. Sir, you can't tell me you fell down and cut yourself in the kitchen. I'm not going to believe that." Although he'd heard plenty of much stranger stories.

"I don't care what you believe."

"What's your address?"

"We're from out of town."

Sam crossed his arms. "I can get all this information from reception or the registration on your car, which I assume is the Prius parked in the loading zone. I didn't ticket you."

Leslie lit up. "Thank you. That's my car. We're neighbors." Officer Richer reminded her a little of Jimmy Stewart, her mom's favorite actor.

Sam gave Ethan a long, appraising look, keeping his face blank. "Friendly neighborhood."

"Screw you," Ethan snarled.

"Sir, she gave you a ride after you somehow got a nasty cut on your arm. I could site you for barking at me like that but I'm a nice guy so I'm not going to. You've lost a lot of blood and should just shut your pie hole, okay?" He kept his tone friendly.

Ethan rubbed his bandage, nodded several times. "Got it. Sorry. Bad night, to say the least."

"Moving forward, what's your address?" Staying calm in these DA situations was crucial. People lit up like Christmas trees if you looked at them the wrong way.

Ethan lowered his head. "Fourteen twenty-eight one Crescent Ridge."

Sam knew the neighborhood immediately. When Finn Hill had been annexed, he'd cruised around, exploring his new territory. Crescent Ridge was a shallow cul-de-sac with large, majestic houses, sweeping lawns. Boats in the wide driveways, European cars in every garage. "Your wife still there?"

Ethan nodded. "Probably. I don't think it's a good idea to go there now. It's late; she's pretty upset."

Sam put away his notebook, told them both he might be in touch. He wouldn't though. The peckerwood's wife had taught him a good lesson. As he pushed his way through the ER double doors into the lobby he felt a grudging respect for the wife. Good for her. Seventeen stitches. She wasn't going to take this sitting down.

3.

"It is not lack of love, but lack of friendship that makes unhappy marriages."
Friedrich Nietzsche

At 9:45 a.m. Jackie charged through the front door without knocking, her hair twisted up in a wet bun. "Where's Henry?" were the first words out of her mouth. As a psychologist, she knew that Henry, being young and male, was the least equipped to deal with the situation. In her practice she'd seen parents battle it out furiously while their kids sank.

"At Carol's. Probably 'till ten." Meryl barely had the energy to rise from the table. Jackie poured herself a cup of coffee, kissed the top of her sister's head.

Pulling out Ethan's chair from the breakfast table, Jackie put her feet up, took a long sip of coffee, focusing her bright blue eyes intently. Of the two, she looked most like their mother. "Good. Now tell me everything."

"I cut his arm…" Meryl began. "With a champagne bottle."

"You're kidding, right?"

Meryl shook her head.

"That's very ghetto."

Jackie set the gears for listening, settling back with her coffee. "I wasn't wielding it like a weapon, if that's what you think but I did throw it."

"Where was the girl?"

"Believe it or not, in my closet." Meryl recounted the evening with clinical precision, wincing at the worst details.

When Jackie told Meryl that she'd chosen the nearby University of Washington Hospital for her residency, Meryl wasn't pleased or disappointed, just wary of all family. Her mother, after getting drunk with Ethan's gay cousin at Meryl's wedding, told dirty jokes before suggesting to Meryl's new mother-in-law Betsy that she take the stick out of her ass. That had made it easy to cut all ties. Faye had shown up once when the kids were little, clutching a huge ToysRUs bag. Meryl had slammed the door in her face.

Betsy, her mother-in-law had few requirements: show up at her charity guild events and Christmas parties, dress the children and herself well and keep her mouth shut. This she was eager to do, once she found out that Ethan Senior was going to bankroll the majority of Ethan's start up: Inspire. He'd bounced around stockbroker jobs but none of them ever stuck. He needed to be his own boss.

Meryl quit teaching after Nathalie was born. Eventually, a few months into her residency when Jackie came up for air, having her around was fun; a window into another world outside the cul-de-sac, even if she did make fun of her straight-laced sister sometimes. This morning, as Meryl recited the entire story, she thanked God for the millionth time for her efficient, intelligent, vibrant younger sister.

While listening, Jackie fetched a second cup of coffee, opening the fridge. "While you were raising money for sick kids, he's screwing the neighbor?" She opened a Tupperware, sniffed. "Is this lasagna?"

"Yes and yes. Don't eat it now."

Ignoring Meryl, Jackie scooped a huge serving onto a plate, placing it in the microwave. "I'm hungry."

"Seriously?"

Jackie shrugged, watching the lasagna, which she hadn't covered, pop and sputter all over Meryl's clean microwave interior. "You know I hate breakfast food."

"Me too."

The sisters both spun around. Nathalie, sleepy-eyed and infuriatingly lithe in her yoga pants, sauntered into the kitchen. She emptied the last drops of the coffee into her mug, shaking the empty pot. "Thanks Mom. How much coffee did you have this morning?"

Jackie removed her lasagna from the oven, inhaling deeply.

"Yech! That is a mountain of food." Nathalie wrinkled her nose. "You're inhuman Aunt Jackie."

"Thank you. Coffee stunts your growth."

Nathalie got out the canister to make more coffee. "It's all DNA baby."

Jackie shot her a proud grin as she settled back down at the table. "Good girl. Science wins every time."

The words "good girl" brought Meryl back to last night. She heard a car and the front door. "What were you doing coming in at 2:30 this morning?"

Nathalie scooped coffee, not missing a beat. "Denny gave me a ride home. He's Lana's older brother; kind of a weirdo but nice. I went to her house instead of Zoe's at the last minute after volleyball." She ignored her aunt's laser beam eyes, concentrating on her mother, who seemed more exhausted than usual, if that was possible.

To throw her mom off-track she added, "How was the guild auction? Raise a bunch of money?"

"Almost seventy-two thousand," Meryl said dully, staring into her empty coffee cup.

Jackie knew her niece was lying; she'd used five words too many explaining Denny, besides she'd heard Nat talk about him before. Nathalie had a heavy lidded sensuality that no doubt left a string of boys in her wake. Girls like Nathalie liked a challenge. Jackie would have to talk to her but for now, she'd let it go. Now wasn't the time.

"Listen honey, your mom has had kind of rough night. I'm going to hang out here today while she gets some rest."

Nathalie pulled the pot early from coffee maker, spilling a little as she poured. "Details please."

Meryl shook her head. "Jackie, it's okay. We can just go for a walk or drive or something once Henry gets back. I can't sleep."

Jackie shook her head. "No, I'm going to call in some medication for you. I really think you need to sleep."

Nathalie left the puddle of coffee, plopped down at the table. "Is anyone going to tell me what's going on? Is this about Dad? Or Henry? Are they okay?"

Meryl stared at her daughter, dark hair winding over her shoulder, skin glowing. Meryl could hear her phone pinging. Probably more messages from Ethan. Meryl put her head down on her folded arms. "Maybe I do need to sleep."

"Would someone please tell me what is happening here?" Nathalie demanded.

Meryl made a weak effort. "I'm okay; just tired. We'll talk later when I feel better."

Nathalie turned to her aunt. "She's like, turned into silly putty and I'm supposed to ignore it?"

Jackie raised an eyebrow. "No. It's just…"

Wearily Meryl lifted her head from the table, pushing back her hair. "There is no easy way to say this honey. Your dad has temporarily relocated. We're having some marital issues."

"It's that bitch next door, isn't it?" Nathalie said.

4.

*"If we men married the women we deserved, we
should have a very bad time of it."*
–An Ideal Husband, Oscar Wilde

Surprisingly, it felt good to hear her daughter call
Leslie a bitch. Very good. For a moment. "Don't talk that
way," Meryl said, her head a bowling ball on the kitchen
table, seemingly too heavy to lift.

Jackie rolled her eyes. "Meryl, she wasn't exactly
collecting for Unicef."

"Sorry Mom. I'm just, you know, right."

After a dull moment recalling that she'd called
Leslie a whore, Meryl dragged her heavy head toward
Nathalie. A painful red circle tattooed her forehead. "You
knew? How much worse can this get? Does Henry?"

Nathalie shook her head, smoothed her hair back
into a high pony tail and fastened it in a gesture painfully
reminiscent of last night. "No, of course not; he's clueless,
as per usual. Diane doesn't know either because I made a
few comments to Zoe and she didn't say anything.
Remember on Halloween, Leslie was dressed as a sexy
pirate wench and Dad took Henry trick-or-treating over
there? That was a tip off. Anyway, it's not like I knew, knew
but all summer long, while you were doing the auction
stuff, Dad would leave work early and just kind of be here,
you know? Dad is, like, never here. Or if he is, he's holed

up in his office on the computer or phone. But he'd just go outside and sit on the deck. Leslie was out there reading and I'd hear them talking, you know. She totally rocks a bikini."

Jackie held up her hand. "TMI Nat."

Nathalie shook her head. "No, I didn't mean it like that... it's just...you know... Mom's like queen of the tankini and I kind of get why Dad liked talking to her. He's a bald dude with a paunch. I thought he liked the attention..."

Meryl moaned. "Oh God..."

Jackie put up her hand. "I think your mom and I should discuss this by ourselves."

Nathalie shook her head. "No, no. I just want to say one more thing. Last night when he called me, Dad was acting really weird, like he wanted me to come home. He told me to skip my volleyball game. But when I wouldn't do it, he seemed, you know, relieved a little bit. It's so weird. Now all this other stuff makes sense. When I totally think about it-"

Jackie reached out, clenching Nathalie's arm. "Please stop Nat. Let your mom rest."

Nathalie shrugged. "Whatever. What a total freakin' douche." She climbed the stairs with unusual haste. By the time she reached the landing, she'd typed her text. MY DAD IS A TOTAL MAN WHORE. LESLIE THE FLIGHT ATTENDANT AND HE ARE-

"Hey Nathalie?" Jackie called from the kitchen.

Nathalie scrolled down to Zoe, hit "send." She turned around on the stairs to face her aunt. "Yeah?"

"Nat, obviously don't tell anyone. At this point let your mom have some privacy, okay?"

"Okay. But I have a right to tell my friends, okay?"

Jackie nodded. She wished she could remain loyal to her sister; tell Nathalie to grow some compassion. But keeping this in was the wrong thing. "You do. But pick someone whose family doesn't know your mom well, just for now, okay?"

Before Nathalie could answer, the doorbell rang six times. Knowing what was coming, she disappeared upstairs.

Henry, bright-cheeked and full speed, barreled in the door. Without bothering to shuck his parka, he dropped his overnight bag, going straight for his aunt in the foyer, nearly knocking her down with his hug. She held him tightly, stroked his crew cut. "Hey Hen-boy. Looking good. You have fun at your friend's house?"

"It was okay. We had pancakes."

"Sounds good. Bet they weren't as good as mine."

"Naw. Max's mom always puts bananas in. Barf."

They went into the kitchen. Meryl had grabbed her phone and deleted all Ethan's texts, repeating her daughter's words in her head as she lightly tapped. "You are a douche Ethan. A total douche." Henry frowned when he saw his mom's face. She forced a grin, causing her to look even sadder.

"Mom?"

Jackie crouched down, blocking Henry's view of his mother. "Hey, your mom is having a hard time sleeping so we're going to let her rest, okay? Run on upstairs and get your board. I'm taking you to that new skate park downtown, alright?"

"The one in Redmond or Kirkland?"

"Which one's better?"

"The one in Kirkland blows."

Meryl said weakly, "Don't talk like that."

"Then we won't go there," Jackie replied. "Go on, get your board."

Henry thudded up the stairs two at time. "Cool, pancakes and skate boarding in the same day. Wicked."

Jackie leaned over, smoothing her sister's dark hair. "Want me to call in some Ambien for you?"

Meryl shook her head. "No, I have some. Do you think it's a good idea to take one during the day?"

Jackie sighed heavily. "You have to face some really terrible stuff Mer. You can't do it on one hour of sleep."

Meryl stood up, hugged her sister. They clung to each other for a moment. Meryl whispered, "I haven't gone into my room. I can't."

Jackie let go. "Where are the pills? I'll get them."

***

Amazingly, she slept until morning. Nathalie's voice dragged her, unwilling, from the black hole of sleep. "Mom, wake up. There's a cop here who says he has to talk to you." Meryl drifted lazily out of her dream. It was a strange one: lawnmowers and hedges gossiping, neighbors flying overhead. She clung to the last downy puffs of sleep, her brain foggy with sleeping pills. "Mom! Come on. He says he has to talk to you now!"

When the words assembled themselves into meaning, Meryl sat up. Hair stuck to the side of her face. Make-up from last night shadowed her eyes and skin.

"Whaaa? A cop?" She blinked directly into Nathalie's bright blue eyes. No matter what she did, or how fast she ran, she couldn't escape Faye's blue eyes. "What have you done?"

Nathalie laughed. "Me? Nothing. He wants to talk to you. I swear to God." She did a "scouts honor," finger salute. "He said he wanted to talk to you alone and I should probably stay in my room. I don't have to, do I?"

Thick with sleep and Ambien, Meryl shrugged. "Are you sure you're not in trouble?"

Narrowing her eyes, Nathalie disappeared into her room, leaving the door open a crack. Her plan was to creep down the hall when it was safe enough to eavesdrop.

What Sam expected and what Sam saw that morning were two entirely different things. In a house like this, he expected a perfectly manicured, high maintenance, semi-pro snob, who'd treat him like an underpaid civil servant. She'd justify throwing a bottle of champagne at her husband the same way she justified spending $350 on a pair of shoes or a $5 latte or whatever she felt like consuming at the moment. Instead, he saw a tired, beautiful woman in a bathrobe, coming down the stairs with the best posture in the world.

"Thank you," she said as she descended.

Sam shifted in his boots. Most people didn't thank the officer standing in their doorway, preparing to tell them they'd done something wrong. "For what?"

She reached the main floor. "For telling my daughter to stay in her room. She wouldn't have listened to me."

Sam took off his hat, played with it. "I have a son just a few years older. Same story." It wasn't really true, Kevin was very respectful and polite but Sam was a big believer in building rapport, especially with beautiful women.

She brushed her scraggly hair off her forehead. "I'm thirsty. Do you want a glass of water? Please, come in." He stared at her back, straight as a nail. Where did a woman her age learn to do that? Some kind of fancy gym?

Unaccustomed to being invited into a home without stating his business, he blurted out. "Sure but I'm not making a social call. Your neighbor and your husband were in the ER last night."

He followed her into the kitchen, bewildered. By now, with most people, he'd heard about their innocence or mitigating circumstances, the unfairness of the system, marriage, family or life in general. Either that or they slammed the door while they hid the evidence. This woman was getting him a glass of water.

Taking two glasses from the cupboard, she filled one after the other at the fridge. Outside it was drizzly and cold but her kitchen was a sunny yellow that seemed to absorb light from the frigid Northwest morning. The glass-fronted white cupboards were neatly stacked with dishes, family photos tucked in the glass.

"Well, I'm glad he went to the ER. I don't want him to bleed to death. Yet." She yawned. "I'm sorry, please sit down."

Sam was charmed by her lack of vitriol. He couldn't recall such a calm domestic abuse call. Ever. "Okay."

Meryl sat across from him, trying to focus her eyes. Maybe taking another sleeping pill at two a.m. wasn't such a good idea. She drank down the entire glass of water and, before she could help it, loudly burped, then laughed. "Excuse me."

Her pupils were the size of poker chips. "Are you on something?"

She thought about lying but the drugs just made her nod, without worrying about being judged. "My sister is a shrink. She gave me a sleeping pill. My tongue feels like a splunge."

A splunge? "Okay, I'll keep this brief. Do you want to tell me what happened last night?"

"Not really. It's kind of personal."

"That seventeenth stitch is when something stops being personal and starts looking like a domestic altercation. I know it might be painful but you really need to tell me your side of the story."

"What did Ethan tell you?"

"How about you tell me your version?" He was kind, patient.

She drank the rest of the water, giving herself time. She took off her wedding ring, rolled it back and forth on the table with her fingers. "You know what I hate the most about this?"

He shook his head. "Your husband?"

She shook her head, then nodded. "Well, yes, with intensity that scares me. I mean, I threw a champagne bottle at him and didn't even care if he bled to death. I got a lot of texts from someone using his phone. He's alive, I take it?"

Sam nodded. "Very."

"Good. Because I need child support. What I hate is becoming like my mother. That is the worst thing about this whole situation. My mother was the drama queen. My mother is the one who threw things and had men literally jumping out the windows when their wives or girlfriends or in one case the Sheriff showed up." She raised a finger, waving it around her lovely kitchen with its granite countertops and stone farmhouse sink. "I am not that person. And then suddenly, I am. I am the shrieking, melodramatic woman who throws things and hurts people."

"I'm sure you're not normally like that," he said, thinking she sure was sharing a lot for someone who didn't want to talk. Her sleeping pill, he was pretty sure, was doing a lot of the talking.

She was crying now. "Oh but I am. I go around dressing and talking and acting like someone else but in a very intense situation like last night, well, the real me comes out. And it's my mother."

Sam didn't know quite what to say yet felt something was required. "Women really hate becoming like their mothers, don't they?"

Meryl nodded so enthusiastically her head seemed ready to roll off her slender neck. "Yes. Well, except maybe Chelsea Clinton. She probably wouldn't mind. My mother is no Hillary Clinton. She's more the Monica Lewinsky type."

Again, Sam had no idea how to respond. It was all very well and good for someone to disparage their own mother but Sam knew better than to jump on that bandwagon. Besides, he had to remind himself, he was at work. "So I need to take a statement from you about last night."

She seemed to be having trouble focusing her eyes. "Here's my statement: you ready?"

He nodded, ready for the onslaught. "Simple is better."

"I came home, found my husband in my bed, our bed, with the thirty-two year old next door neighbor, who is a flight attendant, on top of him. And do you know what he said?"

Sam shook his head, wincing. "No idea."

"He said: This isn't what it looks like. I mean honestly, what did he think it looked like? Charades?"

"So you threw the bottle then?"

Meryl shook her head. "No, Leslie, ran into the closet. At some point I threw the champagne. I called her a whore." She finished her glass of water. "I know it's horrible but it felt good."

Having encountered the working variety of whores Sam knew that Leslie was a long way from your average garden variety hooker. "I'm sure it did."

"I can't believe I am sitting in my house, telling a police officer the details of the most humiliating night in my life."

At moments like this, Sam wished he'd paid more attention to his psychology classes at U of W. Usually he just went with his gut. "But you didn't do anything wrong. He did." Minus the seventeen stitches.

Tears welled up in her eyes. "Then why do I feel so bad?"

Sam flipped his book shut. He'd sum up her statement later. He knew the gist of it. Wronged woman; got angry, husband not pressing charges, end of story. "Listen; there is only one thing that is going to make all this feel better."

"Vodka?" She laughed. "Because sleeping pills aren't cutting it."

"Time. That's it." Since his wife died, he'd become a better cop. Not much of a silver lining but what the hell. Death had a way of leeching things down to the elemental. If someone is in pain, be kind. It was that simple.

She got up from the table, found some Kleenex and blew her nose. "I'm so sorry. Normally I'm a very private person."

He got up from the kitchen table, stuffing the notebook into his back pocket. "You're going to do fine. Do you have someone to talk to?"

"My sister."

"Good."

She slipped the wedding ring into her pocket. "Was it an artery?"

"Uh, his arm? Yeah, I think so."

"There was a lot of blood."

"So I heard." Leslie had expressed a wish that Meryl serve hard time.

Sam put on his hat, stood up. "Is your sister here?"

"No, she's coming back."

"Good. Listen, you get some more sleep and well… don't throw anything else at your husband."

"I can't promise you that."

His laughter came out as a snort. He should have been long gone. "Okay, fair enough but no witnesses." *What kind of dumb ass cop says that? You're flirting.*

"You got yourself a deal."

"I'll show myself out." *Finally, you moron.*

"Good. And I'm sorry. I will get some sleep."

A vague discontent washed over Sam. He'd never see her again. "Good luck."

As he closed the door, she yelled out from the kitchen, "Thanks, I'll need it!"

As Sam walked to his squad car in the drizzly late fall morning, he had a thought that often occurred to him when he was on duty: he hoped everything was going to be okay. More often than not, he'd learned, things were going to get worse. A lot worse.

5.

Skateboarding had been fun. Although it had been drizzly and icy cold at the skate park, Henry was hot, sweaty and tired. A glass of orange juice sat next to his computer. Normally he wouldn't be allowed juice in his room because of the Great Cherry Gatorade Incident but today all bets were off. Something was going on. No one would tell him. Everyone, even Jackie, was tired and cranky and kept giving him treats every time he opening his mouth to ask a question. He was day-after-Christmas sick with Starbucks hot chocolate and Top Pot donuts.

The house was quiet. Everyone was sneaking around like a bunch of spies, whispering about Leslie, the nice lady next door. Dad and Leslie had a sleepover. Although Henry knew that grownups didn't do sleepovers and whatever had happened between his dad and Leslie was very bad, he wasn't sure about the Very Bad Thing. Did they kiss? See each other naked? Did their thingees touch?

Of course he knew what sex was. Boren Fischer, who had an older brother, filled him in on the details in third grade. Boren, explained it in terms of thingees. The guy's thingee went in the girl's thingee, like a prong in a socket. For a while Henry went around imagining grown men with three extension cord prongs and women with giant outlets *down there*. Sex was both revolting and fascinating to Henry. Like a traffic fatality.

Last year, his mom had dropped off Henry for a late dinner to meet his dad, after work, at the drive-in Burgermaster. By the time Henry got into the car, the food hung off his dad's window on a tray. His dad handed over a greasy bag with all his favorites, the black and white shake sweaty with cold. Un-wrapping their food, they watched the headlights streaming down Interstate 520 toward the floating bridge, Seattle bound. His dad gave him a slightly more detailed, boring version of Boren Fischer's speech. No prongs. Penises. No outlets. Vaginas. Henry had concentrated on dipping his fries into his shake. Now that was an awesome combination. In the end Henry remembered more about the waitress, who had six earrings climbing one ear, than the conversation.

Mostly, Henry didn't want to think about his dad and any girl, not even his mom, doing It. Whenever he did, hot chocolate, donuts and pancakes swirled around in his stomach threatening to violently defy gravity.

After his computer finally warmed up, Henry went to his favorite website: Super Penguin Camp. Kirkland rarely had snow so it was fun to pretend to be a penguin and sled, ski, ice skate and hang out in igloos. Besides, you could dress your penguin any way you wanted. After hanging out with a bunch of penguins from Canada, Henry found another penguin that had a SEA, WA next to him. They could be neighbors, in real life.

Fuzzy Boy was his name. He wore matching purple earmuffs and a scarf. Henry's penguin, Squidge, decked out in a black leather jacket and shades, followed Fuzzy boy to an ice camp where it was only the two of them. Fuzzy Boy lit up with a smile. Squidge, with a few key strokes, smiled back.

"Whassup?" typed Fuzzy Boy.

":(" typed Henry.

"B cuz?" typed Fuzzy Boy.

Henry put his hands in his lap. His mom and dad always said that you never knew how old someone was online and who they could be. He wasn't even allowed to enter KIRKLAND, WA, as his home, just SEA, WA, for SEATTLE. Fuzzy Boy could be some kind of weirdo.

"B cuz??" Fuzzy Boy typed again. His scarf changed colors three times. He lowered his silver fishing pole into a stream.

Henry got a good feeling about Fuzzy Boy. Right now he was bright blue with a purple scarf and was nibbling a little green fish. It took a lot of skill playing games to earn enough tokens for a silver fishing pole at the Penguin Post. Henry decided to trust Fuzzy Boy. Aunt Jackie said his mom and dad would work everything out, eventually, and he could talk to her or his mom and dad as much was he wanted but Henry really wanted to talk to someone his own age. He couldn't do it at school. No way.

"I think my dad just left our family," he typed, with no misspellings. Henry was good at school.

Fuzzy Boy shed a purple tear. "That stinks. My dad walked out two years ago. It's awful."

Henry knew, as soon as he saw Fuzzy Boy's prompt response, with no misspellings or typos, that this was wrong. Two kids shouldn't be talking about personal stuff on a website. He'd been warned by Mrs. Maberly the librarian at school, his mom and dad, even Nathalie, who told him he'd be a moron to share on his stupid websites (even though she practically posted her every fart on Instagram.) Now Henry knew why everyone had warned him. Although it was wrong, it felt good to have someone listen. Really good.

Henry got up and shut his bedroom door.

***

"You have to talk to Ethan." It was late, after dinner, which had become a forced family ritual where everyone moved the food around on their plates. Jackie was at the door of the bonus room, saying goodnight to Meryl.

"I can't. I just need a little time to process things. I feel like I'm the Titanic. Not a survivor but the actual boat itself." Meryl looked better. She'd eaten a sandwich at lunch. The kids watched TV upstairs.

"You're much thinner than the Titanic."

"Thank you. You always know the right thing to say."

Jackie smiled her crooked smile. "Are you sure you don't want me to stay?" She hung on the door, itching to lock herself in the car and call Rob. It felt wrong to be obsessing about a guy right now but she couldn't help it. Her brain was split between feeling horrible and empathetic to her sister and mooning like a teenager over her new crush.

"No, I want to keep things normal."

Jackie smiled. "Good luck with that."

Meryl rolled her eyes. "Yeah, thanks Ethan!"

"Maybe instead of making snide remarks across the driveway you should go over there, make them to his face."

"I'm going to wait until I can be mature and adult."

"Because he was so mature and adult last night."

Meryl hung her head, thinking of his bleeding arm. She'd responded to his latest two e-mails with "Drop dead" and "Piss off." How could she face him? Jackie didn't quite understand what she'd seen last night. Her sister could barely commit to a breakfast cereal, let alone a man. She once had a guy ask her to move in and she told him she wasn't even ready for a dog.

"Do you want my bed? I paid nearly three grand for it at Restoration Hardware."

"Ew, no. Put it on Craig's list. Or better yet, burn it."

"You're not thinking like a therapist."

"You're right. Hire someone to burn it." Jackie's face grew somber. "But really, you should cancel book club."

Meryl shook her head. She wanted a shower but the idea of entering her room or even her closet for fresh clothes was daunting. But it seemed too weak to ask anyone else to get her clothes and make-up. She'd do it. "No, they're my friends."

"Please don't try and make this normal. This isn't one of your to-do lists. It's messy and ugly and no one cares about book club."

"Oh they care."

"Your friends will understand. Please?"

"Would you like to come?"

Jackie slouched, hands jammed in her jeans. She'd never have Meryl's great posture. When Faye offered personal dance lessons, she'd refused. For some reason, although they both agreed as kids that there would be nothing worse than learning dance from show-off Faye, Meryl had agreed to the lessons. And she'd loved them, for a while. At fourteen, she'd quit. No explanation. Finished, just like that. "No. Do you want me to?"

"Only if you'd like to."

Jackie met her sister's eyes dead on. "I'm sorry that Ethan is being a complete dick but I would not enjoy a night of juiced-up suburban moms blathering about *The Mermaid's Chair*."

"We don't talk about the book."

Jackie threw up her hands. "Well then, what time?"

Meryl cracked a grin. "Six. Bring wine."

"Nice to see you smile. My last client is at six so I'll be late. Don't drink, okay?"

"Isn't that what you're supposed to do when your husband leaves you for a younger woman?"

"I don't know. Carrie Underwood thinks you should beat up his car with a baseball bat but I'd recommend a lawyer. See you tomorrow."

Meryl's eyes filled with tears. "Thank you."

Jackie wrapped her short, muscular arms around her sister, who had five inches on her, patting her softly on the back.

"It's okay. It's okay. I swear to God. We've gotten through worse, right?"

6.

"Rituals are important. Nowadays it's hip not be married. I'm not interested in being hip."
John Lennon

Nathalie rattled the house with thunderous double door slams. Nothing happened. Her father wasn't around to listen. Her mother, seemingly zoned out on anti-depressants, sleep deprivation or possibly shock, didn't seem to give a rat's ass. She was getting ready for book club as though everything was hunky dory. Nathalie, who'd thought she'd slipped through the earthquake-sized cracks of her family's upheaval, was grounded.

It was a slap in the face after the free-wheeling days when Mom was chasing the chairmanship of the auction. It got even better when she was buried under the details of the auction itself. Nathalie came and went as she felt. Her parents were ciphers, more roommates than authority figures. What a rude freaking awakening this was. No cell phone, computer time or contact with the civilized world. Shit.

Tired of being ignored, Nathalie went into her room, dug out her old Ipod and listened to music on headphones for a while, emerging a half hour before the book club arrived. Never contrite, Nathalie simply decided to find another crack and slip through. It wouldn't take long.

Sitting on the second floor with a bird's eye view of the front entrance reminded her of 5th grade, the book club's inaugural year. She missed the days when she thought her mother knew, if not everything, then at least how to manage their lives. Routines were simple back then: play volleyball, do homework, eat snacks, play. Mom's voice was the radio playing soothing tunes beneath it all. And it had worked.

High school complicated things exponentially. Her first two years at Forest Ridge had passed in a blur of hard studying, volleyball championships and her parents, puffed with pride. This year, for reasons that remained unclear, she'd hit a wall. Denny was the first serious boyfriend she'd ever had. From that first summer night on the Houghton Beach raft, he made her laugh and unlike her parents, he was clearly interested.

Although Denny didn't belong to the straight toothed crowd of kids with access to speed boats and waterfront homes, he was included because he had what they wanted: drugs. So while he was grudgingly invited to tag along, there was an undercurrent of resentment, subtle slights that he pretended to ignore. These heightened when he snagged Nathalie. And no one hated him more than Zoe.

Zoe usually arrived to book club early with her mom, Diane, but had called, saying she was going to finish her homework before she came over. Nathalie skipped hers, so she'd been free to spy on her aunt helping her mom find an outfit.

Nathalie spent an amusing half hour lying on the master bedroom room floor eavesdropping as the two women argued inside the walk in closet with the door conveniently wide open. Jackie managed to dig out, from all Mom's preppy, droopy duds, what sounded like an amazingly cute outfit: narrow jeans, fitted orange tank, short navy blazer and stacked heels. Her mom dragged out loafers, pressed slacks and a baggy cotton sweater.

"This is more my style."

"Flannel trousers? Didn't Winston Churchill wear those?"

"Thank you for your kind words but I'm still in the pajama phase of grieving for my marriage."

"You're 37. There is no pajama phase."

"When did you get so mean?"

"When you started dressing for the early bird special at Denny's."

Nathalie heard her mom groan, the squeak of the plush pedestal chair she kept in her closet. "Fine, I'll wear your outfit."

Nathalie imagined her Aunt Jackie rubbing her mom's shoulders as Meryl spoke. "You know what my worst fear is? That I'm like Mom."

"Don't worry about that; you're the anti-Faye. But you have to stop pretending that everything's okay. You're like the textbook child of an alcoholic: zippedy-do-dah everything's fine and dandy."

"You really think Faye was an alcoholic?" Meryl asked. They both exploded with laughter. This was followed by a long, thoughtful hush.

Nathalie waited expectantly. They never talked about their mother. Ever.

"But what about the kids?" her mom finally asked. "I can't exactly fall apart."

Nathalie could practically feel her ears stretching to hear her aunt's reply. "You won't. But you can't hide everything. They're a lot tougher than you think." She waited a moment. "And you should call Mom."

"Yeah, I'll invite her up. She can get drunk and burn down the house with a cigarette. Perfect. Just what I need."

"She's different, she's in AA."

"Mom used AA to pick up men."

"Maybe so but it's sticking this time."

"Uh-huh. How many times do you have to get thrown before you find another horse?"

Aunt Jackie didn't take the bait. "Don't laugh. She's found God."

"Ha! Of course she has because God will forgive you for absolutely everything! Remember when she told us to lie about going to church to the social worker from CPS? We picked Harmony Unitarian out of the phone book because it sounded friendly. Normal people do not have childhood memories like this. They just don't."

"I'd forgotten about that one."

"Not me. I wish I could. I wish I could forget about a lot of things."

Her mom and aunt were quiet for a very long time. Finally Aunt Jackie said, "Let's get you dressed."

***

Fifteen minutes after six, Zoe arrived with her mom, Diane, and two plates of brownies. Jackie answered the door, welcoming them with an odd stiffness and a premonition that this night wasn't going to go well. She told them, although they already knew, to place their coats in Ethan's office. Everyone paused awkwardly at the mention of his name. Jackie moved things along, commenting on the freshly baked brownies as she took both plates from Zoe.

Zoe stepped back nervously, holding onto one of the plates; the green one. There was a strange little tug of war.

"It's okay Zoe, I'm not going to eat them all," Jackie said.

Zoe laughed nervously. Something about her was completely off. "Oh, yeah. I know."

Jackie tilted her head. "You can let go now."

Zoe waited a beat, her face twisted in agony. "Uh-huh. Okay then. Right." She let go, dashing upstairs frantically. By the time she reached Nathalie on the upper landing, she was hyperventilating. She threw herself onto the thick carpet next to Nathalie. "The, the, the..." She sputtered hopelessly.

"Spit it out." Nathalie felt like slapping her but got her a glass of water instead. It was nothing short of a miracle that Nathalie, who could fabricate elaborate lies while higher than the Goodyear blimp without missing a beat, could be friends with Zoe, a kid incapable of lying to her own mother about the smallest of transgressions. Zoe was one of those kids who'd chastise their parents for going 3 miles above the speed limit.

Nathalie waited until Zoe finished drinking. "Spit. It. Out."

"The brownies!" Zoe's eyes welled with tears. "Oh my God, what do we do? I can't believe it. I never thought..." She continued dithering on in this vein.

Nathalie flicked her long brown hair over one shoulder, annoyed. "What about them?"

"Denny, gave me some Berkley Bum and I put it in the brownies."

Nathalie didn't know which was more shocking: that Zoe had accepted pot from Denny or that she had baked it into a freakin' dessert. Jealousy got the best of her. "Denny? What was he doing at your house?"

"He wasn't. He called and asked if he could drop something off for you. He pulled up in our driveway and handed me a bag of pot. He said you needed a break; that your phone got taken away, that it was almost legal, and given what was going on with your family, it would help you relax. I put the drugs in my pocket but I got so nervous carrying it that I baked it in the brownies for tonight!"

Nathalie screwed her eyes shut. "Jesus, Zoe. You're not manufacturing meth for God's sake, although I do have to say, I'm a little shocked here. What made you suddenly decide to be a pothead?"

"I'm not! I wasn't going to eat them; they were for you." Zoe had a long history of assisting Nathalie get in trouble. It had all the high drama with none of the pitfalls. Nathalie never gave up her bagman so Zoe never paid the price. Yet.

"And now they're downstairs?"

Zoe was nauseous. Baking drugs into sweets was easily traceable. "Your Aunt Jackie grabbed them from me. I tried to hold onto the platter but I just couldn't. She's incredibly strong."

Nathalie snickered. "She probably knows. She's a shrink on TV." She opened her hands like a book. "I swear to God she can read people like that."

Zoe bent over. "I'm going to throw up. They'll kick me out of Honor Society."

Nathalie bent over, rubbing her friend's back. "I'm sorry but you're being, like, a total idiot. Do you think Honor Society is like Big Brother?" Nathalie had read *1984* her sophomore year, comparing, in her essay, George Orwell's dystopian society to her parents' house rules. It was her last A. "Relax. Nothing's going to happen. Did you bring your phone?" Nathalie nodded sickly.

"Cool, fork it over. I'm going to call Denny."

Zoe handed Nathalie the new I-Phone 5-S she'd bought with babysitting money. It had a white plastic case, a black and white photo of her terrier, Petal, as a screensaver.

"Thanks." Nathalie dialed, praying Denny would answer.

Zoe dashed into the bathroom, closed the door and threw up.

***

Although Meryl had arranged for Henry to watch a movie at Max's house, which he normally loved, Henry got bored. The movie had lots of car crashes which only made Henry think about his dad's car. The car, which his dad called *the Mercedes*, became increasingly important to his dad. He thought about how his dad spent time outside in the summer, without his shirt, washing the car when he'd normally used the carwash near their grocery store.

Before buying this car, Henry had seen his father shirtless outside exactly once, when he'd spilled a platter of hot ribs on himself at a barbecue. The car, Henry thought, had something to do with his dad's sleepover next door. Cars did, he knew, have something to do with attracting girls. Maybe this even applied to married people. A link was formed that ate away at Henry's conscience. The car. The girl. The trouble.

Riding his skateboard down to Max's house, Henry saw his dad's car, parked in front of Leslie's house, gleaming and smooth. The car. The girl. The trouble. You didn't park in front of a house in the cul-de-sac unless you were visiting or lived there. The car. The girl. The trouble. He couldn't stop thinking about it.

The movie was boring. By the sixteenth cinematic slow motion car crash, Henry left, pretending he was going to the bathroom. Max, engrossed in the clashing metal and spraying glass shards, didn't notice. Outside, Max shivered, put on his coat. As he walked past Leslie's house, stars peeked out from fat rain clouds. The moon vanished.

Carefully opening the front door to his house, Henry snuck down the open hallway into the laundry room. It was amazing, really, how no one saw him. The only thing between him and all those chattering ladies was three pillars. They were waving their arms, deep in discussion, nearly yelling. He hadn't bothered hiding. Yet not one of them noticed. Had he been older he'd have attributed it to Chardonnay, not magic.

He slipped into the garage. It smelled of gas, lawn clippings and chemicals. For years the Garcia brothers had tended their yard.

They always said, "Hola little bro," before firing up their machines.

The summer after Leslie moved in, Dad let go of the Garcias to save money. It made sense. Dad was, Henry knew, worried about money. But the car, girl, and trouble connection demanded action. Something. But what?

The first time Henry had seen Leslie, he was mesmerized. In high heels and bright lipstick, a roll-aboard trailing her like a well-trained pet; she was perfection itself. She never bummed around in yoga pants unless headed to the gym. She flew all over the world in a trim navy blue uniform, making sporadic, sensational appearances. Her blonde hair was never limp or greasy. She was a rare exotic bird. A flamingo.

A couple of weeks ago, she'd winked at him. He'd been poking his hand in the boxwood hedge bordering her driveway.

"Hey Henry," she'd said, rolling down her car window as she pulled in.

He'd grasped his basketball, not sure what to say. They'd never been introduced. She came and went at odd hours, didn't have kids. He'd never even seen her move in. Poof: beautiful girl next door. How did she know his name?

Henry was flooded with sadness. The garage was Dad's place: his lawnmower, his good natured irritation at how the bikes always fell down. Henry wouldn't mind being scolded anymore. He did put his bike away wrong. Tears welled. Holding two fingers over his eyes, he forced himself to stop. He should be at Max's house right now, stuffing himself with microwave popcorn.

It was all so confusing. Questions flew around in his brain like Frisbees. Why were all the neighborhood women yelling at each other? Was Aunt Jackie moving in? What made his dad decide to stay at someone else's house? Would his parents get a divorce like Cameron Abelson's parents? (Cameron said the only upside was that her dad bought her pretty much anything she wanted.)Could Henry knock on Leslie's door and talk to his dad?

No. That much was clear.

Sitting down on the narrow cement garage steps, Henry went through his various options. He could go back to Max's house. He could talk to his mother. He could sneak upstairs and message Fuzzy Boy on his computer. Or he could do something different: something angry and rebellious and completely wrong, just because he felt like it. Henry looked at his watch: 8:56 pm. He gave himself until 9:00 to decide.

7.

*"If you don't have anything
nice to say, sit by me."
-Lillian Hellman*

Sandy Chen, who lived next door, blew in like a tornado, short hair spiked with haste. She threw off her damp wool poncho, smelling of Issey Miyake perfume. "I'm so sorry Meryl. I heard what happened from Mike. I'm just sick. Seriously. That rat bastard." She shrugged at Carol, who detested swearing. "Sorry," she said, forming her thumb and pinkie into a phone, which she placed against her cocked ear. "When you are ready to talk, call my office. Do it before Ethan." Sandy, a divorce attorney, poured herself a healthy slug of Merlot, shoving her tiny nose deep into the glass. She sniffed, thought for a moment, took a small sip. "Men are such pigs."

Diane patted Sandy on the back. "Maybe Meryl doesn't want to talk about it. We are a book club. We might actually discuss the book. What was it called? I read it so long ago…"

"*Beloved*," whispered Carol, taking a tiny sip of wine.

Meryl took a bite of brownie, letting the hushed conversation drift, like snow. After a glass of wine and a brownie, she felt calmer, almost dreamy. The reoccurring image of Ethan and Leslie blurred. She waved a hand. "I don't care. I'm fine. Talk about whatever."

Lorraine Fuller, who lived across the street, squeezed Meryl's arm. Fingers bright with ten silver rings, she wore a long tunic over faded jeans. "Embrace your sadness darling. The sooner you let go, the sooner healing begins." Her droopy spaniel eyes glowed. "Your spirit will rise, stronger, like a phoenix from the ashes." She demonstrated with raised, chubby arms, bracelets jangling.

Meryl wiped oniony spit from her ear. "Thanks Lorraine. I'll remember that."

Jackie sipped her cranberry juice, less bored than she'd anticipated but anxious to get home and talk to Rob.

"Screw that," said Sandy Chen. "After all these years together some tramp bats her eyes... I mean you'd think-" Her head whipped around. "Is that him?"

All eyes swiveled to the broad, eastern two-storied window. Across a large expanse of lawn, shadows moved inside Leslie's house. The book club, silent as spies, murmured. *Weird. Speak of the devil. Would you look at that? Is she naked? No, look, she's got on workout clothes, see the shorts? More like diapers. How old is she?*

After the figures disappeared from sight, everyone quietly located their wine glasses, drinking thoughtfully.

Lorraine anxiously blurted, "*Beloved,* the book was boring, so I rented the movie. What a weird story. Thandie Newton's walking around naked and Danny Glover and Oprah are having sex. If Thandie was the ghost how come she got pregnant? Once you're a ghost, can you get pregnant?"

Jackie was the only one who registered the comment, chuckling. Their minds were next door.

Carol dabbed her lips with a cocktail napkin, addressing Meryl firmly. "From what I've read about mid-life crises he's going to come around. You just have to be patient." Her eyes darted nervously. She'd been criticized for her Christian perspective. Diane sometimes backed her up against the pagan Lorraine and Sandy, who was either an atheist or Buddhist, depending upon how much she drank. "And pray," Carol added, somewhat boldly, she thought.

Diane snorted into her wine glass. "For what? Ethan has gone way beyond the coveting phase with his neighbor. I'm pretty sure that morally, he's stepped so far over the line, he's like, in Mongolia or something."

Carol's mouth was dry. "For guidance?"

Meryl poured Carol a healthy slug of white.

Lorraine chewed on a stuffed mushroom. "Many cultures don't believe in monogamy."

"Thank God ours does or I'd be out of business," said Sandy Chen, raising her glass. "And thank God for whoring around."

Carol choked on sip of wine. "That isn't something you should thank God for."

As Sandy continued arguing with Carol, Meryl leaned over for another brownie, speaking her thoughts in a dreamy monotone to no one in particular. "Do you know what the worst part was?" She took a large mouthful of brownie, speaking loudly through the food, "They were in our bed; on my side."

"She never was very friendly," said Carol, seeking relief from Sandy. "I took her some pumpkin bread when she first moved in and she didn't even invite me in."

Lorraine shook her head. "She didn't make any effort to get to know any of us."

"Except, apparently Ethan," Diane snickered, immediately feeling badly.

There was an awkward silence. Glasses were refilled, food examined.

Jackie sat down on the hearth, kicked off her boots and crossed her legs. "So who actually read the book?"

Only Diane and Meryl smiled at the comment. Sandy toyed with the idea of pushing Jackie into the fireplace. This was Meryl's sister. Where was her sisterly outrage? Her anger?

After forty-five more minutes of discussing Ethan's behavior, contrasting and comparing it with other philandering husbands, both local: Ronnie Abelson and Juan Formosa and celebrity: Pitt, Kennedy and Trump, emotions and blood alcohol levels increased. Even Carol took repeated, bird-like sips of chardonnay. As their fury grew, becoming hard and focused, Jackie and Carol formed an unlikely alliance, trying to dissuade the group from venting their collective rage. Neither woman, for separate reasons, could see this ending well.

It was like trying to force an angry swarm of bees back into their hive. Sandy and Lorraine thought they should march right over and confront Ethan. *We totally should. When he got into bed with her, he spat in every one of our faces. We need to tell him exactly how we feel.* Jackie knew that drunks tended in two directions: they either became terribly remorseful and full of self pity or angrily righteous and full of wrath. Clearly this group was trending to the latter.

Jackie waved her hands over their heads, trying to forestall a collision. "No you don't. Drinking a bunch of wine and telling people how you feel is never, ever, a good idea. If any one of you has drunk-dialed then you know what I mean. You'll regret it in the morning."

Carol frowned. "What is drunk dialing?"

Jackie cocked her head. "Exactly what it sounds like."

Carol shook her head. "What?"

"She went to a Christian College. They signed a pledge not to drink, screw or have any fun," Sandy informed Jackie.

Carol winced. "We had fun."

Sandy winked at Carol. "It's okay. I was having enough sex for both of us." She leaned over to whisper to Lorraine. "I'm Asian. Everyone thought I was at the library."

Carol, frantic to change the subject, cleared her throat. "Jackie's right. Please, think of your children. What kind of example are you setting if you charge over there?"

Sandy took a gulp of wine. "The kind where you don't take shit sitting down. You say something!" She drained her glass. "I always feel better when I tell people off. It helps me sleep. I swear to God."

Carol pleaded with Sandy not to take the Lord's name in vain or lead the group into any kind of action. "I suggest that we all take a deep breath and join hands and pray. Who is with me?"

"Boooo!" yelled Sandy with a thumbs down.

"Anyone else?" asked Carol.

Lorraine's bracelets shook as she spoke. "Carol, I do believe that prayer and meditation have a place in healing but a group of women, joining their friend in a collective release of anger…. Well, it's quite organic. And fun."

"I have a sitter until 10 o'clock. Let's do this," said Sandy Chen.

Diane, well beyond her limit of 2 glasses of wine, thumped Sandy on the back in agreement. "I believe," she slurred a bit, "in this day and age, when people hide behind their computers and break up via text, it's good to tell Ethan exactly how we feel. Eye-to eye. Face-to-face." Her voice grew deeper. "Man-to-man."

"Technically, it's not man-to-man," Jackie said.

Diane pointed a drunken finger. "I meant, figuratively."

"It's not that either," Jackie mumbled.

After three seconds of heavy silence, there was a rush to find coats, hats and rain boots. Diane, raised with the motto: "Never deliver bad news without lipstick", dashed into the bathroom.

In despair, Jackie turned to Meryl. "This is insane! Do something!"

All her life Meryl had strictly limited her alcohol consumption. Losing control was not part of the plan, although, now, for the life of her, she couldn't think why. A slight buzz might have helped. Her neck muscles swung gently on a deep red ribbon. Zoe's delicious brownies lifted her into the clouds. She walked her fingers, tip toe, up the imaginary clouds. Her fingers could still dance. Yes, they could. And did.

A goofy smile lit Meryl's face. She turned, fingers dancing in the air. "I'm single. I can do what I want, when I want, how I want."

Gulping the last of her wine, the glass slipped through Meryl's fingers, shattering on the floor. She hardly noticed. Pushing her blazer sleeves up to her elbows, her arm shot upwards. "Come on ladies, let's go visit the neighbors!"

***

Henry was in the garage, siphoning gas from his mother's car. Each year (except this one) Ethan made a big production of dragging the stainless pot, big enough to hide a small child, into the backyard. He filled it with canola oil and deep fried the Thanksgiving turkey over a gas flame in the backyard, huddled with a glass of something. This he presented, deep golden brown, to Ethan and Betsy, who were always unsure of how to react. It was just a turkey.

It was cold but Henry wasn't shivering because of the temperature. Placing his mouth on the siphon to create a vacuum was nerve wracking. This violated any number of lectures he'd endured in his short life.

For a fleeting second, Henry missed the grandmother he'd never met. This happened sometimes. He made up stories about her life. They involved nocturnal sightings of Burrowing Owls, 10 inches high. Aunt Jackie said Grandma Faye was a "hoot" and a "pistol," sparking images of Faye blowing smoke off a handgun, Annie Oakley style. Grandma Faye, Henry decided, was a bird-loving, gun-toting lady who would understand her only grandson with silent cowboy sympathy. She would love tarantulas.

The siphoning went smoothly until the laundry room door opened. It was Aunt Jackie, who stopped on the garage stairs. Henry could see her through the windows of his mom's car. Folding the hose, he stopped the gas mid-flow. The slightest noise would alert her. He waited, crouched, legs aching after all that skateboarding.

Aunt Jackie spoke into her cell phone. "I need a freakin' reality check. You know how I told you about my cheating brother-in-law and that whole mess? Now Meryl's entire book club is all liquored up and ready to go confront him next door." Aunt Jackie laughed. "I know, right? It would be if it weren't so sad. My niece is already a semi-train wreck. I don't know what the hell her brother is thinking." Aunt Jackie listened for a moment.

"There are six of them, counting my sister." She was quiet again. "Yeah. Okay. I know. I'm off duty, right?" More silence. "Yeah, I had a good time too." She listened for a while longer. "I'm not sure you know what you're asking. My family puts the fun in dysfunction." She listened again. "I know. Okay. I'll call you."

She turned off the phone, staring at it. "Sheesh. Whatever happened to men who just wanted to get laid? If I wanted emotional intimacy, I'd get a dog." Sighing heavily, Aunt Jackie pocketed her phone, flicked off the garage lights and went inside.

Henry sat in the dark, wondering why Aunt Jackie talked to her phone. Adult were so confusing. I mean, why say all these things after she'd hung up? Then again, he was learning that more and more things were better left unsaid. He imagined that as he became an adult; that spot would expand, where you kept unsaid things. It would have to.

It was nearly pitch black. He couldn't see his own hand. Worse, he couldn't siphon; that would be dangerous. Meanwhile, he was stuck in the dark with a half-filled turkey frying pot of gasoline. Awkward.

Jackie's words ran through his head, "I don't know what the hell her brother is thinking." *Girl. Car. Trouble.*

Removing the siphon from the pot, Henry made sure to shake off the gasoline drips. Feeling his way through the blackness, he bumped into some bikes and his own skateboard. Inside, the front door loudly slammed. Maybe the party was over. He turned on the light, hoping it wouldn't spark a fire. Gasoline fumes clouded his eyes. Fumbling for the switch, he opened the garage door. There were voices in the driveway; loud voices.

Henry was not given to panic but the thought of every neighborhood mom ambushing him, when he was supposed to be at Max's, did him in. He darted out of the garage, straight towards the four women scurrying in the lead. Gas fumes shot up his nose. The women bundled in hats and coats were grey silhouettes. But Henry could easily discern their shapes.

Aunt Jackie, short and fast and Max's mom Carol, skittering daintily, chased the lead four, yelling, "Stop you idiots!" and "Ladies, please, think of your children!"

Eyes squeezed shut, Henry waited for someone to ask him what on earth he was doing. *Didn't he know gasoline was poisonous? Flammable?*

Ten feet away, the four women who had harassed him at every juncture, questioning the safety of every skateboard jump, sharp object and slingshot, trotted past him like an angry gaggle of geese. It was as though he was invisible. Blinking in the fumes, he waited until Jackie and Carol chased the others through a gap in the laurel hedge. He dragged the stainless pot into a cluster of desiccated brown hydrangeas.

What in the Sam Hill was going on? Were they going to invite his dad and Leslie over to book club? Why was his aunt calling his mom's best friends idiots? Yes, they were making as much noise as a troop of Howler Monkeys but still. He'd wait and listen. There was plenty of time to carry out his plan. Besides, a kid could learn a lot hiding out in the hydrangeas.

8.

"A journey is like marriage. The certain way to be wrong is to think you control it."
John Steinbeck

As soon as the book club left, slamming the door three separate times, Zoe and Nathalie thundered downstairs. The living room was a wreck: broken glass, empty wine bottles, half-eaten plates of appetizers. Nathalie held up a blue plate heaped with brownies.

"Problem solved."

Zoe returned from the kitchen with an empty green plate. "Wrong plate. I color coded them." She fell onto the couch. "I'm doomed."

Nathalie dug into the pockmarked hummus with a cracker. "Would you relax? They don't know they're stoned. They've been drinking."

Zoe shook her head. "Are you serious? Lorraine grew pot on a commune in Astoria."

Nathalie's eyes widened. A smear of hummus streaked her chipped black nail polish. "Lorraine, the naturopath?"

Zoe nodded miserably. "And Sandy followed Phish."

"Fish? How can you follow fish? I don't get it."

"It's a band for hippies, or something. Where were you? Have you forgotten the Butt Sack Club's motto? 'We spy! Here's why: We get the dirt!'"

Nathalie slathered a cracker with the remaining Drunken Goat cheese. "I remember that. Only you would come up with a motto for a two person club. What a dork."

"Remember when Andy's dad went on that long 'business trip' and only we knew he was in jail? And how Monica's dad didn't know he wasn't her biological father until they had that car accident and she needed a blood transfusion? Weren't you listening? The book club knows everything."

Nathalie shook her head. "They're boring."

Zoe sighed. "They are now. They didn't used to be."

"If I grow up to be as boring as them, I'll commit suicide."

Zoe covered her eyes with one hand. "If I get busted for pot, I'll commit suicide."

Nathalie ate a blue plate brownie while pouring the dregs of each wine bottle into an empty. Clearly she'd done this before. "Whatever. It'll all work out."

"That's easy for you to say. You don't even care if you go to college."

"And you act like you're thirty. Lighten up already. You're a teenager. You're supposed to do stupid stuff."

"I think you've got it covered for both of us." Zoe wrinkled her nose at Nathalie's careful ministrations with the wine bottles. "What are you doing?"

"I'm being creative. Denny's coming to pick me up. The moms ate all the pot brownies…"

"First of all, that's disgusting and second of all, you're grounded."

Nathalie carefully corked her full bottle of Char-Merl-Syrah-Grigio. "First of all, Ms. Middle-Aged Career Drone, I'm not going to a wine tasting and second of all, look around - do you really think my mom is on top of things? She can barely handle a dirty spoon on the kitchen counter, let alone her husband playing spin the salami with the neighbor."

"That's disgusting. He's your dad."

"Life is disgusting. I'm going to have fun while things are going seriously bat shit. My family is in the full moon phase."

Zoe sighed, surveying the wreckage. Bending to pick glass shards off the floor, she realized Nathalie was right. Things were going crazy. Her mom, who always made such a big deal about her 2 glass limit, had sounded drunk. What if her mom was high too? A gust of cold air followed by a slammed door made her jump.

"Nathalie?" said Zoe, straightening.

But Nathalie was gone. Zoe's eyes stung with the realization that she'd been used, again. Her new Iphone was missing.

***

"Don't answer the door," Ethan repeated, looking up from his computer screen at the kitchen table. Typing with one hand was infuriating but using both made the stitches in his arm throb. Making matters worse, Leslie had rules for everything. He had to squeegee out the shower every morning. Meryl might be a control freak but at least he could eat cereal in the bonus room.

"They're not going away Ethan. Every woman in the neighborhood is out there. They're drunk," Leslie said.

She'd just flown in from LA, a quick turnaround with cranky passengers and a quarreling crew.

"It's your house. Don't do it."

Leslie pulled her wet hair into a pony tail, turning off the gas under her eggs. Two eggs and nine hours of sleep was all she wanted. Those drunken bitches were keeping her from enjoying both. Her first attempt at uncomplicated sex with a married man had gone terribly awry. Instead of being her hot distraction, he was her hot mess. Then he followed her home. Tying her pale blue robe firmly, she padded barefoot to the door, throwing it open.

The wet November air hit Leslie like a damp towel as she shouted. "He's not here!"

Sandy Chen's fist hung in the air, mid-pound. She unfurled her fingers into an awkward wave. "Hey Leslie!"

"Hi Sally."

"Sandy."

"Right." She nodded at the rest of the women, whose anger diminished when they saw her wet hair, the purple rings under her eyes. "Book club tonight?"

Meryl waved sheepishly. It wasn't that hard, she thought, seeing Leslie again. As long as she didn't have to see her naked. Ever.

Jackie cleared her throat and stepped forward. "They'd like to talk to Ethan, if you don't mind." She felt like a chaperone on a field trip that had gone horribly awry.

Leslie shook her head, mulishly. "Again, not here."

"Bullshit Leslie. His car is parked out front," said Sandy Chen.

Jackie admired her approach. She made a mental note to hire her should she ever need a divorce attorney, thinking this type of reasoning didn't make her Grade A relationship material.

As Jackie wrestled with her demons, the book club turned, gazing down the lawn. Ethan's black Mercedes gleamed in the dark, glittering with dew.

"He took the bus."

Lorraine crossed her arms, her words slurring. "Okay then, who was that we saw trotting through your living room, someone else's husband?" Her purple alpaca jacket had developed a wet goat funk.

Leslie rolled her eyes. "Oh for God's sake, you're spying on me?"

Carol leaned forward, whispering softly, "You might want to invest in some nice thick curtains."

Jackie stepped to the front. "Look, I'm really sorry. We'll go home. Come on." Turning, she took Meryl by the arm, dragging her away.

The door opened wider. Ethan stepped into the light, his handsome face thin and haggard. Wearing an old flannel shirt and Levis, he held his bandaged arm close. "Hi Jackie," he said. "Thanks for coming over and…" He searched for the right word, "…helping."

Rolling her eyes in frustration, Leslie threw up her hands, muttered some dark curses and disappeared into the hallway.

Meryl turned at the sound of his voice, her eyes filled with unexpected tears. "Ethan!" There was far more emotion in those two syllables than she'd intended. Seventeen years of loving was a hard habit to break.

Sandy puffed herself up, pointing a finger at Ethan's chest. "You cretin! How dare you bring another woman into the bed you and your wife shared? That's not only violating your marriage vows it's rolling them in dog poo and throwing them in Meryl's face."

"Nice imagery," Jackie quipped.

Lorraine wrapped her goat-smelling jacket closer. "It's primitive. Violating the symbolic primacy of your union in the space you shared!"

Ethan allowed himself a small grin. "Okay Lorraine. Got it. I'm a bastard. Sue me. Wait, Sandy can sue me. Now can you let me talk to my wife?"

Carol rose to her full height in her sensible heels, placing her hand, with its simple wedding band, over her heart. "She doesn't…" she began tremulously, gathering strength. "You should be listening, Ethan. You are the one who should have knocked on her door. You do not have the right to call her 'wife' right now. Like it or not, we are involved. Meryl is our friend, this is our neighborhood."

Ethan's eyes filled with tears as they wandered over the six women, looking for a trace of compassion. "Carol-" he began but Carol turned her head, shut him out.

Diane wrapped an arm around Carol, who trembled with emotion. "Well said."

Ethan turned to Diane. She'd always stocked his favorite brand of bourbon; never failed to ask about the business.

"No." Diane shook her head, fighting back tears. "I'm not buying it. Whatever you were going through, this is…" She choked up.

"And for good measure, might I add: fuck you!" Sandy said.

Diane patted Sandy on the back. "That's what I was trying to say."

Ethan fought for composure, looking up at the night sky. "If anyone needs to vent further, I'll listen. I didn't realize I had wronged six women."

"You have wronged all women," Lorraine said, shaking her fist.

"Geez," said Ethan. "I'm in deeper shit than I thought." He tried to catch Meryl's eye.

"Enough with the fecal analogies. Anyone want to say anything else?" asked Jackie. "Get it all out ladies. You've come this far."

A few women sniffled, their drunken energy dissipating. Lorraine blew her nose. Meryl hiccupped.

"Okay," said Sandy. "That was depressing."

Jackie drew Meryl away by the arm. "Come on." She glanced at her brother-in-law. "She'll call you tomorrow."

Meryl jerked her arm away. "No. No. I do have a question: just one." He lifted his chin, waiting for the punch. "Why? Why now?"

As Ethan spoke, no one heard the front door of Meryl's house slam. Nor did they notice Nathalie running down the street. If they heard the guttural thrum of the Camaro as it pulled out from Sandy's house, they didn't care. No one peered beyond Leslie's porch at Henry, staggering down the laurel-flanked driveway with an enormous pot. He hid in Diane's yard, scaring the cat.

Henry saw his dad, a tall figure at the open door of Leslie's house. All six ladies listened intently for three minutes, grouped like strangely silent carolers. His dad wore a UW sweatshirt. Henry hoped, if his grades were good enough, to go there. After that he'd probably become an astronaut or a garbage man. After the women left, his dad shut the door. The porch light went out, leaving the sloping lawns black with glints of thickening frost.

Henry watched the six women shuffle back to the damp sidewalk, talking thoughtfully. A few took each other's arms. They each hugged his mother, whispering something private before leaving. Henry was sure he'd be caught. A few scraggly boxwood hedges weren't much protection and the gasoline fumes were strong. Diane disappeared into her house. So did Lorraine. He'd have to hurry up and finish. His Mom would go berserk if Diane called saying he was missing.

After Sandy Chen's door thudded shut, Henry waited a full ten minutes, which was easier for him than most kids. For some reason his mind went back to the desert, to his grandmother Faye. She probably had a pet rattlesnake or maybe a tarantula. She'd save the skin after the tarantula molted. When he'd visit she'd say, "Don't tell your sister. Look at this." They'd bend over the terrarium in the back of her house, examining the ghostly arachnid husk next to the living black spider.

Although he grew cold, ten minutes sped past. Henry braced himself, lifting the stainless pot with his scrawny arms. Placing it on the hood of his dad's car, he steadied it as he climbed. Widening his stance, he took a moment to enjoy the view from the higher elevation. Through a brief opening in the sky, he identified Venus, something his dad had taught him, years ago.

Warming up, he blew on his hands before slowly, carefully pushing the pot up the windshield, scraping the glass. Although he knew the car was very expensive, the screech of metal on glass didn't bother him. He concentrated on not drenching himself with gas.

Finally, when the pot was on the roof, he scrambled up the windshield. Although the car was slick with frost, Henry wasn't worried. His mind fixed stubbornly on the task at hand. With the pot safely centered on the car roof, he tied a string to the handle, hopped down to the sidewalk, trailing the string in his hand. He stood, carefully surveyed the cul-de-sac. The only illumination came from his house. His mom must be cleaning. He'd better hurry before she called Diane.

One firm jerk of the string and gas spilled over his dad's car. The roof rack stopped the pot from clattering to the ground. Delicately teasing the string brought down the empty pot. Henry sat down on the overturned pot to think.

It wasn't too late to change his mind. The gas had ruined the glossy finish but that was nothing compared to what would happen next. As he ran down the various outcomes, he returned to the same facts: 1) He'd come this far. 2) He was an object in motion. 3) He couldn't stop now unless an unbalanced object interfered.

He was the unbalanced object.

He dug the lighter out of his pocket.

Car.

Girl.

Trouble.

***

For the first time in two days, Meryl entered her own bedroom without reliving That Horrible Night. Shucking her high heels, she quickly undressed, folding herself into her plush robe. The white robe she'd bagged for charity. Or burning.

Before washing her face, she decided to check on Henry, make sure he was home. Carol would have called if he'd asked to spend the night. Sometimes Henry went straight to his room after playing with Max, forgetting to check in. Sure enough, he was tucked into his bed, snoring soundly. Shutting the door as quietly as possible, she walked down the hall toward Nathalie's room. Light spilled out from under the door. Meryl took a deep breath, not up for one more confrontation. Besides, she was still pretty tipsy.

She tapped lightly on the door. "Nat, get some sleep. You've got school tomorrow. 'Night."

There was no reply but it didn't surprise her; Nathalie usually wore ear buds. Meryl stood in the hallway, dizzy from sleep deprivation and the chemicals flooding her system. Tonight she'd lie on her own bed. Even if she couldn't sleep, she'd reclaim her space. As she quickly stripped the bed, trying very hard not to think about Ethan and Leslie, sirens whined in the distance, growing closer.

***

Tucked into bed, Henry heard the fire trucks groaning, heavy with machinery, into the cul-de-sac.

It was unbelievable. He'd set his own dad's car on fire. *What a disaster. This is what Michael McGearty means when he says that kid is going to hell. Hell is lying in bed, thinking about all the bad things I've done and all the bad things that are going to happen. But I'm going to hell. The real one.*

Stiff with anxiety, he denied himself the pleasure of rushing to the window, watching the fire truck spray his dad's car with foam. Henry loved fire trucks with a passion. Someday, if the whole astronaut thing didn't work out, he even wanted to be one. But how could that happen if he set cars on fire? If he became a fireman God would probably crush him with burning scaffolding. That's what Michael McGearty would say.

Michael was Catholic and firmly believed in God's giant hand coming down from the sky and smashing people like bugs if they misbehaved. This didn't feel at all like he thought it would. It felt like knowing he was going to throw up in class.

Jumping out of bed, he sat at his desk, turned on his computer. *I'm not even in my pajamas. What a liar.* Through the window, he watched the lights of the fire and medic trucks flash, bouncing red and blue against his white bedroom walls. He'd never seen such a long hook and ladder in hilly Kirkland. Could it even back its way out of the cul-de-sac? Finally, his computer warmed up.

Henry went to Super Penguin Camp, looking for his friend Fuzzy Boy, from Seattle, WA. He wasn't at the Watering Hole Igloo, the Fishing Spot or the Ice Arena. After ten minutes of searching other igloos, Henry gave up. Next time he spotted Fuzzy Boy, he'd get his e-mail address. It was against the site rules but did it matter now that he'd set a car on fire? A whole lot of things that once seemed important no longer seemed important.

Logging out of Super Penguin Camp, Henry's thoughts turned to his mysterious grandmother. Mom never talked about her childhood, except for one funny story: the neighbor lady who lived in a nearby trailer with eight cats. Sometimes his mom and Aunt Jackie would have dinner there when their mother worked late. Mom, who'd never had a pet, still remembered each cat's name: Penelope, Rose, Angel, Violet, Sky, Peter, Warner and Daddy Warbucks, who ate cantaloupe rinds.

Danetto - that was Grandma Faye's last name. Dan-etto, little Dan. Aunt Jackie said that one time she'd used every finger on her left hand counting her mother's names.

Henry went onto the Dexknows.com, chose the PeopleFinder tab and typed in Faye Danetto, Las Vegas, Nevada. There were three Danettos but only one F. Danetto: 21 El Camino Circle Drive #31, Las Vegas, NV. Phone: (702) 641-8879. Henry reached out, stroking the number on the screen with a finger. Could that really be her? He searched on Google Earth, typed in the address. The perspective flew towards earth like a heat seeking missile. Twenty-one El Camino Circle was a ring of trailers

neatly partitioned by a sagging lattice fence. Number
twenty-one was tiny, ringed in turquoise gravel. Spindly
orange trees grew on either side. A shutter hung perilously
from one window. Clearly this woman was in dire need of a
grandson.

Henry dashed down to the bonus room, grabbed
the phone. A police radio squawked loudly in the street.
Henry carried the phone to the window. His dad talked to a
tall, gangly police officer. Max's dad joined a group of
neighbors in bathrobes huddled near the foam-covered car.
Lorraine was talking to Sandy, who wildly waved her hands.
Carol and her husband watched from their front porch,
hunched deep in their matching parkas.

A wave of terror hit Henry. He needed to talk to
someone. Anyone. His finger touched the phone icon. The
digital tone clicked along, carrying him closer to what-
another mistake? He steeled himself for a man's voice; an
angry man who didn't like late night phone calls, a Frank or
Fernando or Felix.

"Hello?" It was a woman's scratchy voice. She
didn't sound irritated or angry or even all that old. It was,
Henry thought, a good voice for the desert.

Henry's throat constricted. *What am I supposed to do
now? Even if it is Faye my grandma what should I say? Do you own
a pistol? Do you know that the Burrowing Owl lives in other animals'
dens and is only 10 inches high? By the way, I just set my dad's SLS
Mercedes Roadster on fire. He special ordered it from Germany.*

"Hello? Is this Donnie?" The lady inhaled, deeply,
as if smoking. "Honey I'm your sponsor. If you're using
you'd just better out and say it. If the good Lord took out
all the sinners I reckon Vegas would be pretty lonely place."
She waited, tapping what sounded like long fingernails on a
table. "Donnie? Is this - who the hell am I talking to here?"

Henry hung up.

9.

"Marriage: A word which should be pronounced 'mirage'."
- Herbert Spencer

Someone was at the door. Meryl wrapped her bathrobe tightly, preparing for Ethan's anger before she answered. *I don't know and I don't care who set your stupid car on fire.*

Or maybe she should just pretend she didn't see it. That would be a hard sell given the sirens and flashing lights.

Revved up, she threw open the door. It was the same tall, rangy uniformed Kirkland police officer who'd been here two days ago. Officer Richer.

"Sorry to bother you Mrs. Howe. I know you're going through a lot but it seems that your husband's vehicle spontaneously combusted. I glossed over the incident the other night but this one..." He cocked his head, raising an eyebrow.

Meryl's hand went to the neck of her bathrobe. She couldn't see his eyes under his hat but his voice was rather bemused. "Do you really think I set Ethan's car on fire?"

He smiled, which was charming and supremely irritating. "You know, in detective school, they teach us if it looks like a rat and smells like a rat, then it probably is a rat."

"Are you calling me a rat?"

"No ma'am, I'm calling you an arsonist."

"Don't you yes ma'am me. We're the same age."

"It's called being polite."

"You think it's polite knocking on someone's door and accusing them of arson? I call that rude."

This was not the same woman he met the other night. Same face, same body but good lord almighty, when her back was against the wall, this woman fought. "I'm just doing my job."

"So was Hitler."

Sam shook his head. "I don't really get the connection there so I'm just going to ignore it." He stepped back, nodding toward the street. "I just interviewed eight people who told me about the confrontation in front of Ms. Keller's house. In case you've forgotten, in some grim twist of fate, I also saw your little signature on your husband's left arm. So I am here, Ms. Howe, wondering what you're going to say about all this."

Half way through, he took off his hat, tiredly running his hand through his thick reddish hair.

Meryl felt like slamming the door in his face. "My signature? Are you crazy? I might be mad at him and yes, in the heat of the moment, I did throw a bottle but that ridiculously expensive car is half mine. Why would I set it on fire?"

Sam cocked his head. "He's living next door, isn't he?"

Meryl rolled his eyes. "This is insane!"

He cocked his head. "I do have to have a statement here. And the word insane isn't going into the report so come up with something else, alright?"

Meryl looked him directly in the eyes. "Don't boss me around."

He had to laugh. "I'm a police officer."

"Well, bully for you. I bet your mother is so proud."

He put his hands up in defeat. "I'll tell you what. I'm leaving now. If you weren't..." he was going to say, "So pretty," which would have been nearly the stupidest thing he'd ever uttered on duty.

"If I wasn't what?"

He spoke through gritted teeth. "If you weren't obviously under a great deal of stress I'd cite you for impeding an investigation." He turned, talking over his shoulder as he left. "We'll talk later. At the station where it's safe."

She ran outside, tiptoeing gingerly on the bitterly cold pavement. She dashed in front of him, blocking his way.

"I didn't do it. Honestly. That's my statement. I saw the car burning and did not call 9-1-1, which is probably wrong. I should have. But seriously, put yourself in my shoes. The car was a ball of flames."

Sam couldn't help but grin as she danced around in the bathrobe, trying to keep warm. "I didn't hear that last part. You didn't do it. That's what goes in the record. By the way, I left out the part about the seventeen stitches in his arm. You can thank me later."

This time there was no hesitation. "I did do that. And I'm glad."

Sam shook his head. "You're really hell bent on incriminating yourself, aren't you? Why don't we talk about that one tomorrow?" He fished out a card. "That's my number at the precinct. You can come on in or I can come back here."

Meryl felt a sudden urge to explain herself. Before her tired brain had time to catch up, she blurted, "Do you want some coffee?"

Sam eyed her robe, shaking his head. "No, I've got to finish things up outside."

Meryl made a quick calculation about how fast she could get dressed, clean up the living room and make coffee. "I know this all looks really bad but this actually is the best time for me. The kids are asleep. Tomorrow I have to start looking for a job and figure out if I can keep this house." She wrapped the bathrobe even tighter. "I even have a couple of brownies left over."

Sam scratched his neck. "You do realize that it's nearly midnight?"

She hopped from foot to foot to keep warm, her breath fogging. "I do. But my life just got very complicated and I'm trying to keep my head above water." She pulled the robe tighter. "I need a cup of coffee too."

She was appealing, no doubt about it. She had a sort of a steel magnolia kind of thing going on. Keeping his head above water was exactly how it felt after his wife died. But he'd been warned, after the budget cuts hit and he lost his partner to the recession, never to put himself into precarious situations with lonely, vulnerable women. And this one was beautiful. *Oh what the hell. It'll save me a trip tomorrow.*

"Alright, gimme twenty minutes. I might bring someone with me."

"Thank you." Meryl dashed inside.

Sam approached the last two neighbors. They were watching the firemen clean up. As he walked, he came up with five solid reasons why he should get into his car and call it a night. After questioning Diane and Sandy, he could list five more.

***

It was fun. That's what struck Sam about sitting in Meryl's living room, listening to her, eating brownies and forgetting, for a little while, his own problems. She spoke eloquently and with insight, about things she had just realized in the last few days. While she'd been furiously raising money for Children's Hospital, her husband's company was dying. Deals failed, partnerships ended. Nothing he tried worked. Exhausted, he'd stopped talking. She'd quit listening.

Meryl stared at Sam, her pupils glowing black velvet in their green orb. "You don't need to hear this. I'm sorry."

He took another brownie, thinking he should steer this back onto professional ground but he was losing himself in something other than fishing or football. He was enjoying a conversation with an intelligent, attractive woman. This happened – never.

"No, I want to hear it." This conversation was wrong on so many levels but he was tired of being the anchor. Sometimes it felt good just to float.

Now she was talking about her daughter, who was in an expensive private school, Forest Ridge or something. She didn't know how she'd pay tuition.

It was funny. Over twenty years working the night shift the sad stories had never been interesting, not really. It was work. He always kept a close eye on his watch, aware of being back in his car, available for the next call, the next possibility. Sure, he felt compassion and sometimes even moved but it wasn't personal. This living room, with its stone fireplace, white-curtained windows, felt like an island. The flickering fire, the heavy carpeted silence, Meryl balancing a coffee cup on her knee; they could be in a snowstorm, sharing something private.

He didn't want to talk but something in his mind melted, as he ate one brownie after another. Watching his wife die of cancer had left him angry at first but now he saw life differently. He could afford to be philosophical, he was a cop. He wasn't the one in trouble anymore.

"You sound like you almost knew this was coming." His tongue stuck to the roof of his mouth.

"Yes, well, sadly, I come from a long line of divorcees. I just thought," her voice caught, "it wouldn't be me." She didn't mention that the long line of divorces were all one person.

"Maybe it won't." The words came out like peanut butter, extra chunky.

She avoided his eyes. "Do you want some water?"

He laughed although he didn't know why. His mouth was parched, stuck. "Please. Yes. I'm sorry. I sort of drifted off a little bit back there."

She shook her head, giggling. "I know. This is such a pathetic drama. I feel like the oldest, ugliest Kardashian." She returned from the kitchen with two glasses.

He drank the water at once, wondering what to do with the empty glass. This wasn't the kind of place you could just plop your glass anywhere. "What is a Kardashian?"

She laughed. "Never mind."

"Cut yourself some slack. You didn't do anything."

"I threw my husband a hell of a curve." She mimicked throwing the champagne bottle with a hard right. "Who knew Pilates would lead to seventeen stitches?" He thought maybe Pilates had something to do with Kardashians. They both giggled, relaxing into the deep cushions.

"Okay, okay. Too much information. Despite appearances to the contrary, I am on duty." He stood up, straightened his uniform. "I should go." They hadn't discussed the car fire but he was in no shape to talk now.

She handed him another brownie. He swallowed it in two bites, laughing so hard he had to brace himself on a chair.

"You should go!" Her scream was hysterically high. Clapping a hand over her mouth, she whispered. "Shhhhhh. The kids. We'll wake up the kids."

"The kids." He leaned over her, whispering. "Do you know I run an anti-drug program at Juanita High School? It's true. It's very good. I show these horrible after meth pictures. Get it? It's like aftermath but-"

"Got it." Her nod was that of a Bobble Head.

His face grew serious for a moment before another wide smile appeared. "Those poor meth heads. One bad night and poof, there goes your brain." He pointed to his straight white teeth. "You should see what it does your teeth. They turn black." He couldn't stop laughing. "And your skin. Wait, not your skin. Their skin." He tried for a straight face. "This is a serious, tragic subject. I'm sorry. Why am I laughing? Drug addiction is sad." He attempted to arrange his face into something sober but sputtered into gales of laughter.

Meryl laughed until she fell off the couch. They both managed to keep it together until she repeated, "One bad night and poof, there goes your brain!" with wide eyes and a staged, hoarse whisper. "You sound like a bad documentary." She made her voice sound theatrical. "This is your brain. This is your brain on drugs. Remember that? The fried egg?"

They both laughed so hard, leaning on one another, shoulders touching. When the laughter trailed off, they'd wipe their eyes and look at one another, setting off another bout of laughter.

"This is soooo not politically correct!" Meryl wailed.

"I know!" Sam wiped a tear from his eye. "It's terrible! I'm a police officer."

When they both managed to stop, Meryl was holding Sam's arm for support. He looked down, suddenly aware of the pressure. She was staring at him, intently. Her eyes were so pretty.

She removed the arm, picked brownie crumb from her knee. "When did you know that you wanted to be a cop?"

He snorted with laughter. "I was seven. Can you imagine? What kind of kid decides on a career when they still believe in the tooth fairy?"

"Little tiny cops?"

He showed her his size. His pot-addled brain reckoned that he was about two inches. "Tiny ones. Yeah. I got caught shoplifting a candy bar and the Korean guy who owned the store ran outside screaming in Korean and brought back this cop. I can still remember what the guy looked like. Big black guy, Officer Wayne. Officer Wayne said 'son, there's two kinds of people in the world, those that take for themselves and those that give. What kind of man are you gonna be?'"

"That's all it took?"

"No. Get this: someone tried to rob the place. Can you imagine? A thief so dumb he doesn't notice a six foot tall 250 pound uniformed cop?"

"And you saw the whole thing?"

"Like it was in slow motion. It was just like TV. Or at least that's what I told all my friends. Seeing Officer Wayne take down the bad guy with one hand on his gun, cool as an ice cube, saying he'd do what he could for him if he put his gun on the counter by the time he was done counting to three. The guy listened and that was that."

"So you became a cop." Her eyes were glassy.

"So I became a cop."

"That's a good story," she said, barely aware of what she was saying.

"I think so." He leaned into her, mesmerized.

Their heads were a few inches apart. He lowered his head and without thinking, kissed her. She tasted like brownies and wine. He had no idea how long the kiss lasted but something in his brain fought for control. She was kissing him back. He put his arm around her. Somewhere in the back of his brain his training asserted itself. He was at work. She was married. He pulled back, heart thudding.

Sam tried organizing his thoughts but they flitted around like barn swallows. "I'm sorry." He stumbled toward bathroom where he drank several cups of water, washed his face.

After a few minutes, he stepped into the foyers warm yellow light. "I think I'm coming down with something, which would explain-"

Meryl stood alongside a slight teen whose hair glistened with raindrops. The girl wore a fancy jacket and ripped jeans. No piercings or weird jewelry.

"Nathalie this is Office Richer. He's just leaving." Ethan called this her teacher lady voice. "You and I are going upstairs to have a chat. You were grounded and you left without asking young lady."

Nathalie rolled her eyes. "Okay..." She drew out the word with sarcastic flippancy.

The cop, Nathalie noticed, was blinking a lot. Under his hat brim, his eyes were red; he wiped them with the back of his hand. Her mom was going on about her dad's car but Nathalie wasn't paying attention. She moved

slightly to the left, until she could see into the living room.
On the table was a plate with a single remaining brownie. A
green plate. Her face paled, cockiness evaporating.

"Nice to meet you," she muttered to Sam before
bolting up the stairs two at a time.

"Nice kid," Sam lied.

"Thank you." Did she really kiss him? Or was her
unreliable brain telescoping into the future? And Nathalie,
dragging herself in from God knows where with God
knows who. *What a mess.*

Sam fidgeted awkwardly with his radio buttons.
"I'm doing the arson investigation for your, um, your
husband's car, so I guess I'll be around."

She coughed, unsure of what to say. "I hope you
find out who did it."

Cross-legged on her bed, Nathalie sent a text to
Denny: Mom & random cop 8 Berkley Bum Brownies.
Fried. 2 funny. She thought about forwarding it to Zoe
before realizing she was holding Zoe's Iphone. Just for
laughs, she sent it to Zoe's old Disney phone. She knew the
number which was crazy. Three years ago was ancient
history.

10.

The pinging of Zoe's phone woke up Nathalie. Denny's text: Three words: random drug testing. Of cops. DO NOT TELL ANYONE!!!!" Nathalie threw on her sweats, rushed downstairs, out the door, towards Zoe's house. As she pounded on the door, she realized she was overreacting. Zoe wouldn't have checked her old Disney phone any more than she'd be wearing a Miley Cyrus t-shirt. Diane opened the door chewing on a piece of toast.

"Hey Nat, you just missed Zoe. She had a teacher meeting before school."

"Oh." Of course she did. Suck up.

Diane cocked her head, taking in Nathalie's frazzled appearance. "I'm running late. Is everything okay?"

"I've got Zoe's phone."

Diane's car warmed up in the driveway. "Oh, it's fine. We forgot to deactivate that old Disney phone. She took that for today." She held out her hand. "I'll give it to her. Thanks."

Nathalie remained immobile, hair curling from the early morning drizzle.

"Nat, the phone?"

"Oh, right." She quickly deleted Denny's message before handing it to Diane.

She glanced at Nathalie's bare feet. "Are you sure you're okay honey?"

When she opened the front door, Meryl waited: arms crossed, brows furrowed. Nathalie was tempted to march on by but something made her stop. It was the second time in twelve hours she'd been ambushed at the front door. *What happened to the good old days when nobody was ever home?*

Note to self: use the back door.

"I just went to give Zoe her phone."

"Here." Meryl held out Nathalie's I-phone, in its shiny crackled purple and black case.

Was this a trick? Nathalie took the phone as if it were going to explode. "Um, thanks?"

"I expect you to check in with me before and after school. You're grounded until the end of the school year."

Nathalie's face flushed. "Are you serious?"

"Very."

"But Christmas break is coming up. I can't stay home for a month. I'll go insane."

Upstairs, Henry's door opened, followed by the familiar creek of hardwood, the toilet seat being raised. The noise of him peeing assisted by the acoustics of the open, two-storied foyer, left little to the imagination.

Nathalie bellowed, "Hey Niagara Falls; you ever hear of this thing called a door? You shut it when you pee."

Meryl waited for Henry to flush. He didn't. He thudded into his room and slammed the door.

"Oh grow up Nat," she spat out. "I'm not telling Henry but since you think you're an adult, here it is: your dad's company is bankrupt. We're up to our eyeballs in debt. I'll be lucky if we can scrape up the tuition for your senior year at Forest Ridge, let alone stay in this house."

Meryl clamped a hand over her mouth. She'd said too much. Tuition. Bills. Tuition. Her head throbbed.

Nathalie's shook her head, bewildered. "Are you freakin' serious?"

"Don't talk like that." Meryl raked a hand through her tangled hair. "We're not going to lose the house. I'll borrow money…" She'd been on the computer all night, checking their banks accounts, IRA's, money market funds, anything. He'd plundered it all, taking out lines of credit. Had she really signed them all?

"I'll figure it out. Don't worry. But in the meantime I need your help, alright?"

Nathalie set her jaw the same way Ethan did when he knew she'd disagree. "I'll go to Juanita High." *Hello silver lining: I can still see Denny. Public school will be cake compared to Slaves-R-Us.*

"No." Her mother's face was grim. "They owe me for last year's auction and they know it." The Forest Ridge Family Auction had been last year's obsession.

Nathalie pressed her hands together. "Mom, listen: it's perfect. Christmas break is in two weeks. I can transfer then."

Christmas? Two weeks? Ethan's timing was impeccable.

***

"One, two, three and a one two three. No, kick that back foot behind on the beat. It's a cha-cha rhythm, not ballroom dancing. Sexy, sexy. Lower that shoulder. Look straight in the mirror, like this…"

At four o'clock in the afternoon, the desert sun fought a losing battle with the office blinds. The area rug was rolled back, leaving room enough, barely, to dance. Faye's therapist, Lee Ann Varnsley, in t-strap dance shoes, a maroon leotard and dangly silver earrings frowned at Faye, moving with exquisite grace for her age. For any age. It was odd to have a client barking orders but Faye had been right; she'd come to love these lessons.

"Okay, I got it," Lee Ann said.

She waggled her hips, lowering her eyes. The carefree flower child lived again.

Faye clapped her hands excitedly. "Okay, now we're talking. Show me a grapevine with that kind of sass." She spun her index finger. "With a sashay at the end. Ready?"

Lee Ann dropped into her leather office chair, drinking deeply from a water bottle. She wiped her face. "I'm done."

Faye checked her watch. "You have another ten minutes."

Lee Ann shook her head, earrings glinting in her salt and pepper hair. "We're fine. Let's talk about you."

Faye stood, tapping her glittering high heeled sandals. "Uh-uh. You need the full hour of dance lessons, otherwise I feel like I'm ripping you off."

Lee Ann's face split with a grin. "I'm tired. You've more than held up your end of the bargain. Please, sit down. Tell me more about this phone call."

Faye settled on her therapist's couch, taking a pack of cigarettes from her white knit purse. "Okay, if you're sure then." She toyed with a cigarette as she talked. "Whoever it was didn't say 'boo'. They hung up. I hit the star six nine and it's a 425 number. My daughter, Trixie, up in Seattle, I figure. But she doesn't talk to me so I figure she's reaching out and she lost her nerve or something."

So I call my other daughter, you know, the shrink on TV, Jackie. She tells me that Trixie's husband has dumped her and run through all their cash. I figure Trixie is calling because finally, after all these years, she needs her mama. She was always the stubborn one. Even changed her name; I told you that."

Lee Ann nodded, took another sip of water. "Why would she hang up?"

Faye re-crossed her legs. The rhinestones on her sandals reflected tiny glittering spots on the wall. "Probably she's embarrassed. She was always on me about the men: how they cheated, took advantage. Now she's in a bad way herself. I don't know. Just a theory."

"How about this theory: she was testing you to see if you were sober."

Faye blinked furiously, snapping her cigarette in half. "What kind of BS is that? I been clean and sober for five years. You and the good Lord know that."

"But does Trixie know?"

Faye took out a stick of gum, grinding away on it angrily. "How the hell would she find out? We don't talk. She don't call. Nothing. She's got a boy, Henry. He's twelve and I never even laid eyes on him. Saw her little baby girl for a split second. I told you about that. She's a hard one, that girl."

"Have you reached out to her? Made your amends?"

Faye checked her watch. "What a bunch of hog wash," she thought. An iced peach Snapple and a smoke sounded like two kinds of heaven. "You sure you don't want those last ten minutes of dance lesson? This barter stuff's got to be straight up."

Lee Ann measured her words slowly. "Don't avoid the question."

Faye played with her platinum pageboy wig.
"Alright, I did call. When I was working on making amends
I left a message for her. She didn't call me back."

Lee Ann's eyes narrowed. "How long ago?"

"I don't know. Sometime after my ninety days. So
what's that? Four and a half years ago?"

Lee Ann raised her eyebrows. "Over four years
ago?"

"Jackie talks to her. Jackie has told her everything
she needs to know. You ever watch that tape I gave you of
Jackie on TV? She's pretty good, huh?"

"Stop changing the subject."

Faye paced the room, heels clicking. "I'm not
changing the subject. I'm talking about my daughter
hanging up on me and suddenly we're back five whole years
and what do you know? It's still my fault. I don't buy it. I'm
five years sober. I have Jesus in my life. I am one helluva
happy woman."

Lee Ann leaned back, keeping it slow. Dust motes
floated in the murky air. "Are you?"

Faye leaned over the couch, hoisting her purse like
a weapon. "What did I just say? I'm sick of your question
this, question that. Is that what I get for a one hour dance
lesson: a bunch of lousy questions? How come you never
get right out and say what you're thinking? Go on, I'm a big
girl; I can take it!"

Lee Ann's eyes softened. "Faye, I want you to
realize your own truths."

"So my kid hangs up on me. Where's the truth in
that?"

"What do you think?"

"I think I'm tired. I'm tired of coming in here and
wasting my time and having you ask me a bunch of
questions."

Lee Anne was unflappable. "What do you think about your older daughter?"

"Another question. I'm gonna die right here, which is good timing 'cause I wanna be buried in these shoes." She held out a manicured foot. "They're cute, huh?"

Lee Ann stood up suddenly, talking very quickly. "It's night. Trixie calls. She's going to hang up. What do you say?"

Faye clenched her fists. "I'm sorry."

Lee Ann sat down. Faye froze, eyeing herself in the mirror. The office clock ticked. A car drove by. Lee Ann watched Faye's reflection, hoping she'd speak first. Faye stood up abruptly, slung her purse over her shoulder and left, slamming the door, which was light and very unsatisfying from Faye's perspective. Lee Ann parted the blinds in time to see Faye shakily light a cigarette. She exhaled a white plume into the purple desert sky.

"Therapy can kiss my ass," Faye said to herself.

11.

*"If you made a list of reasons why any couple got
married and another list of the reasons for their
divorce, you'd have a hell of a lot of overlapping."*
-Mignon McLaughlin

The holiday decorations at the Kirkland police
headquarters were one of the most depressing aspects of
the season. A bedraggled silver tree and an angry looking
reindeer greeted Sam when he entered, followed by the
office manager's Christmas sweater. Where did she even
find those things? Was there a Super Ugly Sweater Store?
Normally Sam didn't pay much attention to clothes but
when they stood up and hit you in the face it was hard to
ignore.

Grabbing his mail from the wall of cubbies, he
wound his way through the cluster of desks and found his
own.

"Don't forget to vote on the holiday party!" Monica
called out as he poured coffee. As office manager it was her
duty to remind them of any number of things they didn't
give a shit about.

"You bet." He hid behind the half wall bordering
his desk.

"Hey Sam, glad I caught you." Manfred Wilson
poked his head over the top of a file cabinet. Manfred was
from Redmond Precinct, in charge of internal
investigations.

"Hey there Man. What's up?" Sam winced. He should vote for an upgrade in coffee instead of a Christmas party.

Man waved a little plastic bottle in front of him. "Pee time."

Sam laughed, shaking his head. "You got a sick fetish there dude."

Man smiled. "That I do. But this ain't it. Keep guessing my friend."

Sam took another sip of his coffee before standing, taking the bottle. "You're in luck. I'm on my second cup of coffee."

Man followed him down the hall toward the bathroom. "You older dudes are easy. After 30 ya'll leak like a sinking ship."

Sam offered him the middle finger before disappearing into the bathroom. When he opened the door, he handed Man a bottle of urine. "Merry Christmas!"

Man rolled his eyes, taking the bottle. "Mazeltov!"

***

Sister Mary Louise's office was suitably dark and austere, smelling of furniture polish and a musty funk coming from the worn Persian carpet. Through the large windows a foggy dusk descended on the twinkling lights of Bellevue. Beyond that was Microsoft, churning out the salaries that paid the hefty tuition bills. Meryl, in a chair facing the nun's desk, had finished recounting all her hard work as a Forest Ridge fundraiser. Sitting before the principal, Meryl had a momentary sense of solidarity with Nathalie, which soon evaporated.

Sister Mary Louise, who'd been gazing thoughtfully out the window for the last few moments, turned to face Meryl. "Mrs. Howe-"

"Please, call me Meryl." As long as she knew that Meryl was a Howe. As in, the Howe's who donated heavily to Catholic charities.

"Thank you. Yes, Meryl, do you think Nathalie is happy here?"

The question threw Meryl. She was a teenager. Of course she wasn't happy. "I do." When the sister didn't react, she added, "Of course. She loves Forest Ridge."

Sister Mary Louise lifted a sheaf of papers. "Her grades have dropped dramatically. She doesn't participate in class. Last semester she missed eighteen days of school."

Eighteen days? Doing what? Meryl scrambled for an angle and found one: last year Nathalie helped the volleyball team get to state. She was the star. "She loves volleyball."

The nun let a little time elapse before stating flatly, "She quit at the beginning of the season."

A small gasp escaped Meryl. "Quit?"

"She hasn't suited up in months."

Meryl's pulse quickened. What had Nathalie been doing instead of practice?

"To be honest Mrs. Howe, I'm sorry, Meryl, we have a waiting list of thirty-eight girls with 4.0 transcripts, some of them scholarship students who are just dying to get into Forest Ridge. It might be an adjustment but maybe a public school would be a refreshing change of pace. To be quite blunt Meryl, Nathalie grades disqualify her for a scholarship. Although her grandfather donates very generously, she's not doing well."

A refreshing change of pace? "Can I please see her transcript?"

The nun handed over her daughter's grades. Meryl inhaled deeply before looking down. She could not believe her eyes.

***

"Is this Mrs. Howe?"

She'd been sitting in her car in the Forest Ridge parking lot, trying to stop panicking before she drove. Dusk was falling and the traffic would be horrendous. Already she could see the red taillights on 405, like a string of fireworks.

"Yes, who is this?"

"I'm calling from American National Incorporated to discuss a payment plan for your Visa bill Ms. Howe." He sounded young, energetic, the antithesis of how she felt.

Her heart thudded to her feet. "I paid the Visa bill last month."

"Your husband took a secondary line of credit out last year. When can I expect your first payment of $2,300 on that debt before we take further steps?"

Meryl's throat went bone dry. "What further steps?"

"Trust me Mrs. Howe; you do not want to go there."

She stared at the phone for a moment. What should she say?

"Mrs. Howe, are you there? Mrs. Howe?"

"Who is this?" she asked in a friendly manner, as if fundraising. "Your name?"

"I, uh, well, Derrick ma'am."

"Derrick what?"

"Derrick Smith."

"Sure it's Smith. Listen Derrick, the truth is, I don't have any money. None. So can you work with me?"

Derrick didn't miss a beat. "If we don't receive $2,300 by December 14th, we're going to sue you for money owed. We'll probably put a lien on your house and foreclose."

"Are you serious?"

"Yes ma'am. Have a nice day." He hung up.

12.

"The majority of husbands remind me of an orangutan trying to play the violin."
—Honor de Balzac

Leaving Las Vegas had been depressingly easy. As she crossed the pea green Columbia River at Kennewick/Pasco, Faye saw how her life had narrowed: six boxes and one cat, farmed out to a neighbor. She lit a cigarette to celebrate entering Washington State. Opening the window, she took in the flat grey terrain, punctuated by silos and towering cottonwood trees. Damp air filled the car, smelling of river, minerals and dirt.

If AA had taught her anything, it was to enjoy the moment. Nobody but God knew when the proverbial shit was going to hit the proverbial fan.

Jackie had tried to talk her out of this trip. "It's terrible timing."

"I think it'd be a fun surprise."

"Mom, you two haven't talked in sixteen years. You don't just show up on someone's doorstep after that."

"It's a spontaneous gesture." Even Cosmopolitan Magazine said impromptu trips were a good idea. But there was no use telling Jackie.

"You should warn her."

"You make me sound like a hurricane. I can visit my own daughter, can't I?"

Jackie sighed. If her mother argued this long, she'd lost. "At least call her first. Please? Mom?"

Faye took her time, chewing on a nail. "What if she tells me not to come?"

"Seriously? Do you really need me to answer that question?"

"Promise me you won't tell her."

"Mom, I can't do that. It's dishonest."

"It ain't dishonest if you don't tell her."

Jackie could hear her mother snort. "It's lying by omission."

Lying by omission? What kind of jumped up hogwash was that? If she hadn't let certain things gone unsaid she would have chased off more men than Elizabeth Taylor had husbands. Nobody wants the whole truth all the time except judges and nobody gave them that. "Don't tell her."

"I'm not promising anything."

Faye chuckled. "Why thank you Miss Smartykins."

As she reached the I-5 Interchange heading north, Faye wondered if maybe Jackie was right.

And then there was the dream.

The first dream was six months ago. Jesus appeared at a convenience store where she was buying Snapple and a pack of smokes. Jesus wasn't dressed in a familiar way. Not hardly. Far from the tortured man on the cross, he was a God in a John Deere trucker's cap, threadbare Levis and a form-fitting white t-shirt. He had a nice set of pecs under his t and filled out his Levis as well as any headlining country singer.

Faye felt strange, being attracted to Jesus. You weren't supposed to lust after the son of God. Even in her dreams she knew this.

It was Jesus who struck up the conversation. He was partial to raspberry Snapple. She showed him the little fun facts on the inside of the lid. He thought that was cool. He liked trivia and used the knowledge when playing board games. Faye was impressed that Jesus knew slang. But of course he had to reach modern worshippers so he would have picked up on such things in the last two thousand or so years.

There was an awkward silence while Jesus stared at her. Faye felt the sweat rolling between her breasts, self conscious that she was showing off a lot of cleavage. But then again, she never thought she'd run into Jesus. He was gazing at her with those warm brown, very kind eyes. Normally when a man looked at her for this long, Faye squirmed and flirted. But his eyes bathed her in warmth and security. Being looked upon by the son of God with such kindness made her want to stand in the refrigerated aisle for eternity.

After a while she couldn't let Jesus rest without conversing, although the man did seem perfectly comfortable with silence.

"You're shorter in person," she said, immediately embarrassed by a comment more appropriate for Tom Cruise. "But you're not short. That's not what I meant."

Jesus laughed, lifting a hand. It made him look like an image in the bible, which was comforting. "It's okay. There are a lot of large statues of me. Don't worry. It takes a lot to offend me."

"So you are…"

He nodded. "The son of God? Yes."

"What are you doing here?"

"I wanted to ask you the same question, Faye."

She loved the way he said her name. With love. She raised her drink. "Getting my Snapple. I like a Snapple and a smoke this time of day. It's kind of my thing."

"Think about the dropping the smoke part."

Now Jesus was telling her not to smoke. That was a hard sell. "Yeah, I know. It's just that I quit drinking and it's sort of my crutch, you know?"

"I'm very glad you quit drinking. I didn't ask what you were doing in this store, I meant, what are you doing in this city?"

Faye was puzzled. "I live here."

"Your family is in Seattle." His way of talking made everything sound like a revelation. There was great significance to her family's location. Now she knew. For months it had been a tick she couldn't locate under her skin.

Still, she wasn't getting it.

"And Tennessee but they're all a bunch of drunks down there. I left home when I was a kid. There wasn't nothing there for me but heartache."

"I know why you left home."

Tears sprang to Faye's eyes. She brushed them away before they ruined her careful make-up. "It hasn't been a day at the park, has it?"

Jesus nodded and drank his Snapple. Faye wondered if he was going to pay for it himself. Lord she'd love to buy Jesus a Snapple. That would be one of the highlights of her life. "And what about your children?"

Things got a little trickier when it came to her girls. She bragged about Jackie a little before telling him about Trixie's marriage. She said she felt bad for her because she knew how hard it was to have a cheating man. She'd like to help but things weren't too good mother-daughter wise. In fact, they were awful. No contact at all. Not even a lousy Christmas card. His face grew cloudy. For the first time he looked away, staring into the parking lot, shimmering in the heat.

When she was done, he said, "You miss her." It wasn't a question, just a fact. "And you miss her children."

"I don't know them."

"And you accept that?"

She shook her head. Both Jesus and her therapist had a whole lot of questions. "It's not up to me. They're her kids."

The Pakistani clerk appeared in their aisle. "This isn't a meeting hall you know." To Jesus he said, "You have to pay for that."

Jesus smiled and nodded. "We're done here sir. Thank you for the use of your store. We do appreciate it."

The clerk trudged off to the register, muttering in Urdu.

"He doesn't know that you're the son of God, does he?"

Jesus shook his head. "It doesn't matter."

"Jesus is right here in his store and he don't even know it. Oh I bet he'd just die if he knew."

Jesus winked. "That's not how he dies." He looked outside again. "Well, I have to go. Think about what I said."

"I will. I will. Thank you. Listen, I'd like to buy your Snapple for you."

Jesus nodded in the direction of the register. The clerk had the till open. "I bought yours. My treat."

"But I didn't see you pay. You've been right here."

Jesus winked again. "The Lord works in mysterious ways."

With that he strode out into the parking lot, climbed into a battered old truck and drove away. Faye noted it was American made, which made her feel good.

Jesus appeared in her dreams several more times, always as she was running errands. He always had the same message: mend those fences. Put your prayer to action. It felt like a highly evolved AA meeting without all the tears and smoking.

When she awoke, she felt secure and happy until she remembered that she hadn't done what Jesus asked. The warm glow of his love evaporated into the funky air of her claustrophobic bedroom. She'd light a cigarette, think about the past. Trixie was a tough nut, that kid. When she'd finally left for college, Faye had been relieved. Being found wanting 24/7 was exhausting.

This request, straight from the lips of Christ was in many ways harder than quitting drinking. As a drunk, she'd been crawling down the road of life, beaten and empty. On April 16th, 2008, which she did not remember, she hit a family of tourists from Germany in their rental car. If the two little girls in the backseat hadn't been wearing seatbelts, they would have died. The parents didn't sue. Deeply shaken, they left Vegas as soon as their daughter was discharged from the hospital. The judge made a deal with Faye: rehab or jail.

It was a crossroads. To the right: GET SOBER. Go left: DIE IN A POOL OF VOMIT. Four years later, her life was calm, stable. Sometimes it felt as though something were missing, a deeper connection but whenever she felt the urge to have a drink all she had to do was recall the morning she woke up beside a corpse. Later she learned that he'd died of a heart attack. She didn't know where she'd met him or who he was. Those were the kind of situations alcoholism brought into her life.

Now her life was a placid, if somewhat shallow pond. She had God, a steady income and a cat. Why push things?

When she told Lee Ann about the dreams, Lee Ann said Jesus was her subconscious. Lee Ann's theory was that the older she got, the more Faye needed her children. Faye rolled her eyes and accused Lee Ann of being an atheist.

"I'm not saying Jesus didn't appear to you in a dream. I'm saying his voice comes from inside you."

"You are making this so complicated. If the man can walk on water and multiply fish why can't he show up in my dream?" Faye argued.

"You're missing my point."

The dreams kept coming.

And yet, she waited.

***

Nathalie knew something was up the moment she entered the kitchen. Her mom slumped at the table, hair held back with one of Nathalie's old junk drawer clips. A glass of amber liquid rested at her elbow. Whiskey?

"Welcome home. You must be terribly tired after a long day of maintaining your 1.3 grade average and skipping volleyball. Tell me, how do you manage to do it all Nathalie?" Her mom slammed her hand down on a piece of paper. "I visited Sister Mary Louise today." She took a sip of her drink. "She's a bitch." She laid her head down. "Sorry. Wait, no I'm not."

"Are you drinking?"

"Yes, I am. Turns out my mother was right. When the going gets tough, the tough get drinking. What have you been doing from 3:30 until 6:00 instead of volleyball? Who is giving you a ride home?"

"I've been hanging out with friends."

"What friends?"

"New ones."

"I see. Sister Mary Louise told me that if your grades were better, there might have been a chance that you could stay at Forest Ridge."

"I don't want to stay there."

"Obviously. Apparently one of the best high schools in the state isn't good enough for you."

"It isn't that." The walls of the kitchen seemed to be closing down on her. She hated seeing her mother like this. It made her want to run.

"Then what it is?" Meryl didn't wait for a response. "I am going to ask your grandparents for the tuition. You would think since Ethan Senior paid for half the gym, they'd let this one slide but oh no, Sister Mary Brass Balls goes by the book. And the book says you're out."

"Good. Yeah for me!" Nathalie turned to leave but Meryl wasn't done.

"You're still enrolled for one month and you are going. Start showing them you belong and I will find the money even if it kills me."

"I don't belong. I hate the nuns and uniforms and the fact that there are only girls there. Life isn't on a hill with a bunch of Catholic girls and Bill frickin' Gates' daughter."

"Oh I see. It's at some public school where they have metal detectors in the hallways and drug dealers in the parking lot?"

"This isn't about me. You love Forest Ridge. You like telling your snobby Guild friends that I go there. That I was captain of the volleyball team, although you never bothered to come to one game, did you?"

Meryl took another sip of whiskey, blinking hard, as if slapped. "You know that chairmanship is full time job."

"How many Mom?"

"You've made your point. I was preoccupied; raising money for very sick kids without insurance. But last year-"

Nathalie's hand formed a circle. "Not one. Last year you did the auction. You were at the school doing place cards during the semi-finals, trying to decide who would be close to the Gates' table. And I realized: who am I doing this for? Who wanted this school anyway?"

"I wanted it for you."

"Oh my God, listen to yourself. Newsflash Mom: I'm not you. I don't base my entire life on going to the right school. I'm going to Juanita High where I can just be normal. Average. I know you hate that word but I don't mind it." She thumped her chest. "I'm average."

Meryl finished her whiskey. "I don't agree."

Nathalie was half way up the stairs before turning back and yelling: "Dad came to six games this year. I counted."

***

"Senior's not here," Betsy, her mother-in-law, said coldly. She must be thrilled, Meryl thought. She'd finally been proven right; her son's marriage was a tragedy.

Meryl didn't budge.

Betsy toyed with her pearls. Meryl had never seen her mother-in-law in jeans. She wore full battle regalia to the grocery store: St. John's suit, good jewelry, Chanel purse. Her nightgown was probably made of tweed. "Anyway, we're going to dinner."

"It's five o'clock."

"I'm getting ready," Betsy snapped.

"I need to talk to you and Senior."

"I said: He's. Not. Here." Jackie's first impression of Betsy had been a pit bull in pearls. At this moment, Meryl agreed.

"My car's in the driveway Bets. The girl has eyes." Senior appeared, looking floridly prosperous in pressed khakis, pale yellow shirt and deck shoes. He always looked as if he'd just stepped off his yacht.

"Come on in Meryl, although I don't know what we can do. Ethan's not here, if that's what you're after."

"He's not what I'm after," Meryl said acerbically.

Betsy shot her husband an irritated look as she pulled open the door. "We're going to be late," she snapped, marching into the hallway. Meryl stepped into the slate entry. It was the first time she'd ever been there alone. It was as elegantly appointed and polished as a five star hotel, with flower arrangements delivered weekly.

The house opened to the west with an emerald green lawn. It rolled gently down to the choppy grey waters of Lake Washington and the dock. Across the water was Laurelhurst, dotted with waterfront estates, their docks poking into the water. If things had gone well, Meryl would have moved into a similarly grand spread. If things had gone well Ethan would have brought home take-out instead of Leslie.

Stop it, she thought. Feeling sorry for herself would only make things worse.

"Have a seat," said Senior, his normally placid face grave. He opened a silver filigree box, removing a cigar. Betsy frowned pointedly. He let the lid slam to show his displeasure.

Betsy smoothed her tweed skirt as she sat. "Meryl, I think you're being very hard on Ethan."

"I came home to another woman in my bed, Betsy." No sense in beating around the bush.

Senior took a deep breath. He opened the cigar box again, seemed to remember his wife was in the room and slammed it shut. "Our son is devastated."

"He should be." Meryl couldn't help it.

"When a man strays-" Betsy said.

"Betsy!" Senior barked.

"Well, I don't want to be the one to cast stones," Betsy said. "However, you were very wrapped up in the auction. I told you that it would be too much."

"I see. Because I spent too much time out of the house, Ethan ruined us financially and cheated on me." Meryl's voice shook. "Uh-huh. Might I remind you that your son is shacked up with the next door neighbor?"

"Maybe he needed a sympathetic ear," Betsy said.

"He used more than her ear!" Meryl shot back.

Betsy's face went grey. "There is no need to be vulgar."

"Drop the good breeding thing Betsy. I've seen you gossiping with your friends at the club. This is a vulgar situation and your son has put me in it."

Betsy lowered her head, shaking as if ready to charge. "Ethan, are you going to just sit there and let her talk to me like this in my own home?"

Senior glared at his wife. She'd never liked her daughter-in-law but this was ridiculous. "Ladies! Please! This isn't getting us anywhere."

Betsy seemed to hold back whatever barb she was ready to launch. Meryl desperately wished she'd approached Senior by himself. He was old school, which helped, if you wore a skirt.

"Let's cut to the chase," Senior said. He found Betsy's dislike of Meryl baffling but years of marriage had taught him that nothing would change. It was best to treat this like a business meeting and move on. Besides, he needed a stiff drink.

"You want money. Is that it?" Senior asked, relaxing visibly. Money was a language that Senior spoke fluently. They'd settle the terms and part ways. He'd enjoy his single malt scotch and dinner all the more. And Betsy would have plenty to talk about.

Meryl's voice quivered. "I sat outside your house for an hour working up the nerve to knock. If I had known I'd need money, I would have kept up with my teaching credentials."

"As if a school teacher's salary would solve anything," Betsy sniffed.

"Let her talk Betsy," Senior snapped.

After explaining her finances and how Jackie could help on a limited basis, Meryl worked up the nerve to meet Senior's stern gaze. "I'd like enough to get by on until I can figure out what I'm going to do." She wiped her damp hands on her skirt, turning to Betsy. "I'll pay you back as soon as I possibly can."

Betsy jumped in before Senior opened his mouth. "What my son did wasn't very..." she searched for a suitable word, "...pleasant but as you may or may not know we also suffered our own, not insignificant loss when Inspire became Expire. I'm sure, as family, you can understand that we simply cannot be put into the middle of this."

Meryl's mouth dropped open. This was the last thing she'd expected. "How would helping us out financially put you in the middle? We might lose our house. We're so far behind in our tuition payments, Nathalie will have to leave Forest Ridge." She kept her face expressionless, as if any rippled would reveal Nathalie's real problems.

"If you can't see why then there isn't any point in discussing this further. The answer is no." Betsy stood up, fingers at her pearls. "Now if you'll excuse me, I have to get dressed for dinner. We're meeting the Marchands at Sea Star. Love to the children."

Love to the children? But let them lose their home? No wonder Ethan was so screwed up. This woman could refuse them help and go enjoy a $200 dinner.

Sunk deep in his chair, Ethan Sr. watched his wife clatter into the hallway darkness. He'd always liked that she stood on principal but right now it made his jaw ache. Betsy turned to remind him that they didn't have much time to change and get to Bellevue. The Marchands were always late. They didn't want to lose their reservations, did they? He didn't answer. After a moment, he rose, went to a large antique desk in the corner. Sitting down, he removed a large leather-covered ledger filled with checks.

He sighed unhappily. "I don't really want to do this but for the children, I will."

Meryl was light-headed with relief. He was going against the old dragon's wishes. Thing were going to work out all right.

"Thank you," she said gratefully, padding over to the desk across the thick Persian rug. She crossed her fingers, silently praying that Betsy wouldn't return and ruin everything.

"If you can find it in your heart to forgive Ethan," he looked up at her, pen poised over a check. "I'm prepared to be very generous. Enough to give you two a fresh start. You can get caught up with the house payments and keep Nathalie in Forest Ridge."

Meryl's heart plummeted. "But-"

Senior held up his hand. "I know. I know. He was wrong. But sometimes, in marriages that last, you have to forgive." He looked down the hallway toward his bedroom wing. "You'd be surprised how many long standing marriages have recovered from infidelities."

She was trembling and looked out the window, hoping to keep her composure. "You want me to forgive him, for money?"

Ethan shook his head. "You can look at this any way you want."

When she didn't respond, he closed the check book, slid it back into his desk, signaling that the meeting was over. He stood up. "Alright, you think about it. Call me later. Do me a favor and don't tell Betsy about this hmmmm? She's still upset about the money we lost investing in Ethan's company. She's peculiar that way. Nobody holds onto a nickel tighter."

"You're bribing me." Senior walked towards the front door. She trailed behind, stunned. He had allowed her to feel hope and then calculatingly crushed it.

"No. Merely offering an incentive. There's a difference, you know." He opened the door, pleased with himself. Business and family really were one and the same.

Meryl stood at the front door, trying very hard not to cry. "Is there?"

13.

"Marriage is a feast where the grace is sometimes better than the dinner."
-Charles Caleb Colton

"What the hell are you doing?" Ethan looked up from the front walkway. Meryl was on the balcony, poised like a baseball player with a fat Dan Brown paperback in one hand. In the other was his Itty Bitty night light. On the ground like some yard sale gone awry, were his scattered belongings.

Collapsed on the bed after the disastrous meeting with his parents, Ethan's favorite coffee mug caught her eye. It was from their trip to Nantucket, from the Black Dog. They'd eaten fried clams and drank wine out of paper cups, plunging half-drunk into the ocean at sunset. After showering they'd shared a burger and fried oysters at the Black Dog, their skin warm from the sun. She'd thrown the mug, watching it shatter with great, immediate satisfaction. She kept going. After forty sweaty minutes she'd emptied most of the contents of his walk-in closet.

She threw a Timberland boot at his head. "Cleaning house!"

He dodged the boot, started picking up his clothes. "Come on Meryl. I can't afford to replace this stuff. Be reasonable."

"I am done being reasonable. Look what reasonable got me. You!"

"Will you at least let me bag up the rest of it?" he pleaded, craning his neck.

She disappeared for another armload, reappearing with his jackets. "Sure! Here you go!" The jackets: woolen, microfiber and leather, flew downward, like vultures, landing on the dormant willow hedge. They drooped under the load. It was cathartic. Maybe if she could unload his stuff, she could unload him from the topography of her life.

He raked his hand through his hair, knowing he deserved this but still- "Do you really have to do this in front of the entire neighborhood honey?"

She found herself screaming. "Don't you call me honey! There is a lien on our house! Our home Ethan! I went to your parents to ask them for money and do know what they said? They said I should take you back."

Ethan's face grew stony with anger. "Don't listen to them. They're not going to help us."

"There is no us." She enunciated the word viciously.

"I love you Meryl." With Meryl up there on the balcony he felt like some kind of screwed up middle-aged Romeo. This wasn't a mid-life crisis, this was a mid-life Tsunami.

She bent down and grabbed a running shoe that had slipped out. She lobbed it at his head. "You've got a hell of way of showing it!"

She missed.

She'd ended up helping him carry most of the clothes over to Leslie's yard, dumping them where the kids couldn't see them when they got home. He'd complained about the dry cleaning bill but even she had to agree that he needed those clothes to find a new job. So she'd helped him pick up the clothes.

"Thank you Meryl, I appreciate it," Ethan said, wishing they weren't walking to Leslie's house.

"I'm not helping you. I just don't want the kids to see this," she'd said after they'd carried the last load.

"Have you read any of my e-mails?"

"Piss off," she said, before running back to her house.

***

Two days later, when Nathalie walked in the door from school, Meryl was waiting, purse in hand. "Come on, we're enrolling you in that lousy school down the street."

"Your optimism is overwhelming," said Nathalie but she got in the car.

The assistant principal was friendly and welcoming but did little to cheer Meryl. She had a habit of dropping her pen repeatedly, giving Meryl and Nathalie a view of her plump rear, threatening to burst free of her pinkish brown pencil skirt, which brought to mind a Bavarian sausage with legs. If Forest Ridge reeked of money and privilege, Juanita High School stunk of mediocrity.

The carpet was mildewed and worn, the institutional green paint chipped. The teachers, Meryl surmised, would not be the indefatigable selfless movie archetype but the real life defeated and burnt out variety. Like middle-aged public defenders but paid less.

On one of the lockers someone had spray-painted, "Scool sucks." Meryl had an urge to scribble in the "h."

As Meryl grew brittle with defeat, Nathalie relaxed. A few of the kids milling in the hallway said "hey." Girls in heavy black eye liner and piercings nodded. Boys with thatches of inky black hair, tattoos snaking along their arms, followed her with heavy-lidded eyes. When Meryl asked how she knew them, Nathalie vaguely muttered, "from around."

It made Meryl's skin crawl. Where was "around?" Had Nathalie been hanging around these creatures when she was supposed to be at volleyball? More to the point, what had they been doing?

The low point, for Meryl, was filling out the paperwork in the principal's musty grey office. There were separate spaces for parents' addresses on the forms. She paused; pen poised over the clipboard, thinking that this was a small matter but somehow would sum up, officially, her position. New school, new beginning, as she'd preached to Nathalie in the car.

"This is a chance to reinvent yourself."

Nathalie had given her a dark look from under her bangs and said, "I'm happy with the way I am."

It made absolutely no sense to her mother.

Meryl clicked the pen against her teeth before filling in Ethan's address as Leslie's. The final adolescent flourish was listing the other adult in the household as Leslie Megaslut.

It was cold in the parking lot, a hint of frost in the air. Sam lugged his gym bag to his car, wondering if he had time to run to Starbucks before his class. He'd managed to squeeze in a quick workout in the pool but forgot his lunch again. He threw his bag in the backseat of his unmarked car. He saw Meryl. She was with her daughter.

He watched Meryl for a moment, willing himself to get into the car but he couldn't stop. He knew he should keep things on a more formal basis, in uniform, investigating the arson of her husband's car even though he knew damn well who did it. But he didn't get into the car.

He kept his car door open, propping his foot against the rear foot well, enjoying the sight of Meryl walking.

She was dressed in a long black trench coat, belted at the waist. Her hair fell just to the hood, curling up at the ends. The last time he saw her, it had been tied up in a pony tail. Sam kicked himself for noticing. He was chasing trouble instead of getting lunch.

She saw him and waved. "Hey!"

Her face brightened and he felt two feet taller.

"It's a little cold for short sleeves, isn't it?" she asked. After he swam, he always wore a t-shirt, donning his leather jacket before heading into class. There was some disagreement among his fellow educators about wearing the uniform. Sam felt it added a layer of distance. Besides, Sam now spent half his work life out of uniform, investigating. He knew people would tell him things they wouldn't dare say to a uniformed officer. It didn't make sense but then again Sam had found out that much of the time people weren't logical. Witness: himself, swooning like a teenager over a married woman.

Sam nodded toward the high school pool. "I just swam. I try to work out here before my class.

"You teach here?"

"Horrible pictures of drug addicts?" He raised his eyebrows. "Ring a bell?"

"Oh." Meryl blushed. "Nathalie, you remember Officer Richer?" Nathalie nodded, forcing herself to smile. Her mouth had gone dry. She couldn't look at him. "We just registered her for school."

Sam nodded. "Great, maybe you'll be in my class. It's a real eye opener."

Nathalie wished for a sink hole. Girl vanishes in parking lot, story at eleven. He knew. He could tell that she'd started smoking pot with Denny, in parks, cars, basements, instead of playing volleyball. That she was planning on helping Denny sell drugs at Juanita because she'd be Bonnie to his Clyde. Not to mention that it would be the ultimate FU to her mother. She could do anything under her mother's nose but Officer Sam, he knew something was up. Why else would he mention his stupid drug ed. class?

She calmed herself by thinking of Denny. He dealt with situations like this all the time, worse than this. She was paranoid. How could he possibly know? Keep quiet, Denny had warned her. "Don't say a thing. He's a cop. He'll never figure it out."

After the longest, most curious look she'd ever gotten in her whole life, Sam spoke. "Nathalie, do you think you could give your mom and me a moment to talk?"

"Sure." Relieved, Nathalie grabbed the keys out of her mother's hand. Before Meryl could say a word, Nathalie sprinted to the Volvo, jumped in and slammed the door.

"You got me high Meryl."

Nathalie sunk down in the Volvo's leather seat. Slipping the key into the ignition, turning it a quarter rotation, she rolled the window down a crack, eavesdropping.

"What on earth are you talking about?" Meryl asked.

"I came up positive for marijuana on a drug test at work. Those brownies you gave me?"

Meryl held up her hand. "Sam, slow down. Are you saying those brownies had pot in them?"

Sam nodded vigorously. "Yes. Absolutely.

"How do you know?"

"Process of elimination. The only food I had that night was at your place and the only water I drank came from the precinct cooler, which I'm pretty sure isn't drugged."

"I have never done any kind of drug in my life. And I certainly wouldn't serve food laced with drugs. My God, what kind of person do you think I am?" She remembered the time her mom's friend had gotten her high but decided to skip that story.

Sam rolled his eyes. "You beat up your husband and set his car on fire, why not throw drugging an officer into the mix?"

Meryl glanced over at her car. Nathalie could hear everything. Grabbing Sam by the arm, she dragged him behind a large truck. She squared her shoulders, stabbing his chest repeatedly with her index finger. "I did not set his car on fire and you know it. I don't know who you were getting high with but it certainly wasn't me."

"There was pot in the brownies."

"Prove it!" Meryl snapped. "Prove it. I didn't set his car on fire and I didn't drug you. I didn't even make the brownies."

"Then who did?"

"I don't know who brought the stupid brownies. Someone in book club."

"Alright then, who in book club smokes pot?" He tried to keep his voice impassive, like he normally did but this was different. This was his career.

A teenager walked past on his way to his car. He glanced at Office Richer, giving him a wave. Sam nodded, waited for the kid to get into his car and drive off.

Meryl and Sam stood silently, waiting for the kid to leave, staring into each other's eyes. Meryl smelled the chlorine on his skin, still flushed from the exercise. Sam studied the grey flecks in her green eyes thinking he should run like hell; get someone else to investigate the arson.

When the kid drove off, Meryl finally spoke. "I don't know who smokes pot. I never asked. It's book club not bong club."

Sam smiled in spite of himself. He checked his watch. His class started in ten minutes. "So, you didn't make them?"

Meryl snorted. "No. Of course not."

Sam felt relieved and stupid. "I'm sorry."

"You should be. And I didn't set Ethan's car on fire."

Sam checked his watch again. This wasn't going the way he planned. She should be the one apologizing. "Look, I've got a class to teach."

"So go teach it."

"I will. And tell your book club that whoever made those brownies better contact me."

She shook her head. "You want me to rat on my friends?"

"No, I want you to tell them that a cop ended up eating their handiwork and they should contact me."

Meryl shook her head. "That's going to be a fun conversation. One of the women in book club is an attorney."

"Good, then whoever it is will have representation. This is my career Meryl. I didn't spend twenty odd years on the force to go down as the guy who got stoned on the job." He turned on his heels, marching toward the squat, ugly main entrance.

He made it a few steps before pausing, crossing his arms and breathing deeply, trying to think. She watched him. He turned, walking swiftly toward her until his face was inches from hers. The wind blew her hair in her eyes. His hand itched to move it, to feel the softness of her hair.

If he could have anything on earth at that moment, it would be to close his eyes and bury his face in her hair. He leaned in until their noses nearly touched. "I have never in my life dated a married woman and I sure as hell am not going to start now."

Her eyes flashed. "Especially not some doped up pyromaniac who cuts up her husband, right?"

He drew a line and she was playing tic tac toe. "You said that, not me."

"Alright, how would you describe me?"

He looked up at the soft grey sky. Chubby flakes of snow drifted against the towering cottonwoods ringing the school. "A very brave woman doing the best she can."

Her green eyes filled the tears. "That is the nicest thing anyone's said to me in a hundred years."

"Oh, come on. You don't look a day over eighty-eight."

She laughed, wiping a tear.

His face grew somber. "You're so pretty Meryl."

He leaned in as if he was going to kiss her. She closed her eyes, wanting nothing more but his lips on hers. When she opened her eyes, he was looking at his watch. "I've got horrible pictures of drug addicts to share with young minds."

"You do that." Her eyes remained glued on him as he walked backwards for a few steps. "I'll make sure Nathalie is enrolled in your class."

He nodded, turned and jogged into the school. Watching him disappear, Meryl felt, for the first time since she'd caught Ethan cheating, something akin to happy.

***

More depressing Christmas decorations. Merrill Gardens
was festooned with miles of green plastic garlands, winking
colored lights and a huge plastic tree with drifts of dandruff
snow. Sam, still in uniform, signed himself in at the front
desk, greeting the flirty receptionist. She wore a Christmas
sweater with appliqués of garishly colored wrapped
presents. Clearly she also knew the location of the Super
Ugly Sweater Store.

The third floor was similarly decorated: more plastic
garlands and a tiny fake tree in a hallway alcove. At least in
the residential suites it wasn't so depressingly institutional.
He found his father in the lounge, playing chess with
Sweeney, a retired plumber. Styrofoam cups sat at their
elbows containing the tepid backwash that passed for
coffee in Merrill Gardens. The hall smelled of sour towels
and disinfectant.

Sam put the Dunkin Donut's bag on the table. The
old men's faces brightened like children.

"That's what I'm talking about!" said Arnold, Sam's
dad. "Sweeney, you can throw this swill away." Sweeney
dutifully tossed the cups into the trash; splashing coffee
half way up the wall. Arnold took his first sip, sighing as if
tasting the finest ambrosia.

"You're a good boy, Sammy," said Sweeney.
"Bringing the old men a real cup of Joe. None of that fairy
Starbucks stuff. My granddaughter drinks something called
a caramel macchiato. What the hell is that?"

Sam slapped the old man on the back. "It ain't
coffee," they both said at the same time, enjoying the
private joke.

Sam sat down, watching his father plan his next
move. He found his mind wandering again to Meryl. Not
only was he insanely attracted to her, he wanted to help her.

He could look out for Nathalie at school; maybe even nail that little bastard Denny, keep him out of her path.

"Sam, Sam! Hey son, Sweeney's been asking you about that robbery down at the Swan car wash. Did they ever catch the fellas?"

Sam's brain was reluctant to let go of Meryl. It wasn't like him to daydream. "Yeah, yeah. Bunch of punks. Unemployed losers with marathon rap sheets. They weren't held for long." He went back to Meryl. The way she'd looked in the parking lot, the snowflakes in her dark hair.

Both his dad and Sweeney had turned from their game toward him. "You want to tell us what's going on? Is it Kevin?" Kevin was his son, away at Washington State University.

"No, no. Kevin's fine."

"Then what's on your mind son?"

Sam contemplated denying it but thought it would be a relief to talk. It couldn't get much safer. These two couldn't remember what they'd eaten for breakfast, let alone keep track of Sam's love life or lack thereof.

"I've met a woman."

His dad's face split into a huge grin, showcasing his large, overly white dentures. Sam had tried to talk him out of the large choppers but his dad had insisted that this was a hot ticket with the ladies at Merrill Gardens. He was competing with another octogenarian for the affections of Lydia Smythe, a lissome hottie of seventy-six. "Hot digitty do-dah. 'Bout time son. What's she like? Where does she live?"

"Does she have big hooters?" Sweeney asked, his dentures clicking with excitement. If he were a dog, Sam thought, he'd be panting.

"Slow down. I'm telling you 'cause it's really bothering me. I like her, I really do. But I can't see her."

"Why the hell not?" his dad asked, indignant. "Patty's been dead five years, God rest her sweet soul. Not once in those years have I heard you mention another woman's name."

Sam had, occasionally but his father forgot. "Her name's Meryl."

"A man's name. Huh. Is she built? Built like they used to make 'em in my time?" Sweeney asked.

"Are you really supposed to be this hormonal at your age?" Sam asked.

Sweeney winked. "Some things just improve with age kiddo."

"Enough with Sweeney's pecker, let's hear about this woman!" his dad demanded.

"She's married."

His dad frowned. "I don't like the sounds of this. This sounds like a good way to get shot."

"In the pecker," Sweeny added. "Tell me kid, are you getting laid?"

Sam threw up his arms, exasperated. He was used to Sweeney but today he found him irritating. "No, I am not getting laid. We haven't even gone out yet. I met her on a call. Her husband left her for the next door neighbor. And someone's torched the husband's car."

His dad cocked his eyebrow. "Can't say that I'd blame 'em."

"It's a real mess. And I think the daughter's involved with a kid from the high school where I work. A petty drug dealer. A real little pisser."

"Is she a good woman?" His dad had a way of cutting to the chase.

Sam sighed, running his hands through his hair. "I think so. I barely know her."

His dad moved a chess piece, took a sip of his coffee. "So she's having a bad time. Everything in life is timing. You help her through this and you see what happens. What do you have to lose?"

Sam thought about the grey flecks in her green eyes, the soft purple shadows from lack of sleep and worry. Everything, he thought.

14.

"Love recognizes no barriers. It jumps hurdles,
leaps fences, penetrates walls to arrive at its
destination full of hope."
–Maya Angelou

Faye smoked three cigarettes while parked in front of Meryl's house. She'd forgotten how impressive this spread was. One time Faye had an affair with a hotel executive, Danny Pyle. He'd had a spread like this, although it was Mediterranean with a broken courtyard fountain. Faye had fantasized about Danny divorcing, living in the big house, taking baths in a tub big enough for a small whale. That, like a million other things in Faye's life, didn't pan out.

Meryl was the lady in the big house now. Her husband was a Danny, sneaking in women when his wife was gone. A few lazy snowflakes fell out of the sky. Which house, she wondered, glancing through the bug specked windshield, was her son-in-law using as a hideout? According to Jackie he was right next door although next door here was a much different proposition than a trailer park where you could hear your neighbor snoring.

Faye had gone over her speech a million times on the drive up but as soon as she pulled into Meryl's street the words had flown out of her head like skittish birds. The neighborhood alone made her nervous.

Unlike years ago, when she'd arrived pressed flat by a hangover, she wasn't alone. She had Jesus. Not the painted Jesus from her church but Jesus of the Seven Eleven. He'd progressed from dreams to the occasional daytime visit. It happened so gradually, she hadn't even noticed. She lit another cigarette, blew the smoke out the window. "What if Trixie doesn't want to see me?"

Jesus wore Levis and a clinging red t-shirt over his ripped abs that said Keep On Truckin' in faded yellow letters. "You knew that might happen. She's only human."

"I was a real boozer when she was a kid, you know." She exhaled smoke out a crack in the window, rolling it up quickly. Seattle was a lot colder than Vegas. She didn't have warm clothes. "And there were men." She could have added "a lot" to that sentence but she didn't, out of deference to Jesus.

"I know." There was no recrimination. Still, Faye couldn't help but feel a little embarrassed.

"Look at this nice life she's got. I bet she's got a cleaning lady and gardener. I bet she's got all that." She knew her daughter's financial situation, more or less. But still, the house: that huge, elegant house. It was a statement.

"You're her mother Faye. She loves you." Their breath fogged the windows.

"I know she needs money. That's one thing you learn in Vegas, everyone's got their price."

Jesus wiped the fog, looking over at Meryl's house. "Not everyone."

Faye took an anxious puff. She'd nervously applied two coats of tangerine Coty lipstick. It looked good with her bright red wig. The platinum wig, she'd decided in a highway rest stop, made her look washed out. Her color seemed to have faded as she traveled north. She checked in the mirror, making sure she didn't have lipstick on her teeth. "I know she loves me. What I'm afraid of is that she don't like me."

"Not all women like their mothers. It's a complicated relationship."

Complicated, Faye thought, hell it was like training cats to bark. "Do you know how hard it is to be rejected by your own kid?"

The tiny wrinkles near his eyes fanned out as he smiled. "Have you read the bible?"

"Well of course but-"

"I know. It's not easy. But you are reaching out, and that's the important thing. In a stalemate like this all it takes is one step."

Faye played with her cigarette case. "I think I might drive on over to Jackie's condo and give her a little surprise."

"Faye, you've come this far. Is leaving now the right thing to do?"

Faye stubbed out her cigarette, applying yet another coat of lipstick. "You sound like my therapist."

"Thank you."

"It's not a compliment," she snapped.

***

Henry was on Snapchat with his new friend, Fuzzy Boy, sending each other random funny pictures, when he noticed the battered old Taurus in the street. Probably just someone's cleaning lady, he thought. He'd already told Fuzzy boy that his family was out of money. That his sister got kicked out of school and that his mom was, well, sad.

She spent all her time on the computer looking for work, going to job interviews. He'd smelled whiskey on her breath when she kissed him. His mysterious desert grandma had a problem with drinking. Jackie had said something about it. Henry knew that he shouldn't be revealing such personal stuff online. But he'd already confessed to Fuzzy boy, whose real name was Mark, that he'd set his dad's car on fire. Compared to that, over-sharing was nothing.

Mark had already suggested that they meet, although Henry had ignored it, so far. Something about it felt wrong, although he knew eventually it would happen. It was a relief to talk to Mark online. It was easier than any of his friends. They wouldn't understand.

The car was still there. A lady with bright red hair was in the driver's seat talking to someone. Intrigued, Henry got out his binoculars to spy. She was chatting away as though there was someone sitting beside her but there was no one else in the car. She was gesticulating as if she had an imaginary friend in the front seat.

It was interesting to watch. She was pretty old, Henry thought. About as old as his third grade teacher, Mrs. Fairleaf but this lady wore a lot more make up. She reminded him of someone on TV, sort of larger than life and colorful. The way she talked, waving her cigarette around theatrically, made him want to hear what she was saying. Her shirt was low cut enough that Henry could see her breasts, breaking the surface, like buoys. The overall effect was like watching a movie. A good one.

Henry decided to investigate further. Mark had sent him a picture of a nearby skateboard park with MEET UP HERE...??? Henry quickly logged out. Grabbing his jacket, he ran down the stairs.

His mom was at the kitchen table with a stack of bills. Henry glanced at her for a moment, wondering if he should tell her where he was going. She looked terrible. Usually by this time of year she was baking Christmas cookies and putting up decorations.

He'd even thought about digging the decorations out himself but when he'd brought it up with Nathalie, she'd rolled her eyes. "Dude, have a freakin' clue." So he'd dropped it.

His mom must have heard him coming down the stairs. She looked up, seeing him in the doorway. "Hey Hen, what's up?"

"There's an old lady parked in front of our house talking to herself."

"Oh yeah?" She seemed to welcome the distraction. Her face looked thin.

"It's a Ford Taurus with Nevada plates."

His mother tilted her head. "Nevada?"

Henry nodded. "She has red hair. She's been there at least an hour."

His mother put on the sweater hanging from the back of her chair. "Show me."

15.

"Marriage – yes, it is the supreme felicity
of life. I concede it. And it is
also the supreme tragedy of life."
– Mark Twain

Meryl could see her breath as they walked down the front path, annoyed that she had to brave this cold when what she needed was a hot bath and three Advil. Sure enough there was an older woman in the car. The car windows were fogged and the woman's face was turned so she couldn't see them approaching. A stream of cigarette smoke rose from a crack in the driver's window.

Meryl stepped gingerly across the slick, snow-dusted street, bending down to peer inside the car. The red-head was gesticulating and nodding her head. She was so serious and engaged that Henry found himself searching for another person in the car even though clearly, she was alone.

"I need a Diet Snapple first, that's what I need!" Her voice came through the open window, strangely magnified.

She put her hand on ignition but didn't start the car. Henry wondered if she was crazy. He turned to his mother, slightly afraid.

"Oh shit!" his mom said.

Henry's mouth dropped open. His mother never swore.

Meryl rapped on the car window, hurting her knuckles on the cold glass. "Mom, what the hell are you doing here?"

Henry looked between both women. Mom? Could this be Faye Danetto? He peered inside the car. The red of her hair glowed in the car's interior. A cigarette dangled from her lips, coated with a slick of bright orange lipstick, like Marge Simpson.

The Marge-like possible grandma opened her lips in surprise. The cigarette butt clung to the lipstick for a perilous second before dropping into her lap. Cussing like a sailor, she hopped around the car like a flea, grabbing for the lit cigarette butt as it bounced off her short skirt. It went onto the floor. She lifted her rear end, showing off an expanse of black lace panty.

"Goddamn it to hell! Where is that son of a bitch? I burned my damn leg!" Faye screamed from inside the car.

His mother put her hands over Henry's ears until Faye located the butt, jumped out of the car and stabbed it out under the heel of her white vinyl boot. "You trying to give me a heart attack?"

"You're the one spying on me!" Meryl countered.

"For Pete's sake Trixie, take your hands off the poor kid's ears. He's heard worse on the playground." Meryl's hands remained clamped over her son's ears, although, of course, he could hear everything.

"For God's sake Mom, whatever happened to using a phone?"

"You shouldn't use the Lord's name in vain," Faye said, hurrying around the front of the car.

Meryl snorted. "Are you kidding me?"

Faye yanked up her neckline, trying unsuccessfully to cover her cleavage. She took a deep breath, gazing into the passenger seat of her car as if to draw strength from someone only she could see. Henry crouched down, following her gaze. Meryl looked too, wondering if her mother had a dog. Or God forbid a boyfriend. But there was nothing. Cracked vinyl and McDonald's wrappers.

Both women straightened, staring at one another appraisingly. Her mother had aged well, although she still dressed like a tramp. There was high desert web of fine wrinkles, the lithe dancer's body. Maybe she'd had her boobs done again. Faye thought her daughter looked classy, in her pony tail and diamond studs. No Zirconium here. Tired but yes, very classy.

"I'm here to help you Trixie."

Meryl crossed her arms. "You help me?"

Faye jutted out her chin, remembering Jesus' words: keep it kind. "I'm real sorry about your marriage. Jackie told me."

"You're sorry?"

"Yes, I'm sorry. Is that so hard to believe?"

"Quite frankly, yes, coming from a woman who treated men like Kleenex. I'm way behind you. This is nothing. A glitch."

"Don't be so mean. I've had fewer husbands than Elizabeth Taylor."

"That's not something to brag about."

"My marriages were my problems. This is about me and you."

"Your marriages were symptomatic of a bigger problem."

Faye smiled kindly at Henry, before she addressed her daughter. "And you're just the person to tell me all about them, aren't you?"

"No, I am not. This isn't the time or the place."

Faye went to the trunk of the car, dislodging from the plethora of junk a worn out leopard print roll-aboard, held together with sparkly pink duct tape. "No, we have lots of time, don't we?"

Meryl moved to block Faye's path to the house. "No, we don't. Not right now."

Faye flung her arms out. "I'm here aren't I? I drove all day and night just so I could come up here and be here for my little girl." It was a white lie, Faye thought. An off white lie.

"First of all I am a grown woman. Second of all, I don't see how you could help me. You can't fix your own life, let alone anyone else's."

Faye looked down into the car again.

Meryl had had just about enough of this weird behavior. There wasn't anything in the car but a bunch of empty Snapple bottles and garbage. "What are you looking at?"

"Nothing. I'm just waiting for the third thing you're going to tell me. There's always a third thing."

"There is no third thing."

"Oh come on, honey. No one can list my faults like you. Not even me and believe me, in AA I have done a fearless and searching inventory. Go on. I'm sure Henry here would like to hear about his grandma."

Meryl glanced down at her son. "Now you're being mean."

Faye threw her hands up in the air. "Just like old times."

"You keep looking into that car. What's in the car?"

"I know this is sudden, me just showing up here like this. I been scared to death this whole drive but I came anyway because I wanted to show you that I am a changed woman and unlike all your fancy friends, I am here for you."

Meryl wondered how she knew that most people hadn't bothered to pick up the phone since Ethan left. It didn't take a genius to know that people weren't always there for you in your time of need. "So what?"

"So…" She gave Henry a nervous look. "So I quit drinking. I'm in AA."

"Good for you. I still don't see why that merits a special trip."

"You don't believe me, do you?"

"Mom, it doesn't matter."

"The hell it doesn't. I've been clean and sober for four wonderful years. And I've discovered Jesus Christ."

Meryl stared up at the sky, wrapping her cardigan tightly around herself. "Naturally."

Faye's face flushed red. "I forgive your sarcasm. I forgive you for being such a Class A…" She leaned down toward Henry. "I am your Grandma Faye."

"Faye Danetto?" She had cornflower blue eyes, like Nathalie.

She did a tiny dance move, a quick tap of the feet, amazingly agile on the slippery street. It ended with her arms outstretched. "In the flesh."

Just like that, Henry was enchanted. He stuck out his hand. "Nice to meet you."

"Awww, come on over here. Aren't you just the cutest little thing?" Dropping her colorful suitcase, she gave him a bone crushing hug. Her breasts felt like his mother's yoga mat when it was all rolled up.

Meryl took Henry by the arm. "Hen, go in the house."

"It was nice to meet you Faye," he said wistfully, marching back up the walk.

"Call me grandma," Faye called after him.

"I don't know what you think you're up to," Meryl hissed.

"A fresh start. Can you give me that much?"

"And you thought the end of my marriage was good timing?"

Faye looked up at the sky. "There's no such thing as good timing. There's life. It's messy."

Both women glared at each other in the growing gloom. A few snowflakes clung to Faye's aggressively orange wig.

Faye wanted to push her point, gush about her grandson or sobriety but could sense Jesus telling her to bide her time. Let Trixie come to her. Or Meryl. What the hell kind of name was Meryl anyway?

Meryl buried her face in her hands, wiping away a few tears before crossing her arms. "I know this would be good for you but I am this close to completely losing it." She wiped another tear with the back of her hand. "Try to think about me Faye. Why on earth should I add one more complication to my already incredibly stressful life?"

Faye kept quiet while she thought about it. She fought the urge to light another cigarette. She also fought the urge to say, "Because I am your mother." Instead she said, "Because I love you." The words hung in the soft grey air between them.

"Can we do this another time? Go see Jackie, okay?"

"Lemme just show you what I got in this suitcase." She winked at her daughter. "I think you're gonna be real surprised."

God knows what her mother had inside that garish bag. Whatever it was, she didn't want the neighbors to see.

"Why don't you show me on the front porch where it's dry? Then we'll call Jackie."

Faye, buoyed with hope, fought the urge to touch her daughter. "Alrighty then. The front porch."

***

Nathalie was wearing her knit Ugg boots when Denny dropped her off, so she asked him, for the first time, to drive inside the cul-de-sac.

"I don't want to wreck my boots," she explained. There weren't going to be many $175 boots in her future. Any money made selling pot would be for car insurance and clothes.

He shrugged, giving her the lazy smiled she loved. He pulled into the driveway. "Later dude," he said, giving her a long, passionate kiss. Denny was a great kisser.

"I'll be thinking about it. Constantly."

"I know. You're a guy," she said lightly, trying to avoid the topic. He tossed her an Altoid; the best for masking pot breath. She blew him a kiss and slammed the door.

She walked slowly; hoping the walk to the front door would sufficiently air out her jacket and clear her head. Denny was still sulking that she hadn't had sex with him yet. Several of the girls at Juanita High School were more than happy to oblige, he'd pointed out.

"For free pot," she'd countered.

"Whatever it takes dude," he'd laughed, letting his hair fall over one eye, staring at her like a cat.

Nathalie wasn't stupid enough to think the issue was going to go away. And she wanted to but not without birth control. But if she asked her mom to take her to

Planned Parenthood right now, her mind would probably explode.

Maybe she'd ask Aunt Jackie.

Nathalie was half way up the front walk when she sensed something.

An old lady with bright red hair was on the front porch staring at her. Twin streams of smoke issued from her nostrils. "Oh my God, you must be Nathalie!" She stubbed out her cigarette with her boot.

"Who are you?" asked Nathalie.

***

"You left your own mother on the front porch? It's freezing out there. Jesus, Meryl! You've really flipped out."

Meryl was on the phone with Jackie when the doorbell rang. "She can't just show up and expect me to take her in. Not right now. She's begging me to look at some gift or something in her stupid suitcase but you know what, I'm done with Faye's lousy surprises. This is the same woman that gave you a dead hamster because when she wrapped it, she forgot to leave air holes. I want you to talk to her."

She marched toward the door, flung it open without looking, holding out the phone. "Talk to Jackie, I don't-"

It was Sam, out of uniform, awkwardly holding a folder. "Jackie?"

Meryl looked around the porch, which was empty. She stepped out, peering around Sam at Faye's car in the street. Empty.

"My sister. My mom… oh, never mind." She ran a hand over her head, wishing she'd washed her hair, put on some make-up at some point. "It's nice to see you." She remembered that Jackie was on the phone. "Jackie, I'll call you later." She hung up. "Sorry about that."

He gave her a tight smile. "I'm here on police business."

She ushered him in. "Oh, right. Can I get you some coffee?"

He shifted uncomfortably, hat in hand. "No, thanks. I'm doing a follow up on that arson. Is Henry here?"

***

Henry knew this moment would come. He'd lain awake at night rehearsing his answer. The trick would be to tell enough truth to make the facts line up and enough lies not to incriminate himself. He'd already told Officer Richer that he'd siphoned the gas and carried it out to the driveway. All of that was easy to prove.

"And then what?" Sam asked. They were sitting in an uneasy triangle in the living room. Sam had his folder open. He'd taken a few notes but mostly just talked.

Henry looked at his mom, who was close to losing it. He'd have to be careful with his words. He needed at least one parent around.

"You have to tell me kiddo," Sam said quietly.

Henry shrugged. "I left it there."

The confident, knowing smile left Sam's face. "What do you mean, you left it there?"

"I left the gas sitting in the driveway and I went upstairs to bed."

"So you didn't dump it on your dad's car?"

"No. I was going to fill Matt's go cart, you know, like as a surprise because his dad always pays for the gas but it got too heavy. I left it there until morning when Matt could help me carry it."

Sam sat back on the couch, clearly frustrated. "Was that your plan?"

Henry shrugged. "I always get up earlier than anyone else. Even if someone knocked it over all it would do was kill some plants."

Sam frowned, rubbed his hands together. "So you left a huge cooking pot three quarters full of unleaded sitting on the sidewalk?"

Henry nodded. "I didn't want to tell anyone but Max. They'd think it was dumb and I'd get in trouble. So I went to bed." He turned to Meryl. "Sorry."

Sam ran a hand through his hair, happy to be done. That left Nathalie. And Meryl. "Alright. Thank you Henry." He stood up, grabbed the folder off the couch. "Thanks Mrs. Howe."

Meryl followed him to the door, wondering if he was mad about the pot brownies. "It's Mrs. Howe now?"

"Yes, it is. Good luck."

Faye knew what good luck meant.

***

When Sam knocked, Ethan answered the door barefoot. He was in a pair of jeans and old flannel shirt, pacing back and forth on the phone. He held up a finger and disappeared down the hallway.

The door remained open but Sam didn't know if he was supposed to follow or wait there. Either way Sam was irritated. That was the worst part of this job, being treated like a servant by people like Ethan.

Sam could hear Ethan pleading, requesting an extension on his credit card payment. He shouldn't be eavesdropping. The guy was going through a hard enough time without Sam overhearing him grovel to some junior credit manager. But he couldn't wait at the front door like a UPS driver.

The back of the house was a large kitchen with an attached living area, decorated with overstuffed couches and chairs. A laptop computer was open on the granite countertop. Sam got a glimpse of a resume before Ethan slammed it shut.

"Sending it to collection will not guarantee you payment. Giving me another month will guarantee you payment. Your hands aren't tied. I know this game." He exhaled with frustration. "Yeah, well, thanks for nothing."

He snapped the phone shut, turning to Sam. "I am having the worst year of my whole life and every time I look up, there you are."

Sam's empathy dried up like desert rain. "I'm just doing my job."

Ethan dropped the phone roughly on the countertop, massaging his temples. "Okay, so what's your job today?"

To kick your ass? Sam wished he'd worn his uniform. "To tell you that I'm investigating the arson of your car."

"And?"

Sam cleared his throat. "And it's not looking good. It's looking like someone in your own family did it."

"Who?"

"Henry has admitted that he siphoned the gas. He says he was going to use it to fuel his friend's go cart."

"Do you believe him?"

"I don't know."

"Henry is a good kid."

"Good kids make mistakes."

"Henry wouldn't do something like that. One of those book club women did it. Sandy Chan. She's a divorce attorney. Real ball breaker. Or Lorraine. She's probably thinks it's amoral to own a Mercedes while there are starving children in Africa."

Sam shook his head. "They all have alibis."

"I don't like where you are going with this."

"And neither will your insurance company."

Ethan fell backwards onto the couch. "If you are implying that I set my own car on fire, no I did not. Although I have done some really bad stuff lately, I have not stooped that low." Ethan rolled up the sleeve to his sweatshirt, adjusting the bandage on his arm.

Sam believed him. "Who do you think set your car on fire?"

"Isn't that your job?"

"The victim usually has a pretty good idea of who does this sort of thing."

"Really? That sounds like something you heard on TV."

"Humor me."

Ethan rolled down his sweatshirt sleeve, wincing as the fabric touched the bandages. "Who hates me enough to torch my three hundred and sixty-seven thousand dollar car?"

What kind of prick would drive a car like that and not make his house payments? "Yes."

"I'm not sure who hates me more at this point – my father, whose money I lost, my business partner, who holds me personally responsible for all our losses, or my wife, who walked in on me trashing seventeen good, almost great, years of marriage. Take a number."

Taking a number to punch him in the face sounded good. "Fair enough. Do you need a case number for the insurance?"

Ethan laughed. "The car belongs to the company. It should have been seized months ago. I had it parked outside so the repo man could find it."

Sam nodded. For some reason he still believed him. Liking him was another matter. "Okay, I'll call the insurance company. They'll want the information."

Ethan stood up, shoulders back, a fighter's stance. He was a couple inches shorter, but stockier. "Tell you what, why don't you just drop it?"

Sam crossed his arms, comforted by his Glock, holstered under his coat. It was part of him now, even when he was off duty. He never did that before Patty died. Dealing with cancer made him fatalistic. "We don't drop arson cases, Mr. Howe. They tend to run in strings."

Ethan lowered his head, like a bulldog. "This one is a family matter. My family. So you can quit sniffing around."

Sam placed a business card on the countertop, moving deliberately. "If you think of anything, call me." He headed for the front door.

Ethan called after him, following. "By the way, someone told me you had a little problem with your drug screen."

Sam stopped at the door. The hairs stood up on his neck.

Ethan leaned on the wall. "A little bit of PR problem for the high school liaison officer, don't you think?"

This prick wasn't just well-connected, he was dangerous. Sam steadied himself, opening the door. "I am only doing my job, so back off." If Ethan found out that

Meryl had drugs in her house, he could use it in a custody battle to impugn her reliability as a mother.

Ethan nodded. "Just remember what your job is." He patted Sam on the back. "And try to lay off the ganja."

16.

"A woman is like a tea bag - you can't tell how strong she is until you put her in hot water."
-Eleanor Roosevelt

Meryl answered the door on the second knock, staring at him suspiciously.

Sam stepped inside the house without an invitation, closing the door. "Two things: did you know that your mother is sitting on your front porch?"

Meryl shook her head. "I knew she was in the general area."

Sam nodded. "Nathalie is with her."

Meryl peered out the window. Sure enough, two heads poked over the twin white Adirondack chairs flanking the porch. A white plume of smoke floated above them. "The plot thickens." She sighed. "What was the second thing?"

He fidgeted with the outline of his gun beneath his leather coat. "I talked to your husband."

"What did he say?"

"Not much." He couldn't tell her what a colossal jerk her husband had been. How his adrenalin was pumping from Ethan's parting shot. First he had to take care of the immediate threat. "Will you find out who put the pot in the brownies?"

Meryl shrugged. "I've already asked two of them and gotten two nos."

"Ask the rest of them." He stared at her for a long moment, playing with the zipper on his jacket.

She smiled. "That was the second thing?"

"The second thing is would you like to have dinner sometime? Not a date. Just eating. Food. Together." It all came out awkwardly and too fast. He wondered if he was doing this because it was the right time or because he wanted revenge on the asshole next door. Either way, it was out there now.

Her face lit up. She'd put on lipstick just to make herself feel better. "Sounds like a date."

"It is. But you're married so I can't call it that."

"Separated."

He flipped around the zipper before making himself stop. "I need a yes or no."

Her green eyes widened. "Yes."

Happiness shot through him. He had to get back to work. "Great. I'll call you later. Go talk to your mother." He jerked his thumb toward the porch as he opened the front door. "She's got a surprise for you."

Meryl rolled her eyes, smile dimming. "She always does."

When Meryl came out onto the front porch to assess the situation, she temporarily lost her powers of speech. Between the two Adirondack chairs, in front of the wicker table, on the ground, was her mother's open suitcase. It was filled with bundles of cash. Henry stood with an arm wrapped around a pillar, staring, like everyone, at the money.

The family remained quiet for a good five seconds, posed like a bizarre crèche scene, with baby Jesus replaced by a roll-aboard full of money. Faye stubbed out her cigarette in a planter brimming with rust colored chrysanthemums and yellow creeping Jenny. She was shivering.

"Did you rob a bank?" Meryl nearly screamed after gathering her scattered thoughts, pointing at the open suitcase as if it were a bloody corpse.

Faye cleared her throat. "Yes Meryl, I robbed a bank. I robbed a bank and I drove here. That's exactly what I did."

"How cool would that be?" Nathalie said.

"That is my life's savings; thirty-eight thousand dollars to be exact. They tried to talk me into a cashier's check but I thought it would be easier to keep track of this way."

"You drove up from Vegas with thirty-eight thousand dollars in your trunk?" Meryl asked.

Faye searched for another cigarette, deciding against it when she saw Henry's big green eyes staring her down. "Well, it's better than a dead body, ain't it?"

Meryl wrapped herself in her arms, staring at Nathalie for a second while she gathered her thoughts. "I don't even know where to begin."

"It's money Mom. A lot," said Henry soberly, unable to stop staring at the loot.

Meryl shot Henry an annoyed look before turning to her mother. "Where did you get it?"

Faye smoothed her mini skirt, willing herself not to feel cold. "Tips from InSpa. And I teach dance at the community center. Also, your grandpa in Tennessee kicked the bucket. I don't ever want to touch his money so I'm giving it to you."

"Henry, Nathalie, you need to get inside and do your homework."

"I don't have any," said Henry.

"Mine's done," lied Nathalie, whose fresh start at school had gone stale.

Neither child budged. Meryl returned to Faye. "You can't give me your life's savings." Faye glanced into the growing dark before lifting her chin to meet her daughter's eyes. "I'm giving you half. The other half we're gonna discuss."

"Faye, I can't take your inheritance."

Faye looked into the bushes again, hoping to see Jesus. She took a deep breath; fighting a quiver in the back of her throat. "If you don't take this money right now, I'm gonna dump it on your lawn and burn it."

Always the drama queen. Here she was, dead broke with a cheating husband and it was still all about Faye. "Faye, I really do appreciate the gesture."

"This ain't no damn gesture! This is the real deal." With astonishing agility, Faye scooped up the suitcase, sprinted to the front walkway, dumped out the packets of cash into a neat pile. A Bic lighter appeared in her hand. A second later it glowed in the dusk, illuminating the scene like some crazy painting.

"Faye, this is stupid. You're not going to light all that money on fire."

"I done way stupider things in my life and you know it. I am making my point. And my point is to help you."

"And you think burning up a pile of cash in my front yard is a good way to do it?"

"We were both born poor and if there's one thing that'll get our attention, it's money."

Henry stared with raw fascination. His grandma might not collect tarantulas or know anything about Burrowing Owls but she was her own kind of interesting.

All four of them stared at the flame, flickering in the growing purple dark. The scene, Nathalie thought, got weirder and weirder. No wonder Mom kept them away from this woman. If Mom hated one thing it was anything out of the norm.

"Alright, what do you want?" Meryl sighed.

"What do you mean: what do I want? Can't I give my baby girl a helping hand without her asking what I want?"

Meryl rolled her eyes. "No. You can't."

"Take the money Mom," Nathalie whispered.

Meryl's exhaustion washed over her like a drug. She opened the front door wide knowing she'd regret this later.

***

"She's driving me crazy," Meryl said. She was in her closet, with the phone on speaker, getting ready for dinner with Sam. "Two nights into this and I'm out of Valium. When are you coming over?"

"Look, I'm sorry. I've been working a lot and I'm seeing someone," said Jackie.

"That's great. Yeah well, if you want to hang on to him, keep him away from this mess. Do you know what she did during dinner last night?" Meryl wailed. "She showed the kids all her tattoos. By the way, she's still wearing g-strings."

"Bifocals and g-strings. That's a great combo."

"Did you know that she was planning on showing up with a suitcase full of cash?"

"No. If she's trying to make up for our lousy childhood, I want my share."

"Thirty-eight thousand dollars."

"Seriously?"

"Yeah." Meryl decided her outfit was all wrong and stripped down to start over again. "Some of it's from her dad, an inheritance or something."

"Weird. I never thought they had anything."

"Yeah, apparently the oil rights were worth something. She's keeping it under her bed until I accept it." She held up a silvery blouse on a hanger, wondering if she could wear it with jeans. There was no asking Jackie, who was far too nosy.

"Keep an open mind. This isn't easy for her."

"You haven't lived with her in over a decade. She's still nuts. I always know where she is in relation to the liquor cabinet. Isn't that depressing?" Meryl slid down onto the floor to pull on her favorite high heeled boots.

"It's normal. Give her some time. She has a business plan for the two of you."

The outfit worked, well enough. She grabbed the phone, taking it into the bathroom while she touched up her make-up. "A business plan from the woman who forgot to enroll us in school?"

"Well, there's that."

"I was the only kindergartner who had to prove she existed. What is it?"

"She wants to tell you herself so just keep an open mind. It's not half bad."

Meryl leaned forward to apply mascara. "It's the other half I'm worried about. If you like it so much why don't you go into business with her?"

"I'm not the one that needs help right now. Which is why I am telling you to keep your mind open. Sarah Blakely started a little company because of panty lines."

Meryl brushed on some eye shadow. "Who is that?"

"The founder of Spanx and the youngest female billionaire in history."

Meryl sprayed on perfume, brushed her hair. "The closest Mom will ever come to that is a couple of one night stands with millionaires."

"Don't be mean. Just listen to her."

Meryl took her sister off speaker phone. "I know, I know. I accepted the loan in return for putting up with her for one month."

"Do you think you can last that long?"

"No but she asked for two. And she's distracting the kids. She took them Christmas shopping. What do you want to bet they all come home with matching tattoos?"

"She's turned over a new leaf Meryl, I swear to God."

"Yeah well both sides are exactly the same. You're a shrink. You ought to know. People don't change that much."

"Give her a chance."

"How about we split the month? She's your mother too." Meryl knew she sounded petulant but didn't care. Right now all she wanted was Sam, although it was horrible timing. But what would happen if she waited?

"Sorry hon, she's already got my vote."

Meryl sighed at her reflection. More makeup would only accentuate her fatigue. "Only because you're easy."

***

Bellevue Square, Faye thought, was America on steroids. Jam packed with well-heeled shoppers weaving their way in and out of high end stores. They hefted glossy bags, their exhausted faces blank. It was a parade with no end where the main objective was handing over all your cash. Nathalie perked up as soon as the lukewarm perfumed air hit them, tossing her hair like a pony.

They started at the food court, where Faye handed out cash like an ATM. Henry went off to fetch a Cinnabon. Nathalie drank a venti peppermint mocha chip followed by a Pink Berry yogurt with gummy bears. Faye found a Diet Snapple at a World Wraps, nursing it carefully while playing with the flap on her cigarette case. They sat in uncomfortable iron chairs, their food placed on a wobbly table. Streams of shoppers and crying babies flowed around them.

While Henry wove his way through the Christmas crowds like a minnow, he thought about Faye's wigs. One day her hair was red and shaggy and the next, a severe platinum pageboy. He had asked Nathalie about it. She told him to mind his own business. If it were up to Nathalie, he'd be an emotionless robot. Balancing the carton of sticky cinnamon bun, Henry wondered if he could ask Faye about her hair. She seemed like the kind of person that nothing bothered but with grownups you could never really tell until it was too late.

While Henry was gone, Faye peppered Nathalie with questions about her life: friends, boyfriends, hobbies, tastes. She liked to watch the girl eat, talk, do anything really. She was typical of a girl her age, a brash facade fronting a little kid. She was all long limbs and startling beauty, the kind that young people never appreciate. Nathalie found herself being unusually honest, telling Faye about Denny, how she was glad to be going to the public school because it was easier and the parties were awesome. "Plus I didn't qualify for advanced placement classes so that makes me look smarter, you know, to be in with the normal kids for a change. Most of them are kind of dumb."

Faye took a gummy bear from Nathalie's ice cream, chewing thoughtfully, wondering what kids saw in this stuff. "You know, there's a chance you could be an addict."

Nathalie twisted her lips. "Uh, come again?"

"I'm an addict. I go to AA. First thing I should have done today, instead of promising to take you shopping was to find a meeting. Anyway, I know you've probably had a few beers. I'm hoping that's all it is because the cards are stacked against you."

Nathalie scraped the whipped cream stuck inside her red Starbucks cup with a finger, licking it off. "I don't know what you're talking about."

Henry arrived with his Cinnabon. Faye peered at it, thinking it looked like a glob of fat. "Thanks Faye." He handed her the change.

She shoved the money toward him. "You can call me grandma." She thought about it for a minute. "I mean, if you want. You don't have to."

Henry sat down, stabbing the gooey roll with a plastic knife, holding it aloft, ripping a piece off with his teeth. Frosting smeared across his face.

Nathalie rolled her eyes. "I'm going to be sick."

Henry chomped enthusiastically, opening wide. "Awwww."

Faye smiled. "Cute. Your mom teach you that?"

"How come she didn't come?" Henry asked.

"She's tired. Besides, we're gonna pick out her gifts so she couldn't be here now could she?" Faye said.

Henry took another bite of his roll, wishing he had a glass of milk. It was a lie. He knew by the way Faye played with her Snapple lid and wouldn't meet his eyes. Only the worst kind of people looked you in the face when they lied. His mother was out on a date with the cop. Henry let the sweetness of the icing sink into his teeth as he watched the mechanical reindeer suspended from the ceiling move with robotic grace. If he concentrated hard enough, it almost felt like Christmas.

17.

"Keep your eyes wide open before marriage, and
half-shut afterwards."
- Benjamin Franklin

"I'm so sorry about this," Sam said to Meryl for
what felt like the fifteenth time that night. They were at
Merrill Gardens with Sam's father. Arnold's tiny room
would have been pleasant, had it not been stuffed with ratty
old furniture and a lifetime of detritus. A framed service
award from the Seattle Police Department fought for wall
space with family photos, including Sam's wedding portrait.
Meryl tried not to stare. The dead wife was pretty.

"Don't worry about it," said Meryl, with what she
hoped was a cheerful smile. Sam had gotten the call on
their way to dinner. His father had been roaming the
hallway with a large flashlight, threatening to hit people if
security wasn't improved. He'd broken three windows.

"Will you call Hector's and see if they can hold the
reservation?" Sam asked worriedly.

"Don't worry about it. I'm not even hungry. We'll
eat at the bar later."

Arthur, eating a Snicker bar to get his blood sugar
up, tapped the outside window with his flashlight. He was
folded into his Lazy Boy, momentarily quiet. "They oughta
put bars on these windows. Lock 'em up at night. I'm
telling you Sammy, this place is robbery waiting to happen."

"Dad, you're on the fifth floor. Unless Spider Man goes to the dark side, you're safe."

His dad's eyes flashed with anger. "Of course I am. Fifty years on the force. I'm safe as houses. It's the other people in here I'm worried about."

"They have a night watchman."

"He's no damn good. I caught him taking bribes."

Sam looked at his watch. "No, you didn't dad. His wife brings him dinner. You threw his dinner away, remember?" Mr. Patel, the night watchman, was, thankfully, a kind man.

Arthur looked at Meryl. "Patty you remember. Tell Sam. The night watchman was taking bribes."

"Dad, this is Meryl."

Arthur pointed at Sam. "You just don't like her taking my side." He winked conspiratorially at Meryl. "You know what's going on, don't you?"

Meryl tensed, not sure how she was supposed to respond. She shook her head. "Not really."

Arthur's face crumpled a little. "Where's Patty?"

"She died dad, remember? Almost five years ago." Sam's voice was soft.

Arthur put the candy bar down, his lower lip trembling. "How'd she die?"

"Breast cancer."

Arthur's face was clouded. This was the worst part, for Sam, reliving how hard it was to tell his father. His father had adored Patty. "Oh, right. When?"

"2008. Almost five years ago."

Sam got up, went to the kitchenette where he poured his father a glass of water. "I think you might be dehydrated. You're skipping meals again too. Drink this and promise me you'll go to breakfast."

Arthur growled, staring at the glass of water. "Breakfast, schmectfast. You want to know what the breakfast of champions is? A cigarette and a cup of Joe. That's it." His watery eyes turned to his son. "Why are you all dressed up?"

Pressed khakis and a collared shirt was formal wear in this place. "Meryl and I are going to dinner."

Arthur tapped his cheek. "Aw, give the old man a kiss. You two kids go on and have some fun." Sam nodded. His dad waved the candy bar. "Thanks for the Snickers. See you Wednesday Pattycakes."

Sam felt another twinge. Wednesdays had been Patty's day to visit.

Meryl bent down and kissed the old man's whiskery cheek. He smelled of cigarettes and faintly, urine. "Goodnight."

Meryl stepped into the hallway. She could hear Sam talking to his dad. "No more breaking windows, okay? The security here is top notch."

"No it's not!" Arthur yelled from behind the door.

Meryl waited in the empty lobby of Merrill Gardens while Sam spoke to someone in the office. In the far corner was an empty dining area, presumably for breakfast. A sign posted near the elevators advertised a Seattle Men's Choir Christmas Concert on December 21st. Voices carried across the empty space. Meryl heard Sam promising to pay for the broken windows. There was an angry exchange with the woman, who shut the door. A few minutes later Sam exited; his face red and tense. Meryl joined him at the front entrance, rushing to catch up.

On the sidewalk, Sam pasted a smile on his face. "Okay, let's try and salvage the remains of this night. I know you said I can't apologize again but seriously, this is grim."

Meryl grinned. "Your dad seems really nice."

Sam cocked his head. "Why are you being such a good sport?"

"Because all this makes my life seem somewhat less crazy."

Sam looked up at the stars dully poking through the hazy December sky. "Do you know where normal exists? On TV."

She hooked her arm through his, heading down an alley way. "I used to think my life was normal. Not my childhood but my adult life. I made sure it was government regulated; grade A, capital N, normal life."

"Sounds boring."

She shivered, huddling closet to him as they walked. "Maybe it was."

"Where are we going?" he asked, wondering if he had any future at all with this wonderful creature.

"To find any place that serves food. I'd sell my soul for a handful of pretzels."

So she lied about not being hungry. That was generous, he thought. She was what his dad would call a good egg. He loved the feeling of her arm linked through his. "And beer. That barracuda back there, Ms. Steinman, wants to put my dad in the Alzheimer's unit. She says he's a danger to himself and the community. She made him sound like some crazed gunman. The man spent his life protecting and defending. He just doesn't know when to quit."

"He doesn't seem very dangerous."

Sam stopped to peer into the window of the Tiki Bar, fronted with dried palm fronds interwoven with white fairy lights. Meryl shook her head. The place was a sticky-floored dump.

"He's not. Usually. But one percent of the time he's a loose cannon."

They continued down the sidewalk. Meryl pulled him towards the glass doors of the Wilde Rover, an Irish bar. A Guinness Beer sign glowed in a green welcome. "I think it's sweet that he wants to protect other people."

Sam held the door open for her, the moist air heavy with fried food and hops. "Until he mistakes some old lady for a prowler and brains her with a flashlight. The thing you learn as a cop is that most people aren't dangerous until they are."

Inside the dark interior, a trivia contest was in full bloom. As they searched for seats, Sam leaned into her ear. "Let's talk about something else. I think we both might need a bit of break from reality."

A young waitress carrying two full pitchers of beer passed them. "Are you looking for your team?"

"No, just something to eat," Sam said, eyeing the full bar.

"We're full up but that table is looking for players if you want to stay." She pointed her elbow at a booth across the room. The brown walls were studded with tin European beer labels.

A shaggy haired MC wearing a top hat, jeans and a knit vest spoke from the stage. "This contest strictly prohibits the use of Iphones. Table twelve if you keep looking at your crotches you will be buying the entire room a round of drinks. Okay, number 21: What is the name and location of the world's largest tree?"

Furious conversations sprouted around the bar. Meryl crossed over to the table seeking new players. "Mind if we join you? I've got this one."

"Abso-frickin'-luetely. We suck. Welcome," said a pixie-haired woman, patting the booth seat beside her.

Sam slid in next to Meryl who raised her hand.

"Right here!" yelled a pimply man in a WSU baseball cap, pointing at Meryl.

The MC wove through the tables to Meryl, holding out the microphone. "Tell us your name."

"Meryl."

"Okay Meryl, what's the name and location of the world's largest tree?"

"General Sherman, located in Sequoia National Park."

The MC beamed. "You are correct Miss Meryl. Technically General Sherman resides in the Giant Forest but you got the park right so we'll give it to you. Have you been to visit the General yourself?"

Meryl shook her head, her mind on the bowl of stew being eaten across the table. "No, I used to teach school and I had a picture of General Sherman in my classroom. Actually both General Shermans."

The MC went back to the stage. "Very good. The former school marm captures two points for beleaguered table seven, now tied for dead last."

The MC continued with his next question as the table rushed to thank Meryl. Amid a flurry of introductions and handshaking, Sam interrupted. "Excuse me but the smart lady needs to eat."

Meryl clutched her stomach. "My hero."

Although she'd said it lightly, Sam knew he'd be rewinding that compliment later. "I'll go order for us. What'll it be?"

"A bowl of stew and a glass of pinot noir please."

"Coming right up!" He disappeared toward the bar.

Meryl checked her phone in case one of the kids had called. There was a text from Ethan: Monday December 24, 2:00, 1200 Century Pavilion Ste. 1200,

Bellevue, Dr. Allen Schwartz, marital councilor. See you there?

She texted back: F U.

He responded: I will spend the rest of my life making it up to you.

She texted back: Not enough. Then she shut off her phone.

***

When Meryl came home, she woke her mother up when she shut the heavy oak door.

"Hey," Faye said sleepily, sitting up on the couch, her bifocals at half mast.

Meryl hung up her coat in the hall closet, still thinking of Sam, how handsome he looked, how easy he was to talk to. "Sorry I woke you up."

Faye picked up Us Weekly Magazine from her pert chest. "I wasn't sleeping."

Meryl studied her mother closely, checking for signs of inebriation. Facing her, she sat on a chair, taking off her boots. They pinched. "I heard you snoring."

Faye glared at her through false eyelashes and flashy purple eye shadow. She and Nathalie had a glittery good time at the Sephora make-up counter. Her granddaughter had been impressed with Faye's knowledge of stage make-up. "I do not snore. Never have, never will. Did you have a good time?"

Meryl tugged off the last boot, rubbing her sore foot. "Yes."

"Notice anything?" Faye asked.

Meryl stared closely at her mom. "You have a false eyelash on your cheek."

Brushing it off, Faye pushed herself off the couch, crouching on the far side of the fireplace to plug in an extension cord. The glow of a Christmas tree filled the corner. Its fresh boughs filled the room with a tangy perfume.

Faye, for once, allowed for silence, admiring the tree's beauty. Although she hated admitting it, with her dancer's vanity about stamina, this afternoon wore her out. Traipsing around in her heels through that fancy mall, keeping up with her grandchildren, had gutted her. But then she'd gotten carried away, talked into that high priced mud wallow of a Christmas tree farm. How many years had it been since she'd had a Christmas tree? One pleading glance from Henry, looking like he'd jumped out of a Norman Rockwell painting, and she was a goner.

Meryl was silent, a shadow against the glow of the tree. Faye began to nervously chatter. "Henry wanted to stop and get a tree at the same place you and Ethan used to go, that Red Barn place out in the sticks. Can you imagine, paying to cut your own tree? I took one look at the place and we hot-footed it over to Safeway. It wasn't cheap but it looks real good, huh? You got some really cute little ornaments." Each ornament, Henry said, had a story. But no one knew them like his mother.

Meryl had tears in her eyes when she turned around. "I know you want a do-over. You want to have the happy Christmas scene that we never did have. But what you just did was steal something from me. I wanted to decorate the tree with the kids. I know I should be grateful but it just feels like you're bulldozing me. Again."

"Henry is the one that wanted to do it. I can't say no to that kid."

"You should have asked me."

"You were out on a date."

"You could have called." Meryl didn't realize, until this moment, that she'd been avoiding Christmas like a large box, waiting to be unpacked when she could deal with it.

"Henry was afraid to ask you for a tree. He's too worried about you falling apart because his daddy won't be here for Christmas."

Meryl pointed upstairs. "Lower your voice."

"Why? Kids know everything. You of all people ought to know that."

The Pandora's Box of the past loomed between them but Meryl wouldn't bite. "You really can't you understand that I'd want to decorate a Christmas tree with my kids?"

Faye carefully folded her bifocals. "First of all, Nathalie doesn't give a flying rat's ass. She's sixteen. If you wanted to do it so badly then why didn't you do it? It's December 22nd."

"I have had just a few other things on my mind. Like keeping our house."

"You could have done it tonight. But no, you were out on a date instead of spending time with your family."

Meryl's jaw tensed as she massaged her temples. "Oh my God. I can't believe that you of all people are throwing that in my face."

"This isn't about me. This is about you. We haven't spent Christmas together in twenty-four years. I wanted there to be a tree so I went out and got one. Henry and I had a great time decorating it. We listened to their favorite radio station. I even showed Nathalie some dance moves. We had fun. How about that?"

Meryl had visions of Nathalie twirling on a pole. "Don't you dare show her any of your dance moves. She's got enough problems without learning your tricks."

"Dancing is not dirty."

"The way you do it is."

Faye's anger flared. "I'm not the one throwing in the towel on seventeen years of marriage. Sure, you got some major problems but if you go out there and start something new your past is gonna follow you. It has a way of doing that, trust me."

Meryl placed her hands on her hips, tilting her head. "I suppose being married five times makes you an expert, right?"

Faye held up four fingers. "I never married Sid."

Meryl jerked back, shocked. She tapped the finger formerly weighted with her own wedding rings. "But you had rings. You even brought home a wedding cake."

"Safeway sells them without a license." She couldn't meet Meryl's eyes. "I didn't want you to know that we were living in sin."

Meryl shook her head in disbelief, angry that she was getting stuck in the tangled seaweed of her mother's past. "Your longest marriage wasn't even legal?"

"Don't you try and distract me Trixie, I mean Meryl. God, that's a boy's name. Can I just call you Meryline? It's so much prettier."

Meryl shook her head petulantly. "No! I can't believe you lied about Sid. He was one of the nice ones."

Faye nodded solemnly. "Yes, I believe he was the best one, all told. He begged me to quit drinking."

This was exhausting. Meryl picked up her boots, heading for the stairs. "Faye, as much as I'd like to discuss all your husbands and what you know about marriage, I am not going to talk about mine. I am going to bed."

Faye placed both hands on the back of the couch, twisting towards Meryl. "You are going to have revenge sex with that cop. It ain't gonna to feel nearly as good as you think it will."

Meryl dropped her boots on the floor, marching back to her mother, menacingly towering over the smaller woman. "What makes you think you understand one thing about me?"

Faye didn't back down. She loved a fight. "Because I know a thing or two about being hurt."

"This is my life Faye, not yours! This is seventeen years of marriage not two years shacking up together."

Faye shook her head. "I don't know anything about a scale of human pain but I know what it feels like to be alone." She rubbed the thin skin over her collar bones. "It's the worst feeling in the world."

Meryl flopped down on the couch, defeated. Faye joined her, perched gingerly, as if ready for flight. They stared at each other for a long time.

Meryl sighed. "You want to tell me about your business idea?"

18.

*"I love being married. It's so great to find
that one special person you want to
annoy for the rest of your life."*
-Rita Rudner

It was possibly the worst idea she'd ever heard in her life. A boudoir dance studio in the middle of a wealthy suburban enclave? It was absurd! Still, she hadn't said no. She couldn't look into her mother's hopeful, pleading face and shoot her down. So she found herself at a branch bank with her mother, trying to shove a small bit of cash into the bursting dam of her finances.

"I'd like to make a mortgage payment and a deposit into checking please," Meryl said to the bank clerk, simultaneously relieved and panicked by all the strings attached to this money.

Faye glanced over her shoulder distrustfully. Until she'd gotten her inheritance, she kept her money in a safety box buried on her trailer lot under a scrubby cactus, unearthed on moonless desert nights. Never having been robbed, she had a deep distrust of traditional banking. Of course, there had been times when money went missing but a blackout drunk is used to such occurrences.

"Your account is quite overdrawn Ms. Howe," said the clerk, raising his thick eyebrows. He was milk fed, with sausage fingers.

"I'm aware of that. Which is why I am making the deposit."

The witless clerk waited to be handed sufficient funds. Faye lifted the worn leopard print suitcase onto the counter. The duct tape sparkled in the recessed lighting. The clerk eyed the suitcase as if it contained a bomb. They had all types at the Bothell branch of Chase bank but this was a new one.

As if reading his mind, Faye said, "I bet you don't get many people bringing money in a suitcase. I bet mostly it goes the other way." She winked.

The clerk blinked repeatedly, glancing at the security officer, who approached with the delicacy of a linebacker. Faye batted her eyes. "Look at you, getting all worried about little old me. Here I am with thirty-eight thousand dollars cash to deposit." She raised her voice boastfully, so that the blind man, his dog, the two elderly ladies, and three men in the cold, marble tiled lobby could all overhear. It wasn't a large bank.

Meryl gritted her teeth. "Faye, please."

Faye handed the surprised clerk the first bundle of cash, stacking the money on the counter. "My grandson counted that all. He's so good with numbers. I said divide this thirty-eight thousand into four portions of equal value. He did it no time. Imagine that at twelve. Course, he ran out of rubber bands. Those thick ones are my granddaughter's hair ties. We need 'em back."

"It's very unusual for someone to carry such a large amount of cash around," said the clerk, eyebrows bunched into a frown.

Faye coyly tilted her head until the strands of her red wig hit her shoulder. "Not in Vegas, where I am from. I have friends that have carried hundreds of thousands down the street. Of course, that was back in the day, when everyone carried guns, you know."

The clerk's face went rigid. No, he did not know. He picked up one of the hundred dollar bills, putting it through a scanner. Meryl watched him tensely, not putting it past Faye to be involved in some hare-brained counterfeiting scheme. The clerk plucked a few random bills from different piles. "Just a precautionary measure, you know." He tacked on the last two words as a taunt.

Meryl wondered if he had a pet name for each of his chins.

Faye fiddled with her paperwork, pushing it across the countertop. "Sure. I bet you do this with everyone that comes in with a roll-aboard full of cash. I'm going to open up a business account for me and my daughter, right here. This is my daughter, Meryl." She curled her lips around the name with distaste. "She was born Trixie Louise which we all know is a much cuter name."

The clerk bobbed his head at Meryl. "Nice to meet you."

As each bill passed its test, the clerk grew friendlier. He scanned Faye's paperwork. "Certainly Ms. Danetto. I'll see if Ms. Wood is available to meet with you. She's our business banking specialist. Would you like a cup of coffee?"

"That would be real fine. I take sugar. Four teaspoons. I know I ought to cut down at my age but I don't gain a pound. I weight exactly the same as I did when I was twenty-five. Scout's honor."

Meryl declined coffee.

After the clerk tucked each bundle of money away in the vault, Faye and Meryl opened a business account together. Faye was ridiculously proud, boasting to Mrs. Wood, a fragile 63 year old black woman wearing a small gold cross at her throat, that she and her daughter Trixie, "Whoops I mean Meryl," were going to open the first exotic dance studio on the Eastside, maybe even Seattle.

"We're gonna teach pole dancing, some sexy boudoir dance, which sounds all Frenchie and stuff but it's just plain old showgirl moves. That's more my style. I use props like boas and feathers and gloves. I am a real good fan dancer. You ever seen a fan dance?"

Mrs. Wood, fingering her cross, pushed another paper across the desk. Meryl pegged her for Southern Baptist. "No, I don't believe I have. Sign here and here."

Faye moved her wrists in delicate circles. "It's real pretty. You kind of float the fans in front of the body almost like you're tickling yourself. It's a real tease, you know. Way harder than it looks. The trick is making it graceful. Those fans can be heavy. Not the feathers of course but the wooden part."

Mrs. Wood nodded, keeping her lips pressed tightly together as she took the document from Faye, showing Meryl where to sign. "Here and here."

Meryl was mortified that she had to hide funds from Alliance Mortgage in a joint account. She had requested a cashier's check to make two mortgage payments, hoping that Alliance wouldn't be able to trace the funds.

Her mother prattled on to Ms. Wood, as stiff and unbending as her name when Faye offered her two free introductory dance lessons.

Meryl had no intention of actually participating in the business. Besides, Faye didn't have the money to convince any landlord in Kirkland to rent her a space. So when the next words came out of Faye's mouth, Meryl emerged from her thoughts.

"I need a loan application too."

"Mmmmm-hmmm." Mrs. Wood nodded, shuffling off to find the paperwork.

"Faye, I don't think you should apply for a loan," Meryl whispered.

"Why not?" Faye snapped.

What Meryl wanted to say was that business loans are not given to red dirt Tennessee high school dropouts whose FICA scores stunk, who had at least, to her knowledge, two cars repossessed, a court mandated stint in rehab and an angry trailer park landlord who had tried, unsuccessfully, to evict Faye countless times.

What she said was, "It's a big risk."

Faye played with her cigarette case. "Don't be a fun sucker."

Meryl sighed. "A fun sucker? What is that? Someone who has lived in Kirkland for seventeen years? Someone who has seen businesses come and go and knows that the ones that make it are for people who drink wine, do yoga, enjoy fine art and concerts? These people do triathlons and take classes in how to use knives. Cooking knives not switch blades. They don't want to pole dance or be Rihanna. Do you really think these women are going to dance with feathers or install a pole in their master bedrooms?"

"Yes," Faye hissed. "I do. Sex sells. I know you might think it's everything that's wrong with America but not expressing your God given sexuality is what's wrong with this country. It's trying to kill it that leads to all manner of perversion. Look at Catholic priests."

Mrs. Wood, who had just returned, felt for her cross, suddenly scurrying away to search out another form.

"I'm not saying don't have sex," Meryl snapped. "That is not what I am saying."

"Having sex and feeling sexy are two different animals. Maybe if those ladies felt sexier, they'd have more sex and not need to drink so much wine."

Meryl shot back, "You are crazier than a bedbug."

Mrs. Wood had re-appeared behind Meryl. She stood awkwardly before stepping around to her chair, sliding a fat sheaf of papers across the desk to Faye. "It's a fair amount of paperwork. You can take it home and work on it if you'd like."

Meryl snagged the sheets from Faye's hand. "Thank you. We will." Turning to her mother she spat out, "I've got to get going."

Faye snatched the papers back, ripping the top sheet. To Mrs. Wood, she said, "I could use another cup of that fine coffee. I'm just gonna stay right here and fill this out. You don't mind, do you?"

Mrs. Wood glanced between them, wondering who was going to win this round.

Meryl dug around in her purse. She held her car keys aloft, jangling them in a sure-fire irritate-your-opponent bid. "I mind."

Mrs. Wood had never been so eager to get away from a client. "I'll set you up in our conference room. That's where the coffee is."

"Faye I'm leaving. I have resumes to send out before Henry gets home from school."

Faye followed Mrs. Wood's tiny purple figure across the office. "You go on honey, I'll take the bus."

Meryl trailed her, fuming. "Why can't you just take the application home and fill it out there?"

Faye spun around. "Because if I don't do this right now I might stop believing it could work."

***

St. John Vianney's lobby, like every other church she'd ever visited outside of Vegas, gave Faye the creeps. Vegas chapels were cheery places, draped with fairy lights and dusty silk flowers. Drunken couples could dash in at any moment, say their nuptials and embark on any kind of relationship they deemed appropriate. A church like this demanded something: sobriety, children, and tasteful eyeliner.

Faye wasn't looking for a middle class life, just an AA meeting. And that first step, walking into an unknown church, was always hard. All those statues staring down, judging.

"Yooo-hoo, right over here!" someone called from the dark.

Faye delved further into the narthex. It opened into a tiny chapel on the left, the main nave dead ahead, and a large multi-purpose room to the right. This was reserved for Boy Scouts, bingo and, three times a week, alcoholics who wished, mostly, to remain anonymous.

"Keep going!" The disembodied voice yelled. Faye could smell coffee, a hallmark of AA meetings, who frequently shifted their allegiance from booze to cigarettes and coffee.

She was a bit late, but nobody cared. Seated in hard grey folding chairs, thirty-four of the thirty-six people had announced their names, followed by the ubiquitous, "And I'm an addict."

The uniform proclamation always made Faye want to blurt, "and I'm an Orangutan," or something outrageous, to get a laugh. She never did, mostly because the one thing she'd learned above all at AA was that she shouldn't seek attention. She wasn't extra special or extra anything. She was just another addict.

The meeting was on the large end of the AA spectrum. Like Vegas they were all ages, shapes and sizes. Unlike Vegas, they were better groomed, with corporate logos stitched into their jackets: Microsoft, Boeing, Nintendo, AT&T. Designer purses squatted like small, obedient dogs beside women in tasteful make-up and burnished leather boots. Even the twenty-somethings wore nicer jeans and gold, instead of silver nose rings. There was an absence of tattoos, which Faye found refreshing.

Despite a nagging worry that this was a better class of drunk, Faye found a seat in the back. A few men covertly admired her legs. It was comforting.

A silver-haired man with broad shoulders spoke. "My name is Victor and I'm an alcoholic. I'm happy to say that my twelfth anniversary of sobriety was Sunday."

"Right on Victor!" "Go Victor." "Congratulations!" Some people clapped.

Victor smiled. "I celebrated with Italian food." He patted his stomach. Another escape: food.

Faye found herself wondering if he was single. She wished she'd worn her other wig or bought a new one for the occasion. She'd mentally rehearsed her spiel so that when her turn arrived, she didn't sound stupid. "My name is Faye. I've been sober almost five years. I'm up here visiting my daughter and grandchildren. I'm hoping to stay here and start a new business." She didn't mention Vegas. She didn't say new life. Everyone was here to start a new life.

Victor, arm slung over his chair, smiled kindly. Along with a few other people, he said "welcome" with such genuine warmth that Faye felt tears threatening the nine coats of carefully applied mascara. She pondered telling these nice people that she'd opened Meryl's liquor cabinet a few times, even smelled the bourbon once, as if she could get drunk from the fumes. That she lovingly touched the labels and thought that there was something truly beautiful in the carefully designed bottles.

Only another addict would understand that sometimes, when she woke up in Meryl's bonus room, she felt the booze singing her name in the sweetest, most seductive tones. Like James Earl Jones broadcasting from inside a bottle of Grey Goose. She'd dig her nails into her palms, talk to Jesus, sometimes just zone out on bad TV to get her mind off the shallow promise of oblivion. If that didn't work she smoked, exhaling out the window so she didn't go downstairs, closer to the liquor.

The later it grew, the harder it was shutting her mind against the past. The image of her dad, at the worn linoleum kitchen table in the tired old farmhouse kitchen, reappeared no matter how hard she fought.

The trick was feeling God in her tired body. Sometimes there was only regret, particularly at a certain hour, waiting for sunrise. Finding God in all the darkness was the real trick of sobriety.

Faye let the meeting go on without her, deciding not to talk. It made her feel stronger, knowing that others on this very hill fought the same battle daily.

She didn't need to talk. Just being here tonight was enough. She'd found her new meeting.

One day at a time.

***

"Oh that's rich, you of all people, giving me business advice," spat Meryl.

"Do you know how many small businesses actually survive? And what about health insurance?" Ethan countered.

Meryl thought her mother's idea was ludicrous but Ethan hating it made it sound perfect. "You don't think I can run a business. Is that it? You don't want me to succeed because you failed?"

Meryl wasn't going to come to the therapy session but at the last minute decided she'd use it to initiate a legal separation. She had to tell Ethan that she wanted to make it official. She couldn't let him continue to live a lie. Besides, Sandy said this was the next step.

The therapist sat across from them, his long thin marathoner legs crossed, narrow face attentive and serious. Jackie, asked for a reference, had said they would both like him; he was confident and successful. But Meryl thought he seemed like an effete pansy.

"Okay, stop. Both of you. We aren't going to address specific issues at this session. What we're here to tackle is the direction of this marriage."

"Down. That's where we're headed. Straight down," said Meryl, leaning back.

Ethan pointed his finger at Meryl, pointedly ignoring her last comment. "Do you hear her, calling me a failure?" He turned to the therapist. "She threw all my clothes off the balcony into the bushes. I had a hundred and eighty dollar dry cleaning bill."

"Why don't you just borrow the money from your girlfriend?" said Meryl. She cringed at the way she sounded, like a teenager.

"Whatever Meryl, I have been trying hard to talk to you. And the kids. Who don't want to talk to me either, thank you."

Meryl rolled her eyes. "Now you notice the kids?"

"I have always been a good father. Don't you dare throw that in my face. You didn't even know that Nathalie had quit the volleyball team."

Allen raised his hands like a traffic cop. "Both of you stop right there. Of course there's a lot of anger but I can't see you two if you're going to come in here with guns blazing. You both need to listen. Let me lead this conversation or I'm not going to work with you."

Okay, maybe he's not such a pansy, thought Meryl.

Allen turned to Meryl. "Why are you here?"

Meryl sighed. "Because my sister thought it would be a good idea. She said if the Allies and Germany could reach a truce on Christmas Eve, I should try being in the same room with my-," unable to spit out the word 'husband,' she finished, "-with him."

"You must agree or you wouldn't be here," said Allen. He had a grey goatee and long tapered fingers.

"I don't think this is the kind of conversation you can have in a Starbucks," said Meryl.

"Good point. And you, Ethan. Why are you here?"

"Because I love my wife and I want to work on our marriage." He looked at Meryl. "I'm very sorry."

She sneered. "Screw you."

Allen shook his head, sadly. "Meryl, you can't do this. Do you want this marriage to go forward?"

"I've had two weeks to think about it. Every single time I shut my eyes I see Ethan and Leslie having sex on our bed. It's on a loop in my head."

"In time, that will diminish; maybe even fade entirely if you make new memories together."

Meryl raised her finger. "I'm not done. He lost all our money and didn't tell me about it."

"I didn't lose it. I know exactly where every penny went. It went to trying to save the company. Some start ups work and some don't."

"You could have told me."

"You didn't want to know. Since I've known you, all you've wanted to be was financially secure. You loved the money. You loved the status, the house; you loved being the queen bee at the guild. Oh my God, you couldn't stop talking about meeting Melinda Gates. That meant a lot to you." He turned to Allen. "How do you have that conversation with your wife? Honey, you know how I put our life's saving into this company? Well, the company is going down in flames. And it's my fault."

Allen held up his hand. "I'm sure there were other mitigating circumstances."

Ethan turned to Meryl. "I didn't believe it was really happening. Does that make sense?"

"No."

Allen clasped his hands. His white leather chair squeaked as he moved forward. "Meryl, it's called disassociation. When unmanageable things happen to people, they distance themselves from the event, as in, 'this really can't be happening to me.' It's like their own life is a movie they are watching. There's a level of distance that is direct result of unbearable stress. Not only was Ethan failing his associates, he was failing you, the most important person in his life. It was a coping mechanism."

Meryl got up from the chair to look out the windows. Allen's office had a view of icy Puget Sound. The Cascades were a jagged white fringe across the steel grey water. She leaned her head against the cool glass for a moment to collect her thoughts. Her breath fogged the window. She turned to Ethan. "So how do you disassociate yourself from screwing our neighbor?"

Ethan turned to the therapist. "Aren't we supposed to be talking to each other in a more respectful way?"

Allen nodded. "Yes but it's a legitimate question."

Ethan hung his head. "I didn't. I knew that was happening."

"I bet you did. I've been to the doctor." That last part was a lie, mostly to turn the screw on Ethan, make the consequences of his choice real, in a physical sense.

Ethan spoke to her very gently. "Please turn down the hostility just a notch."

She shook her head. "I'm just getting in touch with my hostility. My mother moved in."

Ethan continued. "Leslie was the person I talked to."

Meryl snorted. "Talked?"

Ethan blanched.

Allen nodded. "I know this is very painful for both of you but she needs to hear this."

Meryl shook her head, tucking her hair behind her ear. "Painful? No, a root canal is painful. This is a tectonic plate shift that registers twelve on the Richter scale and yet only I can feel it."

Ethan stared directly at her. "It's good for me to hear this Meryl. I can only imagine."

Allen waited for Meryl to respond; pleased to see her features soften, slightly. It was a progress, infinitesimally small but movement nonetheless; toward what, he couldn't be sure.

"Okay," said Meryl softly, returning to her seat. She closed her eyes, rested her hands on the chair's arms, tilting her chin up as if preparing for a blow. "Tell me."

Ethan closed his eyes. "Yes Meryl, we had sex. Several times."

She opened her eyes, folded her hands, suddenly all business. "Define several."

"I wasn't counting."

"Give me a ballpark."

Ethan gave Allen a pleading look. "When did it start?" Allen asked.

"Last summer."

"That's what Nathalie said."

Ethan rubbed his eyes. "Oh my God."

Meryl turned to Allen. "Our daughter saw him flirting with her while he mowed the lawn." She turned to Ethan. "You fired the gardener so you could take your shirt off in front of Leslie."

"I fired the gardener because we couldn't afford one anymore."

Meryl thought of opening the door to her cleaning lady, apologizing to her for not calling, saying she had to let her go. The woman had been so angry; she'd marched out of the house with 5 Ralph Lauren towels, cursing in Portuguese. Every day it was something new and horrible. "So you *disassociate* your company's collapse but you talk to Leslie about it?"

Allen surreptitiously checked his watch. "It's a coping mechanism, not a rationally thought out plan."

"This isn't going anywhere," Ethan said. "Are we going to work on this marriage or are you going to beat me up for the rest of my life?"

"You are still living with her!" Meryl screeched, enunciating each word with such fury that flecks of spit escaped her mouth.

Allen looked ready to bolt.

"I don't have any place else to go. You won't let me back in."

"You never asked."

"Will you let me back in?"

"Hell no!" Meryl roared, thinking it felt tremendously good to yell at him. She loved therapy. She loved that someone else paid for it. That Horrible Night in her bedroom was a car crash and she was finally getting a chance to yell at the other driver.

"It's still half my house!" Ethan said.

"You took out a second mortgage without telling me! If you want to take this to court I can have you charged with forgery Ethan." This little tidbit was courtesy of Sandy Chan, who had asked all kinds of practical questions to which Meryl had no answers.

"You did sign it. You just didn't know or didn't care what it was."

"You should have told me!" She was yelling again.

"You should have given a shit. You let me do everything!"

Allen's voice went up an octave as he addressed Ethan. "Is there any place else you might live?"

Meryl turned to Allen. "He can live with his parents."

Ethan slapped his hands over his eyes. "I am not living with my parents."

"You mean your mother. Your mother is a stone cold bitch." It felt good to finally say what she thought about Betsy. Really good.

Allen put up a long fingered hand. "Name calling isn't going to get us anywhere."

"No, it's okay. My mother is a bitch."

Meryl turned to him, her eyes flashing. "What is going to get us somewhere? Huh? What do other women do when they find their husband schtupping the stewardess next door?"

"She's a flight attendant," added Ethan. "How many different ways can you find to describe what happened?"

Meryl gave him a Cheshire cat grin. "Sweetheart, I haven't even gotten started yet."

Allen took off his stylish black and white glasses to rub the bridge of his nose. "Meryl, you are one very angry woman and I can appreciate that but the question I want you to ask yourself is do you want to work at it or do you want to call it quits?"

"What if I just want to torture him some more?"

"You fucking bitch!" Ethan said.

"That's the first heartfelt thing you've said in here!" Meryl snapped.

Allen stood up, slapping his thighs as he rose.. "Okay, our hour's up. Normally at this point I ask you both how you are feeling but I think you've pretty much spelled it out. I'll see you in one week."

Meryl left first, pausing in the plush, modern waiting area to find her car keys. Ethan went straight out the glass door to the elevator. They stood side-by-side, waiting.

"They ought to have separate exits," Ethan said, staring at the elevator door, willing it to open.

"Did you push the button?" Meryl asked.

Ethan punched the button. "I can't even think straight. That was awful."

Meryl applied a coat of lipstick. "I thought it went very well."

"Jesus." Burying his hands in his pockets, he was silent. "I forgot my coat." He ran down the hall, returning a minute later with his jacket. He didn't know if he was happy or disappointed that she was still waiting.

"If you move in with your parents, it would be a show of faith."

The elevator opened. Four business people were inside. Ethan stood next to Meryl, whispering, as the door closed. "You want me to kill myself? That's it, isn't it? My dad is furious about the company and my mother thinks I'm seventeen."

"Emotionally, you are."

Ethan scratched his nose with his middle finger. She giggled, which still, in spite of everything, warmed his heart. "At least we're having a good time."

"Sarcasm is the refuge of cowards." She kept her eyes on the flashing numbers above the door.

He looked up. "I can't help it. You scare me."

"Good!" She snapped.

The business people crammed in the elevator all pretended not to listen but Ethan could tell that they were relishing every word. He just prayed they didn't recognize him. The software community was surprisingly small. They knew that his company was in the sewer; they didn't need to know that his marriage followed. The elevator doors opened. Meryl strode into the lobby, walking quickly.

He marched beside her, pleading. "Meryl, I know you. I know your mother. Don't start a new business. We need to simplify." He reached out for her arm.

She spun on her heels, yanking her arm free as if burned. "Do. Not. Touch. Me." She was pale, shaking and furious.

"I'm sorry; I just wanted you to listen."

"Don't touch me." She repeated softly, her eyes glittering with tears.

Melting down in the lobby near the silver Christmas tree wasn't part of the game plan. Blinking furiously, swiping at any errant mascara streaks, she hiked up her purse onto her shoulder. "I will leave Christmas up to the kids. That's the best I can do." Walking as fast as she possibly could to the revolving exit, her heels clicked on the marble floor. It was a lonely sound.

Watching her leave, Ethan thought he would do anything to win her back. Anything.

19.

The afternoon of Christmas Eve and she was cleaning. Before you covet someone else's beautiful home, Faye thought ruefully, try cleaning the damn thing first. While Meryl went to a job interview, Faye found the cleaning supplies, vacuum and a very strange puff at the end of a telescope stick. It was, according to Henry, for cleaning cobwebs off high ceilings. It could reach every wall in her trailer if she stood in one spot. She'd never cleaned like this in her life and hoped Meryl would appreciate the effort.

Nathalie was at a party with Denny. Henry was wrapping presents. After gamely swiping at all the errant cobwebs, explaining that they'd just be rebuilt in a week, Henry disappeared, leaving Faye to clean a house that grew larger by the minute.

As she lugged the vacuum down the stairs, sweating and groaning, Faye wondered if she'd bitten off more than she could chew. Living in a trailer by her lonesome, rarely having company, she'd had the luxury of cleaning when the mood hit, which it rarely did. Sometimes a beam of sunshine that couldn't make it through the windows or a fringe of cat hair ringing a lampshade set her off. The entire process, from top to bottom, took a slapdash fifteen minutes.

Plus, she thought, as she swabbed the slate entrance, big houses were normally owned by people who could afford someone else to clean them. Both Meryl and her house suffered from lack of time and sleep. A patina of grime and clutter had grown on the stairs, couch and bathrooms. It didn't bother Faye but she could tell that it added to the layer of stress suffocating her daughter. Meryl had yelled at the kids a few times, asking for help. But she'd stopped there, not getting specific enough for kids that genuinely didn't notice the mess. At least Henry remembered which night to put out the garbage.

"Jesus, this place is huge!" Faye yelled up at the ceiling, waiting for Jesus to agree.

She missed him. She was planning a surprise for Meryl and it would be nice to have an adult conversation, someone with judgment about this kind of thing. Nathalie's response, after asking her three times to take out her ear buds was, "Uh-huh, sounds cool," before continuing on her way. Faye could have said "I'm going to wear body paint instead of clothes from now on," and the response would have been the same.

Henry was enthusiastic but Faye was beginning to think he saw her not so much as a grandmother but as a science experiment valued for its unpredictable explosions. Jackie would advise her to mind her own damn business so of course she didn't call her. That girl didn't take a risk on anything.

Jesus, apparently, was booked during the holiday season.

Faye carried the crusty dishes out of the living room, only to find the sink full of breakfast dishes. Meryl had rushed out asking the kids to take care of them. She needed a copy of her resume and was on her way to Kinko's. The ink cartridge was $150 and she couldn't afford a new one. Even looking for a job cost money.

A party was just what Meryl needed to get into the holiday mood. Something to show her daughter that her friends hadn't forgotten her.

Last night, Faye had come home exhausted from filling out the loan paperwork at the bank. It took two hours and many phone calls to Nevada, calling in favors for references. Her InSpa boss, Yvette, had refused to admit that Faye had covered for her, in a managerial position, when an X Factor audition led to an unscheduled week in LA. It took a gentle reminder that Yvette could still lose her job if corporate knew that instead of being stricken with shingles, she'd spent a week tap dancing in front of a panel of stoned judges.

Each reference involved a delicate exchange of blackmail. Both she and her longtime landlord, a former heroin addict named Steve, knew things about each other that could land them in jail. It was exhausting.

Last night, walking home from St. John Vianney after the AA meeting, a drizzle of frigid rain had soaked her thin coat and white vinyl boots. She needed winter clothes, starting, perhaps, with a festive winter coat in hot pink or neon orange. From what she'd seen, Northwest women, bundled in their belted black down parkas, looked like walking sleeping bags. Maybe AA Victor would notice her if she wore something flashy. With any luck she could become what her old meeting called the Shiny New Object. The new old girl.

Her bubble burst when she entered Meryl's house. Meryl had been sprawled on the couch, deep into a bottle of champagne. What was it, Faye thought, as she hung up her dripping jacket, about drunks? They have to wave their inebriation like flags, daring you to spoil their great mood. She sat on the stairs, unzipped her boots. They were ruined.

"If it isn't Fabulous Faye herself! Join me. I found the last bottle of good champagne. It's a hundred and fifty bucks a pop. I looked it up. Seriously. Some expensive stuff we used to serve on New Year's Eve." She wasn't a classy drunk. Her words limped along, falling into one another weakly.

Faye tried to take the bottle away but of course Meryl wouldn't surrender.

"I'm sick of doing everything right. I did everything right and look where it got me."

"Sometimes life isn't fair." Faye was tired. "But you still have to keep going."

"I want a chance to wallow. Isn't that what you call it? Do you think I am wallowing or stewing in my own pain?"

"Both. I'll listen when you're sober." There was nothing more tedious to a reformed drunk than an inebriate. It was like staring at a particularly unflattering photo.

Meryl thumped her chest. "When I am sober, I am not a nice person."

Faye nodded in agreement. "You can be quite bitchy."

Meryl wasn't listening, deep in her own miasma. "It's scary. I threw a bottle just like this one at Ethan. Slashed his arm open like a tomato. I'm this angry horrible woman who is afraid to admit that I shop at a food bank. I do. I did." She threw her arms up. "I qualified with flying colors. They even helped me with my resume. Turns out that former teachers make good salespeople or corporate trainers." She melted into a smile, resting her head on the back of the couch. "Whatever that is."

"You just pretend like you know what you're doing. That's half of life. Hell, maybe all of it." Faye thought about touching her forehead for a long time before she actually leaned over, stroking her daughter's soft brown hair gently, like she'd done when Trixie was tiny, awakened by night terrors. Maybe she hadn't been the best mother but she'd had her moments.

Meryl didn't seem to mind. She closed her eyes, continuing, "Sam is really sweet. You're going to like him. Maybe we should invite him over for Christmas. And his dad. You'd like his dad." Her voice lowered to a whisper. "You know what? If I could have any wish I would go back in time."

"Believe me honey; God isn't in the business of answering drunken prayers."

"I said a wish, not a prayer."

"Same thing."

Meryl looked up at her mother with a crooked smile. "When did you get so wise?"

"When I quit drinking."

"When I quit drinking all I feel is pain."

After much bargaining, Faye got Meryl into bed with a bowl of cereal, promising that she'd bring back the nearly empty champagne bottle once she ate the entire bowl. She trudged back upstairs to find Meryl passed out, snoring like a sailor. Faye sat on the bed and called Jackie.

As soon as Jackie picked up, Faye lit into her. "Your sister is going through hell. She just threw up a hundred dollars worth of champagne all over the couch and lemme tell you it don't clean up any better than the cheap stuff. Where have you been?"

Jackie held the phone away from her ear for the opening volleys. "Hi Mom, nice to talk to you too."

"Oh don't give me that bullshit. Tell me you're at least coming over here for Christmas Eve."

"I'm going skiing." Jackie's voice was blunt, defensive. She'd planned on dropping off presents tonight but the traffic was so bad on the floating bridge, she'd postponed it. Plus, they'd tacked on a toll which meant she had to pay to go get abused by her own family.

"Who goes skiing on Christmas Eve? What kind of horseshit is that?"

Jackie peered into the darkness outside of her condo. Far below strings of white lights hung from barren trees lining the street. "The kind where people get away from their families and enjoy being outside and don't worry about broken marriages and drunken sisters and cheating brother-in-laws. The kind where you don't have to cook or drive or worry about how much you're eating because you're skiing all day. That kind."

Faye sighed. Except for the skiing part, it sounded nice. "You're going to be here for New Year's Eve, right?"

"Yes."

In the master bedroom, Meryl stirred, wiping her nose, murmuring something about Ethan's car burning. Faye squeezed her daughter's foot before stepping into the hallway, shutting the door quietly behind her. She said to Jackie. "I'm sorry baby. I just want to see you. Your sister is kind of a train wreck."

Jackie had moved to her kitchen, gazing at the Starbucks card. Who buys a Starbucks card for $100? And what was less personal than a gift card for coffee? It was a gift that said, "I like you slightly more than the newspaper delivery guy." She picked up the card. "She and Ethan went for their first therapy session today."

Faye was happy to hear this. It was a step in the right direction. "She didn't tell me."

Jackie slipped the card back into the tiny envelope. Maybe $100 was too much. She wanted it to be a real gift, not something her patients shoved at her this time of year, embarrassed and never quite sure of the protocol. It was freaking her out. Normally she broke up with people right before Christmas to avoid this situation. "Look, I'm really sorry Mom but I've got to pack and then I've got a phone counseling session. Christmas is very hard on some of my clients."

Faye sat down at the top of the stairs, staring out the dark windows of Leslie's house. She took off her wig, scratching her limp hair. "Yeah, 'tis the season."

Jackie's voice softened. She slid the tiny envelope into her purse, where it would sit like a bomb. "I love you ma."

"You too baby. Who you going skiing with?"

Jackie hesitated a second. "A friend. I'll call you Christmas morning, okay?" She felt slightly guilty about lying to her mother but really, her whole life had taught her that if it was precious, keep it to yourself. Besides, if the gift card didn't offend Rob, her family certainly would.

Faye hung up. Being a hick with two worldly daughters and no husband could sometimes be the loneliest feeling in the world. The remaining champagne called to her, in a seductive French accent, promising that one little taste wouldn't hurt.

She went downstairs, found the green bottle and sniffed. Taking Meryl's delicate crystal flute to the sink, she poured herself a healthy slug. Holding it up to the light, she admired the tiny bubbles rising to the surface through the pale straw colored liquid. Pretty as a picture, she thought. She recognized the fancy gold label. Rich weekenders in

Vegas drank Dom Perignon. One tiny sip wouldn't hurt a
flea. The glass was to her lips when she heard a car door
slam. It was Henry, coming home from ice skating with
Max. All the neighbors had been very helpful, providing
diversions for the kids, bringing over food, as if someone
had died.

Henry blew through the door, bringing winter with
him, cheeks blazing. Faye put the glass down on the granite
countertop so quickly the slender stem shattered. Ignoring
the mess, Faye hugged Henry fiercely, with tears in her
eyes.

"Boy am I glad to see you kid!"

"Geez, I was like, two point nine miles away,"
Henry said, ducking out of the overly fierce embrace. He
foraged through the refrigerator. Its contents were, lately,
more interesting. When he noticed her staring at him, he
mistook her relief for curiosity. "I always check the
odometer," he said, serving himself a piece of Lorraine's
organic apple pie.

After putting Henry to bed, explaining that his
mom went to bed early with a headache, and that "she'll
probably have it tomorrow too," Faye went downstairs to
clean up the shattered crystal, burying it deep in the
garbage.

Sitting at the kitchen table with a cup of coffee, she
thought about what her first sponsor, Ginny, had said
about backsliding. "Find a project. Throw yourself at
something that is going to take a big chunk of time. Slice up
the hours in your day and make sure each one is filled. Take
a class, start a garden, adopt a dog, bake someone a
birthday cake, take up Peruvian plate spinning. It doesn't
matter what you do just so long as you aren't boozing it
up." Rather than let herself get sucked into the mudslide of
Meryl's depression, she was going to do something.

She was going to throw a party.

***

"Let me get this straight, you want me to go visit my dad at his girlfriend's house?" Nathalie had returned from Denny's house on Christmas Eve with a glazed, vacant look in her eyes. She'd tried to dash upstairs but Faye grabbed her arm.

"Lemme smell your hair," Faye demanded, sniffing her granddaughter's locks like a police dog.

After much effort, Faye had gotten the house sparkling clean. Bowls of potato chips and her famous pigs in a blanket sat on Meryl's fancy plates on the coffee table. The deviled eggs and jalapeno cheese dip hadn't gone so well. They were in the trash. She'd gone to QFC, bought wine with the most interesting labels and hoped for the best. She'd considered buying fancy cheese but could not believe what they wanted for a mildewed hunk rolled in what appeared to be yard clippings. She'd grabbed some spray cheese and Ritz, which always looked festive topped with sliced olive.

What she didn't bargain on was a stoned granddaughter.

Nathalie stepped back. "I'm not high," she sighed. After spending the previous evening quietly peddling two ounce bags of Berkley Bum at Hazel Karr's parent's annual Christmas party, Denny thought the perfect Christmas gift would be her virginity.

"It would be, like, the ultimate," he'd whined after they'd exchanged gifts. He'd bought her a cobra arm bracelet that hurt when she flexed.

"You don't like your skateboard?" she'd countered. "I had it custom built."

He'd pointed at the cobra's beady red eyes. "Those are real freakin' rubies, man. Not garnets."

They'd argued for half an hour. He'd gotten stoned, pointedly not offering her any. Nathalie, left, slamming the basement door without bothering to say goodbye to Denny or his parents, upstairs doing bong hits in celebration of the nativity.

"You're not stoned. I guess there really are Christmas miracles," said Faye.

"Your sarcasm is touching," sniped Nathalie.

"You go tell your daddy Merry Christmas. Whatever mistakes he's made, he still loves you."

Nathalie crossed her arms. "I'm not going. And you can't guilt me into it."

"He made your favorite dinner: corn dogs and macaroni and cheese."

"Which would be perfect, if I were six."

Henry, who'd been upstairs messaging back and forth with Mark, came thumping down the stairs. He linked his arm through his sister's, facing Faye. "I'm not going if she's not. You can't make me."

Faye wondered why Henry was siding with a sister who treated him like a punching bag. She knew he was dying to see his father. Faye pondered the situation, tapping her chin with one frosty white fingernail. She'd bought a new wig for the occasion: brunette and long, very Veronica Lake. Her new gold snowflake sweater dress showed off her trim body.

"Don't do this for your daddy then. Do it for your mom. This is her first Christmas without your daddy and I wanted to have her friends over because she needs to laugh. And if you go next door for half an hour, she won't have to worry about you."

Nathalie shook her head. "We can just be upstairs watching TV."

Faye shook her head. "Your parents might be going through a real rough patch but your mother would be happy if she knew you were spending just a little time with your daddy." Technically this was lie but Faye hoped Jesus was otherwise occupied while she fudged it.

Henry pointed his thumb toward Leslie's house. "Even if it's over there?"

"Leslie is on a trip. It's just your dad." She crossed two fingers over her heart, while gazing directly into Nathalie's calculating blue eyes. "I promise." Ethan had been so grateful to her for coordinating; he would be heartbroken if they refused.

Henry looked up at his big sister. His face had slimmed in the past year, making him look more like Ethan. "I'm doing whatever you're doing," he said to his sister, pulling her closer.

What do you know? Faye thought. Maybe the silver lining was bringing these two closer.

"Get off," Nathalie snapped, pushing Henry. "I have to find my freakin' coat."

20.

"The man who says his wife can't take a joke,
forgets that she took him."
—Oscar Wilde

Meryl sat in the driver's seat, parked in her own garage, both arms folded over the steering wheel, exhausted. She should have known that only a nutcase would schedule a job interview for 2:30 on Christmas Eve. Then again, she'd thought Michael Kippler might be Jewish and therefore didn't have to rush off to shop, or attend a holiday party. If she'd been in the work force all this time, she might have seen it coming.

The fifth floor office had been quiet, nearly empty except for a few cubicle dwellers loading their bags. Michael Kippler's office was open, impressive, with a cheerful view of the festive streets below. Giant illuminated snowflakes on the Bellevue Square façade shone across the street.

After a short interview, during which he described his company's educational software and asked her some questions about her teaching and fundraising experience, he admitted that he really didn't need to conduct the interview that very evening. There wasn't even a job, right now. But there would be very soon when one of the corporate trainers went on maternity leave. He apologized but, nonetheless, was dying to find out, while she was here, what had happened at Inspire, her husband's company.

Then he asked her if she'd like to continue this downstairs, at Joey's, over a drink. That's when Meryl noticed, with a furtive glance, that everyone else in the office had vanished.

For the first time in decades Meryl did the delicate tap dance performed by those needing a job, money and security desperately and also needing to save body and soul by running like hell. A drink, she thought, would dissipate her hangover but hammer her self-respect. Michael Kippler made it clear that he was available to continue this very promising interview, another time, over dinner. Meryl made it clear that she would love to come to the office for a follow up interview, maybe even lunch.

"It's Christmas Eve, my husband is expecting me."

"Is he?" Michael had raised his eyebrows at her empty ring finger. "Tell him I said Merry Christmas," he said at the elevator, leaning in, plucking a piece of lint from her lapel, centimeters away from her breast. "I'll be in touch."

The problem was, Meryl thought as she got out of the car, was she'd really gotten up her hopes. A job at Education First as a corporate trainer might have allowed them to keep the house. At the very least it would given them health insurance. She probably stunk of desperation which, to a creep like Michael Kippler, was intoxicating.

She opened the laundry room door into the living room. Bright lights and mingled perfume assaulted her.

"Surprise!" yelled Sandy Chen, popping out from behind a column wearing an over-sized green and red elf hat with pointy ears. In one hand was a luminous pomegranate martini. She thrust it at Meryl, spilling some onto the freshly cleaned slate. "Merry Blinking Christmas Meryl! Your mom is just awesome."

Her entire book club wore elf hats. Every time they moved, they jingled collectively. It was like being greeted by all the Whos down in Whoville, waiting patiently en masse while she hung her coat. There was a round of hugs and Merry Christmases. Meryl apologized for taking them all away from their families on Christmas Eve but they all insisted that they needed a break. Besides, it was early enough to spend the bulk of the evening with their families.

Who in the hell else would plan a party on Christmas Eve besides her mother?

After she'd made the rounds, they allowed her to dash upstairs and change into jeans. She gulped two Advil, anxious and depressed now that she was forced to act cheerful after being sexually harassed. She stared at her red rimmed eyes in the bathroom mirror, the careful make-up that only highlighted her pallor. She was a mess.

Michael Kippler brought up memories she'd spent a lifetime dodging.

Forcing herself to return to the party, she found a drink and space on the couch. Faye piled a plate with food, leaving it at her elbow before going outside to smoke. She wasn't sure if Meryl, who seemed agitated, appreciated all the effort she'd put into this party. Besides, this was Christmas Eve and she needed a moment to talk to Jesus even more than she needed the nicotine.

Diane sat down next to Meryl, patting her leg. "I made my chicken wings with blue cheese dip: greasy goodness. You should really eat a few. You look thin."

Meryl took a sip of the martini. "I will. Did Faye set up the bar?"

Diane shook her head. "No, Lorraine did. She came up with kale and pepper vodka shots too but no one's drinking those. Who wants vitamins with their booze?"

Meryl picked up one of the chicken wings. "Where's Zoe?"

Diane's face tightened. "At home."

"Nathalie will be back soon. Zoe should come over." She swallowed a bite of the chicken. "I'll have Nathalie text her."

Diane shook her head. "That's okay. She's -" Diane searched for a lie. "Got homework."

Meryl cocked her head. "On Christmas Eve?"

Before Meryl could question any further, Carol joined them, balancing a glass of orange juice on her knee. She wore a wool burgundy jumper and pearls. "Merry Christmas Meryl! I know this must be terribly hard for you but tonight I hope you feel loved. By God and by your friends."

Tears sprang to Meryl's eyes. "I do. Thank you so much. Aren't you usually at the church directing the nativity play?"

Carol nodded, patting her mouth with a napkin. "It's an old story," she said. "I think everyone knows what to do."

"Stick a baby in a crèche and hope for the best," said Sandy Chen. "I played Mary once if you can believe that. Chinese Mary. I said if they didn't, I'd sue them."

"That's the Christmas spirit." Lorraine stood by the bar, eyeing her un-touched vodka shots.

Meryl looked around the room at the women's bright faces. "I'm really moved. I don't know what to say other than thank you. You're all so sweet."

Lorraine threw down a vodka shot. "It was your mom's idea. She wanted to cheer you up."

The martini was helping Meryl's champagne hangover. She'd limit herself to one. "It's working."

Sandy Chen nodded her head enthusiastically. "And her business idea: the exotic dance studio, it's a homerun. I say go for it. There are enough stupid yoga studios in this town. You can downward dog just about anywhere. I wouldn't mind shaking some booty once a week. We're too old to hit the clubs. Those twenty somethings with their tiny butts piss me off. It's a seriously decent idea."

Meryl kept the smile pasted on her face. "In theory." She looked around; making sure her mother was out of sight.

"She's outside," said Diane, mimicking smoking.

"Honestly, I know it's her dream but going into business with Faye would be my nightmare," said Meryl.

"Why?" asked Sandy. "She's a hoot."

"Maybe but that doesn't make her a good business partner. Have you ever worked with your mother?" asked Meryl.

Sandy took another sip of her ruby martini, shifting the jingle bell from one side of her head to the other. "I sold real estate for my mother in college. She could be quite the pit bull in pearls but I learned more about negotiating from her than I did in law school."

Meryl picked up a Ritz piled high with cheese, topped with an olive. Her mother's favorite. "My mom's previous work experience is taking off her clothes for men."

There was an awkward silence in the room. Meryl turned to follow everyone's gaze. Faye stood behind the couch, wearing her thin coat, gazing numbly at her daughter. Jesus hadn't shown.

Lorraine stepped forward, wishing she could jump across the couch, throw an arm around Faye, who was shivering. "One of the best movies I've ever seen in my life was Gypsy with Nathalie Wood. Have you ever seen that Faye?"

The reference to the movie was a misfire, thought Meryl. Her mother saw her stripping as a triumph, not a sad downward spiral.

Faye shook her head, her erect posture deflated, eyes flat and unfocused. "Parts of it on late night TV. Never seen the whole thing." She ran out of steam. "I'm just going to go over and check on the kids a minute."

Meryl stood, following Faye out the front door. "Faye, I'm so sorry. I didn't mean…"

Outside, Faye marched quickly to her car as Meryl protested, begging her to come back. "Honestly, I didn't mean it that way."

Faye spun around, realizing she should have borrowed a warmer coat. "What way did you mean? You're angry and you're looking for someone to blame. Well quit blaming me. I've done nothing but help you from the minute I showed up. Did you even notice how clean your house was? I threw a party for you because I know what it's like to spend Christmas Eve alone."

Meryl bit her lip, looking at her feet. "I'm sorry."

Faye struggled into her coat. "Quit being sorry and start acting thankful."

"Thank you!" Meryl called after her mother. "I was mean and spiteful and I'm sorry."

"You embarrassed me in there," Faye said. "You could tell my story a million ways and make me sound like a mother doing her best. But no, you make me sounds like a sleazy tramp. I am just as good as you. Maybe better because I'm not a snob!"

"I have something to tell you!" Meryl yelled again but Faye had already driven down the street and out of sight.

Meryl gazed at the thin grey clouds, illuminated by a sliver of moon, praying her mother wasn't headed for a bar.

***

"I got you each something," Ethan said, after they'd eaten. He disappeared upstairs, breaking the awkward silence with his purposeful energy.

Nathalie used his absence to study her surroundings. The kitchen, although much trendier than her own, was nearly identical. It was weird, sitting in this alternate kitchen, with no visible Christmas decorations, eating Trader Joe's macaroni and cheese and mini corn dogs. During dinner Ethan kept nervously jumping up from the table, bringing ketchup, forgetting a second batch of corn dogs in the oven.

Nathalie imagined her Dad shopping for this dinner; wheeling his cart around TJ's, trying to remember what Meryl bought. You saw those dads once in a while, trying to figure it out, squinting at items on the shelves, overwhelmed. It was really sad. He was trying so hard.

Henry played with the rim of his glass of sparkling cider, seeing if he could make it sing. Nathalie didn't eat or speak much, picking at her black nail polish, checking her phone in her lap. Cell phones weren't normally allowed at the table but Ethan didn't comment.

Henry reached into the bag at his feet, bringing out two presents and setting them on the table. While Nathalie concentrated on her phone and the text argument she was having with Denny, Ethan returned. He cleared the dishes, bringing back dessert: green and red Oreos and holiday M&M's on a plate. Before he sat down, he tidied up the kitchen.

Nathalie whispered to Henry, not looking up from her phone. "Two presents?"

"One from each of us."

Nathalie texted while she spoke. "I didn't buy him one."

Henry shrugged. "It says it's from you."

Nathalie frowned at something she was reading from Denny. "What is it?"

"A tie."

"Not very imaginative of me."

"Faye says it's the thought that counts."

Nathalie looked up at him; her heavily lined eyes too old for her face. "I think he's a lying douche bag. That's my thought."

They were quiet as Ethan sat down, handing an envelope to each of them. "I'm sorry we're having this kind of Christmas. It's not what I…" He'd already promised himself that tonight wouldn't be dragged down, if possible, by his mistakes. This was about the future. "Thanks so much for coming over here. You don't know how much it means to me to see you both tonight."

Nathalie took the envelope as if handling dirty toilet paper.

Henry offered his dad both presents. "These are from us. *Both of us,*" he said firmly, with a glance at his sister.

"You open yours first," said Ethan.

Henry ripped open the envelope. Inside was a Christmas letter with pictures of him and his dad throughout their lives on Christmas: Ethan holding a Christmas stocking with newborn Henry inside, 3 year old Henry posing with an plastic sword, pretending to cut down a squat pine at the Red Barn Christmas Tree Farm, six year old Henry bawling on Santa's lap, ten year old Henry hung upside down by Ethan on Christmas morning, wearing the Batman pajamas he'd gotten the night before. Beside each picture was a funny, tender caption composed by Ethan: the best Christmas present I ever got, hanging with my favorite bat. At the bottom: From the Luckiest Dad in the World. Happy Christmas 2013. Love, Dad.

Nathalie gazed at her card, thinking that her dad was trying to remind them of what a great dad he was when actually all it did was point out what a crap dad he'd become. Also, her parents used to be much better looking.

Ethan said, "Don't worry, there is a real gift."

He took out his wallet. For a moment, Nathalie hoped he was going to give them a wad of cash, which would have been awesome. Instead he handed them two laminated cards. "I renewed your ski passes."

Henry shook his head. "But Mom said we couldn't afford to ski." Every year until now they'd done a Saturday ski bus. Every year Nathalie said she was too old but was easily persuaded. Secretly, although it was for dorks, she loved it. All of it. The skiing, the French fries at lunch, the sleepy ride back in the dark bus.

Ethan sighed. "She's right. I have a buddy who owed me a favor. His company runs Snoqualmie Summit so it worked out. I'm going to take you guys up every Wednesday after school. If it's okay with your mom." He held up another card. "I got one too."

Nathalie went back to looking at her Christmas card. There was a photo of her and Zoe, the year they both played elves in the school play in those hot, itchy felt costumes. She hadn't heard from Zoe in so long. And there was that Christmas dress she begged her mother for when she was six: the sequined snowflakes all around the hem. They sparkled when she twirled. There was the igloo dad helped them build in the front yard four years ago, rigged up with tiny lights. She'd huddled inside, imagining that she was an ice princess who traveled by jingling sleigh.

The card, and her father's kind words, took her back to a much simpler time: before boys, sex and drugs; before her parent's marriage starting falling apart. The card made her feel worn out. This wasn't what sixteen was suppose to feel like.

She didn't hear her dad talking until he asked the second time.

"What?"

He looked so vulnerable and scared, which further unnerved her. "Do you still want to ski with me Nat?"

Nathalie popped a green M&M in her mouth, ferociously controlling herself. How to act like you don't give a shit when all you want to do is bawl? "Yeah, I don't know. I guess."

Her dad grinned as if she'd jumped up and down in excitement. "I'll take it."

***

"I'm sorry I brought up the whole exotic dance studio thing," said Sandy Chen, her lips greasy with chicken wing. "You're probably right. More businesses fail than make it."

Meryl shook her head, staring into a glass of water. The party was winding down fast. "I am so hard on my mother."

"Um hello, it's called being a daughter," Sandy said.

Carol put on her coat before stopping to pat Meryl's shoulder. "You're too hard on yourself dear. She'll be back."

"I doubt it," Meryl said, thinking her mother had gone back to her old refuge: a bar.

"My family's back from church. I have to run," Carol bent down to kiss her cheek, grasping her hand. "Tell your mother I said thank you for a lovely evening. Just delightful."

When Diane came over to say goodbye, Meryl asked if she could come into the kitchen. "Zoe didn't have homework on Christmas Eve. You can tell me Diane, really. Did Nathalie do something to hurt Zoe's feelings?"

Diane wiped her hair off her face, exasperated. "You really don't know, do you?"

Meryl blinked, wondering what else could possibly go wrong. "What?"

"When you called me asking who put the pot in the brownies at the party, I thought it had to be Lorraine," said Diane.

Meryl shook her head. "No, it wasn't, although that makes the most sense."

Diane clenched her fists, looking out the window, unable to meet Meryl's eyes. "It was Zoe," she whispered.

Meryl chortled. "Yeah, right. Zoe the druggie. Uh-huh. Now you have cheered me up."

Diane's face remained impassive. "I came home one night from work and she was lying on the couch, sobbing, just inconsolable. When I finally got her to calm down she told me that she had been Goggling results for the crime of drugging a police officer and discovered that she could serve jail time. At the very minimum she would pay a hefty fine, do substantial community service and worst of all, get a police record which would prevent her from getting into Stanford or Harvard."

Diane sighed. "She was the one that baked the pot, more specifically a very potent type of marijuana called Berkley Bum. By the end, she was hysterical, practically screaming at me: why would a great college want someone with such bad judgment? Why would they want someone so stupid that she baked pot into brownies that she's wasn't even going to eat?"

Meryl was dumbfounded. "Where did she get the pot?" A pit grew in her stomach.

"From some kid named Denny."

The pit yawned. "Nathalie's boyfriend."

Diane nodded. "He wanted Zoe to give it to Nathalie. So rather than simply stuff it under her shirt, she baked it into the brownies she was making as a favor for me, for book club. Normally she made a batch for the kids. This time she flavored it with Berkley Bum."

"That's disgusting."

Diane could finally meet her eyes. "Yes. And your sister, Jackie, grabbed both plates and served them. If it weren't my daughter's future at stake, I'd find it funny. But it's not."

"And I served the leftovers to Sam."

"Officer Richer?"

"Yes."

"Who got drug tested and wants to know the name of the person who baked the pot in the brownies."

Meryl leaned over the counter, resting on it with her elbows. "Shit."

"Yeah, exactly. She was so stupid. And she's such a perfectionist; it's just eating her up. You know; she's obsessed with getting into a top tier school."

Meryl stood up, hugging Diane. "I'm so sorry. I'm going to talk to Nathalie."

Diane hugged her back. "Don't do anything tonight. It'll all work out."

"Will it? I'm not so sure." Meryl walked her to the door, wondering where her mother was.

Diane squeezed her hand. "I wasn't exactly an angel and I managed." She put on her coat. "Don't forget about Santa."

Faye had told her she'd take care of everything, not to worry. What if she went on a bender? Meryl had no idea where she'd hidden the presents. "Do you really think the boys still believe?"

Diane gave her a tired smile. "I hope so. I could really use a little Christmas magic."

21.

"I tended to place my wife under a pedestal."
- Woody Allen

When the doorbell rang, Meryl was upstairs, digging through the bonus room, feeling guilty about invading her mother's personal space. Wherever her mother had hidden the presents, she couldn't find them. She'd been so excited, asking Meryl to please come look at what she'd bought. But there was never any time. And, if she was honest with herself, she resented her mother's enthusiasm about Christmas.

If things went well, Faye would return sober; they'd make up and finally have a decent mother daughter moment. They'd get ready for Christmas morning after the kids went to bed. But she couldn't find one clue leading to the presents. The doorbell rang again. It couldn't be the kids or Faye, who had keys.

"Coming!" Meryl yelled as she ran down the stairs, irritated that Lorraine, who always, always, forgot something, didn't just open the door and get her glasses or sweater or cell phone.

It was Sam, in full uniform, red-cheeked and holding a huge white poinsettia in his hands, stomping his feet in the chill. "Merry Christmas," he said quietly. Before she could respond, he thrust the plant into her hands. "I'm on duty, so I should go."

"It's beautiful, thank you. I love it," she said, thinking of the twenty poinsettias she used to order every year from Melba's nursery. Christmas past was fragrant garlands, a new Tiffany ornament, and lavish spreads. Tonight even one potted plant was a luxury.

Sam pointed his gloved hand at the window, admiring the glowing Christmas tree. "Nice tree." He stomped his feet, seemingly at a loss. "I was just in the area. I always take the holiday shift you know, for the guys with little kids." He rubbed his gloved hands together. "Okay, I just wanted to see you. I'll get out of your hair now."

"Is your son in town?" The poinsettia's dark pointy leaves brushed her cheek.

"Yeah. He's with my dad. They're watching Dirty Harry and eating popcorn."

"Very Christmassy."

"That's what happens when there are no women around." He worried that he sounded pathetic and lonely, which of course, he was. What kind of a loser knocks on someone's door on Christmas Eve? "We'll go to church tomorrow."

There was a noise in the driveway, voices and the crunch of feet on frozen ground. Both of them knew it was the children, so they said their goodbyes quickly. He leaned in and pecked her on the cheek.

"I know I should have stayed away," he whispered. "But I couldn't."

Walking his children home was strange enough, Ethan thought, without the patrol car in the street and Sam striding away. By the time he and the children reached the front walk, Meryl had shut the door, placed the poinsettia near the fireplace. Henry was first, running in the door, leaving it wide open.

"Look what dad made me!" He shoved the card at Meryl, heading straight for the cookies Diane had brought.

Meryl was reading the card when Nathalie and Ethan entered. Ethan instinctively shut the door. "Can I come in?"

Meryl looked up from the card, "Of course."

"Where's Grandma?" asked Henry, his mouth ringed with crumbs.

"Church," Meryl lied.

Nathalie slouched on the living room couch, watching her parents in the entry. She fiddled with her phone, a ploy to look busy.

"I have something for you," Ethan said, handing Meryl an envelope.

"Thank you. I'll open it later." Tucking it carelessly into her back pocket, she stepped into the living room. "Henry, you'd better run upstairs and get your jams on. Santa's coming."

"Oh yea. Got to get his snack!" Henry dashed into the kitchen.

Nathalie rolled her eyes. "What a moron."

Ethan shook his finger at her. "Santa doesn't bring presents to girls who call their brothers morons."

Nathalie raised an eyebrow. "Um, isn't that like, the pot calling the kettle black or something?"

"Nathalie, that's enough," said Meryl.

Nathalie dragged herself up from the couch, heading to the stairs. At the last moment, she detoured into her father, wrapping her arms around him. "I'm sorry." He held onto her, wrapping his arms around tightly. She leaned back, wiping a tear from her eye, patting her jacket where she'd tucked Ethan's gift. "Thank you for the letter. It's... nice."

Ethan held onto her for dear life, his cheek resting on Nathalie's head, eyes filling with tears. Meryl watched them, thinking that in spite of everything, even what she'd said in therapy, he was a good father. He would do anything for them.

Nathalie pulled away just as Henry came rushing out of the kitchen with a glass of milk and a plate of carrots. He added a few cookies to the plate and ran upstairs. "Holy crow, it's late."

Ethan thought about stepping further into the living room but decided against it. No sense in pushing his luck. "Do you really think he still believes in Santa?" he whispered.

Meryl shook her head. "He's doing it for us."

Ethan nodded. "I'm moving in with my parents before our next therapy appointment."

Meryl was measured, cool. She didn't want to encourage him. "That's good."

"Yeah, in a normal world it would be an epic failure. After what I've done, it's progress."

Meryl stared at the creamy white leaves of the poinsettia. It was in a large sky blue ceramic pot with silvery crackles. Officer Richer had good taste. "I had a job interview today. With Michael Kippler. He said to say Merry Christmas."

Ethan frowned, an uneasy feeling rising in his gut. "I bet."

"Is he as sleazy as I think?"

"Worse. How did it go?"

Meryl nodded, looking at her watch. She needed to go find Faye. "I survived. Look, I didn't get you anything."

Ethan laughed. "That's a relief. It would have been one more thing to make me feel worse. I just came here to say Merry Christmas and I love you." He stared into her jade eyes, thinking he'd never needed her with such desperate intensity. Why did it have to get this bad before he realized how much he loved her? "And I really want, more than anything on earth, to kiss you."

Without another word, he left, closing the door quietly. Outside it was calm and bitterly cold. As he hurried across the driveway toward Leslie's dark house, he congratulated himself on not punching that bastard cop.

***

St. John Vianney was a brash, modern monster of a church. Its tri-sided steeple pierced the sky, lit up for Christmas Eve. The empty parking lot unfolded Origami-like around the church grounds, punctuated by stands of pine and oak. Meryl parked as close to the church doors as possible, looking for her mother's car. It wasn't there. She pulled out, ready to search Bishop's and China Boat. They were the kind of dives her mother favored: places to quietly drink yourself to death unnoticed. Something made her hit the brakes.

Her headlights illuminated a white banner flapping in the wind, draped over the glass church doors: REJOICE. JOIN THE GIVING TREE. Something about the banners hopeful message made her long for a moment's peace; a stillness that the silent church offered. Somewhere she'd read that a church doesn't lock its doors on Christmas Eve. Although she was sure it couldn't be true, she wanted to peer in the large windows, see the nave decorated for Christmas. Although she'd never attended as a child, she'd grown up watching movies where church was a refuge for the troubled. And refuge was exactly what she needed right now.

As she neared, she could see the giving tree: a majestic blue spruce inside the front door. Candy colored snowflakes were printed with the names and ages of the recipients: Thank you from Tiffany, 6. Thank you from Albert, 92. Thank you from Jesus, 14. Thank you from Rufus, 69. As she read, her nose stung with cold and something else: a bittersweet joy. These parishioners gave of themselves to complete strangers. It drew her, compelled her to push the door, expecting it to resist. Miraculously, it didn't.

"Hello?" She stood in the vast empty hall. Dead ahead was the main nave, just visible through an open door. No answer. Fear mingled with curiosity as she took a few steps, repeating, "Hello?"

Checking her cell phone before venturing further, she made sure that Nathalie could reach her, if necessary. Incense and pine mingled with waxy burning candles.

"Oh hello, you're early, come right in," said a cheery man from behind.

Meryl nearly jumped out of her skin.

A plump young priest, double chins straining at his collar, rubbed his chubby hands together. "I'm so sorry. I didn't mean to freak you out. Welcome, welcome." He held his hands out to her in a Christ-like gesture, then, realizing how ridiculous he looked, tried several other poses before locking his hands behind his back. Clearly he was new.

"Early?" Meryl asked.

"For midnight mass. Not many takers in the suburbs but I suffer from insomnia so I do the whole shebang. That way Father Phelps can get some shut-eye for tomorrow. You know how it is. Excuse me; I've got to put on my vestments." He bustled down the aisle toward the vestry. "I'm hoping for twenty people. That would be huge."

Allowing herself ten minutes of peace before continuing her search, Meryl dropped into one of the back pews.

The priest turned around, searching for her in the dim light. "Oh come on, you can do better than that. If you sit way back there everyone will."

Meryl thought about telling him that she wasn't staying but decided it wasn't worth it. She moved up to a front seat, enjoying the sight of the altar, festively strung with holly, sprays of evergreen and huge white and red bows. She bent her head, trying to find an utterly still moment, failing miserably. Images of her mother's hurt face swam before her. This had been, without a doubt, the worst two weeks of her life. And her mother was a big part of it.

Disappointed, she glanced at her phone. Her ten minutes of reflection were up. She stood, crossed herself (movie style) and searched through her purse for her keys as she walked quickly toward the exit, hoping to avoid the priest. She collided with someone in the aisle. Dropping her keys, she looked up. It was her mother.

"Faye, oh my goodness. You surprised me."

Faye's new lime green rain coat glowed in the dark church. She patted her wig, making sure it was on straight. "That was the point. It was a surprise party."

Meryl shook her head. "No, I mean, bumping into you. I didn't expect to see you here."

"I talk to Jesus."

"Yeah Mom, I know you're born again or whatever but I didn't see your car and I thought-"

"You thought I'd be out drinking."

Meryl sighed. "Yes. I'm really sorry. That was a great party and it did cheer me up. I'm just..." She looked up at the vaulted ceiling, black with skylights. The illuminated spires were visible in the otherwise dark sky.

"I'm overwhelmed. I'm not sleeping. I'm worried about money. I was hit on by the guy interviewing me."

Faye nodded, as if this were all expected. "That was my life, when you were little. Except I drank." Faye moved into the entry, pulling Meryl into a corner, near a crèche. The life-sized statues of Mary and Joseph focused on their baby.

"I know why you drank."

Faye crossed her arms. "Is that a fact?"

"Yes. It's hard, dealing with kids, and bills and life on your own. It's like a little escape hatch, that drink. That's why I got drunk on the champagne. I just wanted, for one second to forget that I am married to a philandering liar."

Faye's smile was sad. "Doesn't work too well, do it?"

"No. The hangover stinks.. And then everything that you drank to forget comes back with a vengeance. That's another reason I snapped at you. Please come home and help me get ready for Christmas. I don't know where the presents are. You did buy some, didn't you?"

"Have you forgotten that trailer trash use the car trunk as a closet?"

Meryl looped her arm through her mothers. "You're not trailer trash."

"I don't mind. You're the one that minded."

Meryl squeezed her mother's arm as they left the church, "You're one smart cookie."

"Broad. I'm one smart broad."

"It all means the same thing."

Faye followed her out the door. "Cookies crumble kiddo. Your old lady might have been to hell and back but I've never given up."

Meryl thought, as they walked outside in a light snow, that this Christmas might be salvageable.

Faye paused again, leaning her head back, watching the snow against the church spire. "I got an early Christmas present."

"Yeah?" Meryl tried her best to enjoy the moment.

"I called the bank. They approved my loan. I cannot even believe it. I got a bank to believe in me: little old Faye Lynette Danetto from Hornbeak, Tennessee. I can run my own business, with some help. We can do it. We can do this business honey." She waited for Meryl to say something but was greeted with silence. "I know that I don't have the best track record with you but I really do feel that I've got something to teach people." She paused. "I taught you how to dance. Remember back then? We had fun, me and you. You were a real good dancer, remember?"

Other parishioners began to arrive, their cars crunching on the gravel. Bundled against the cold, they walked around the two women, seemingly transfixed by the monolithic spire. Snow settled lightly on their coats and hair as they stood shoulder-to-shoulder, Faye awaiting her answer.

Meryl thought about the dance lessons her mother had given her. Fooling around in a friend's empty studio was the only time Meryl remembered being free as a child. They were two figures spinning in dappled sunlight, blissfully unaware of the nearby cliff. But she couldn't bring it up. Not on Christmas Eve after all her mother had done.

"Do you want me to put the presents in my car so you can go to church?" Meryl asked.

Faye didn't push. She'd get her answer later. "I'd rather help you set everything out. I'm more excited about giving your two their presents that I ever was with you and Jackie. I could never afford what you girls really wanted."

Meryl squeezed her mom's shoulder. "You always did a good job." They walked back to their cars.

Faye sniffled. "Liar. I always got drunk on Christmas Eve."

Meryl tilted her head, assessing Faye. "Is that a new coat?"

Faye lifted her pocketed hands up. The coat flared around her like a dress. "It's pretty, ain't it? It's stupid but I was saving it for tomorrow morning, my shiny new coat. Tonight I just needed a little pick-me-up."

"It's not stupid," Meryl said, opening the door to her car. "It's cute. See you at home."

Faye winked. "Not if I see you first."

She wanted so little, Meryl thought as she got into her car. But she couldn't give her mother what she really wanted. That was impossible.

22.

"Love: A temporary insanity curable
by marriage."
– Ambrose Bierce

After Meryl had gotten into her pajamas, brushed her teeth and scraped out the last of her costly anti-aging skin cream, she remembered the letter. It was downstairs, requiring her to look once more at the presents awaiting the children, the filled stockings, lit by the glow of the Christmas tree. Near the tree was the huddle of presents for her mother, quickly unwrapped from the surprise party and re-gifted to Faye, minus the Kentucky bourbon from Sandy. She hurried upstairs with the letter, knowing the only gift her mother wanted was the one she was unwilling to give: a business partnership.

She sat cross-legged on the bed, staring at the envelope, debating whether or not to rip it up or open it. Her mother was right. Christmas Eve alone was awful. She felt adrift without Ethan, missing his presence in their bedroom in spite of everything. Their bed seemed so big and neat. Now that he was gone she could have piled it with all the fluffy pillows she loved. But she didn't. She kept the bed the way he liked it. If she didn't open the letter she was in danger of calling him.

Dearest Meryl:

Merry Christmas darling. I know since I started Inspire, I
haven't written much more than birthday cards. I am sorry.
Before, I couldn't face you; couldn't be a failure in your eyes.
You are the only woman who has ever mattered

Believe it or not, I did take a poetry course at UW, thinking it
would be an easy credit. It wasn't and I hated it. But I did
Google a poem I remembered.

<u>I held a Jewel in my fingers</u> by Emily Dickinson

I held a Jewel in my fingers --
And went to sleep --
The day was warm, and winds were prosy --
I said "'Twill keep" --

I woke -- and chid my honest fingers,
The Gem was gone --
And now, an Amethyst remembrance
Is all I own --

From the first time I met you in the Sazzullo library, fast
asleep on your textbook, working so hard to keep your
job and scholarship, you hit me like a Mack truck. Yes,
you were snoring. I know you don't like admit it but it
was the cutest little snore, like a bunny. Here's a secret: I woke
you up. I know you think that it was magic, that this guy just
waited patiently until you woke up but I was running late so I
blew on your face. You couldn't come to the frat party because
naturally, you had to study. I hung around the College of
Education until we bumped into one another. I cut class to
stalk you. Yes, I did. Eight times. Did you really think it was a
coincidence that we kept bumping into one another?

You taught this rich boy the value of standing on your own two feet. You worked like crazy and lived as if there was no fallback, because for you, there wasn't. To this day my dad scares the shit out me. But he's never scared you, has he?

I'm going to bail myself out of this mess one bucket at a time. I know, in my DNA, that our marriage isn't beyond repair. You will always be the love of my life, the amazing mother of my children and the most beautiful person, inside and out, that I have ever met.

Love,

Ethan

      Meryl held the letter in her hands and cried. After going to the bathroom for a drink of water she read it again. And a third time, talking back to the letter as if it were Ethan himself: "Oh you poor thing. Right. You're selling me on our marriage like you sold investors on Inspire. You Googled Emily Dickinson and think it's going to make everything okay? Your honest fingers? The same fingers you ran all over Leslie the flight attendant's little butt? You are a failure. Not at business. Who cares about business? You're a failure at keeping your pants zipped."
      She folded the letter, ripping it up into smaller and smaller pieces, dropping them into the metal wastepaper basket beside her bed. She lay in bed but the pieces of paper burned in her mind. She threw back the covers, picked each scrap out, crumpled them and took them downstairs. She passed through the kitchen, outside to the patio. Her tiny bonfire lasted less than a minute. It was enough time to see her mother's profile upstairs, the puff of smoke out the window.

Passing back through the kitchen, she heard melodic pinging. A text. Despite knowing that she needed sleep, needed to dampen the electrical storm in her brain, she checked her phone. It was from Sam: WHAT R U DOING NEW YEAR'S EVE? The message glowed on the screen like a fresh start. She thought of Faye, who would be just as happy hanging out with her grandchildren on New Year's Eve. She thought of Ethan, whom she would meet that afternoon for a therapy session. A cold wind scraped a branch across the kitchen window, reminding her that this was probably the last holiday season that they'd spend in this lovely house.

NOTHING, she texted.

He replied: EARLY DINNER? I'LL COOK.

YOU KNOW HOW?

YEA OF LITTLE FAITH.

ANSWER THE QUESTION OFFICER.

I'LL LET YOU BE THE JUDGE.

For a moment, she hesitated before typing: IT'S A DATE.

The word "date" hung in her mind like an escape clause in her marriage. She lived in that murky world of "separated," where couples slept without facing each other and ultimately chose their own directions. How could she know her direction if she didn't explore Sam Richer?

"You're still married," she heard her mother say, wondering, for a split-second, if it was her own over-taxed brain speaking.

Startled, Meryl dropped the phone. Faye, sparse hair covered by a terrycloth turban, seemed older without her wig. "Faye! You scared me to death."

Faye opened the fridge, took out a Snapple. It made a pop as she unscrewed the lid, taking what Meryl felt was an annoyingly long drink, and worse, smacking her lips. "I know you're not sneaking down here to text Ethan."

Meryl bent to pick up the phone, rubbing a finger across the screen, making sure it hadn't cracked. Dropping it had sent the message. It was a date.

"I'm not." Although she felt like telling the old bat to drink her Snapple and shut up, she kissed her forehead. Had Faye come down for a Snapple or to raid the liquor cabinet?.

"Good night Faye. I'm glad you're here," she said, not realizing it was true until the words came out of her mouth.

* * *

CHRISTMAS MORNING SUCKED, Henry texted his new friend Mark, who he now knew was also 12 and lived with his mom.

A few moments later a sad faced emoticon appeared on his screen with the words: PRESENTS?

Henry sent a smiley face back. He'd gotten the new skateboard he'd chosen himself and a salt pellet gun to kill flies – from Grandma and the ski pass. His mom had given him a Frisbee golf set, which was cool. Normally she gave him books.

Last night Nathalie had been sneaking downstairs to add some other stuff to his stocking when he'd run into her on his way to pee. He asked, sarcastically if she was going to leave Santa a bag of Berkley Bum. She'd thrown a Nerf Gun and colossal jawbreaker at his head. He ducked. The baseball-sized jawbreaker hit his mom's door, waking her up. It was not fun at all, getting yelled at, again, on Christmas Eve.

CHRISTMAS AND DIVORCE ARE NOT A GOOD MIX, texted Mark.

Henry had promised Grandma that he'd go to church with her, so he'd texted back YEAH, stuffing the phone in his pocket, hoping that she'd let him play Candy Crush during the service.

She didn't.

Maybe, Henry thought, during the long, boring Christmas service, New Year's Eve will be better. Maybe things will go back to normal when the calendar turns. Mark had told him not to be optimistic. The law of inertia, Henry knew, suggested that when life is going crappy it's going to get even crappier. God knew about him setting the car on fire. Sooner or later, Henry thought, God was going to get even.

At home, Meryl made buttermilk pancakes, dreading tomorrow. An e-mail had confirmed that she'd been hired for the day after Christmas sale at Macy's based on a resume she'd submitted online. Her orientation was from 6:00 am to 7:00 am, when the store opened. In a note at the end of the e-mail her supervisor, Melodie, had typed, "Welcome aboard Mel, it's going to be supah crazy!" This was followed by three smiley faces.

Since when had she become Mel?

23.

"Some people claim that marriage interferes with romance. There's no doubt about it. Anytime you have a romance, your wife is bound to interfere."
– Groucho Marx

It was the day of New Year's Eve and Ethan had been stood up. His fury channeled itself into a laser of loathing towards Sensitive Allen, sitting across from him, sipping a murky green concoction. Allen was sweating lightly under his thin cashmere v-neck, as though he'd hurriedly showered after a long cleansing run.

"And how did Meryl respond to the letter?" asked Allen.

Central to Ethan's rage, was the knowledge that Allen was the only person outside the family privy to the lowest moment of his life. He probably coached gay, orphaned, refugees in his spare time, telling them he honored their feelings. "She didn't. The kids seemed to like them, although it's hard to tell." He went back to his hug with Nathalie, a shiny moment amidst the gloom.

Thankfully Meryl burst through the door, twenty minutes late, smelling heavily of perfume. She wore a black smock with a white Lancôme logo stitched beneath a tiny white rose. "Sorry I'm late," she said, sinking into a leather chair with groan. "Ahhh, my feet."

Ethan was relieved and happy that she'd showed. Her beauty wasn't diminished by the utilitarian uniform or frazzled manner. She was here.

Allen took another sip of his compost smoothie. "Ethan was telling me that he moved in with his parents."

Meryl struggled out of the smock, glaring at Ethan. "You must be so proud."

"Again with the sarcasm," Ethan said. "It's what you asked for. Did you read my letter?"

"No, Meryl snapped. "I ripped it up. How are the unsupportive hoarders of wealth? Make sure Betsy tells all her golf cronies that her daughter-in-law is at the Lancôme counter for 3 whole days. If I move enough La Vie Est Belle perfume, I just might have a chance at a permanent position. I'm selling Life is Beautiful. Isn't it ironic?" She raised an eyebrow at Ethan. Their old joke was that Alanis Morissette's smash hit "Isn't it Ironic?" should have been titled "Isn't it a Total Bummer?" Alanis, like most people, misunderstood irony.

"It just sounds bitter to me," said Ethan.

"Enough name calling," said Allen. "This stops now."

"I'm fine with the name calling," said Meryl. "What people forget about name calling is that it's therapeutic." She turned to her husband. "Ethan, besides sarcastic and bitter, what else would you call me?"

"Repressed," jumped out of Ethan's mouth before he could stop. Her face fell. "Sorry."

"Case in point," said Allen. "Meryl, how was your Christmas?"

"Wimpy," she spat out, glaring at Ethan.

"You had a wimpy Christmas?" Allen asked.

Without looking at Allen, she continued, leveling her eyes at Ethan like a gun. "You didn't start Inspire to build yourself up or for our family. You wanted to impress your father. To let him know that you were a player. Because that is all he cares about, isn't it? All that crap about a seat at the big boys' table, remember that?"

"You knew this about me. Remember the story about him making me walk home from my high school football game because I threw a bad pass? The more things change, the more they stay the same. I have a room. I have a fridge full of food. They even let me borrow an old pick up that Margarita used to drive. But I am a failure so I have leprosy." He used quotation around the word failure. "The dog gets better treatment. I have started watching reality TV for self esteem because my own mother has somehow managed, in the same house, to completely avoid me."

"Boo-hoo," Meryl snapped.

"Meryl," Allen said. "He's explaining himself to you. There's a clue in there about his dissociative behavior."

"What? I can't hear. I'm too repressed. My ears are repressed. They don't work properly."

"I take that back," Ethan said, crossing his legs. "You're not repressed with Officer Friendly, are you?"

Meryl thought about it for a moment. Could Ethan possibly know that she had gotten high with Sam? Her anger at Ethan overrode her fear. "No, I'm not. It's very relaxing spending time with someone who hasn't screwed you over."

"Yet," said Ethan.

Allen put down his smoothie, leaning toward both of them. "Wait a minute. You're seeing someone?"

Meryl gulped. "No. Yes. Define seeing."

Allen smiled. "Don't be coy Meryl. I'm not going to judge you."

It was Meryl's turn to smile. "I am having dinner with a man tonight." She opened her arms wide. "Judge away."

Ethan got up from his chair, storming out of the room. Meryl pursed her lips, nodding at the coat. "He'll be back." She counted on her fingers, mouthing, "One, two, three…" Six seconds later, Ethan burst in, snatched the Inspire logo fleece jacket from his chair, without a glance at either of them. The door shut a second time.

Allen took a deep breath. "Ethan got some time alone with me, now I suppose it's your turn. How are you feeling about our session?"

"Judged. And I'm the one that didn't do anything wrong. Yet." She sat there for a moment, thinking it was nice to have someone listen. "The only thing I really, really want to do for myself is the wrong thing. And I'm going to do it. I have a crush on another man. I do. There. I said it out loud." Which felt great, admitting it.

"Ethan said something pretty intriguing to me before you got here. He felt that you two had a performance based marriage."

Meryl shook her head. "What does that mean? If he meant that I held him to certain standards, yes, I did. Our marriage contract did not say, 'no boffing the neighbors,' but it was certainly implied."

Allen shook his head. "No, no. He felt that his performance at work, as a successful businessman, was somehow tied to the reward of your love. Like a paycheck. I'm not saying this was right or rational. Remember how I talked about disassociation? I'm beginning to think, from what I've heard Ethan share today about his childhood, that he associates love with high performance. And if he couldn't perform in business, he feared losing your love."

Meryl looked at her watch. "Aren't we supposed to do this together? He can't even defend himself."

"Do you agree?"

Meryl tried to reach over the hump of her anger, her aching feet, and her desire for Sam Richer. "I don't know. I just think he should have talked to me. We lived in the same house."

"But what if he was raised in a house where they were very good at keeping up appearances and very bad at talking? Where the lines between love and money were blurred?"

Meryl shrugged. "I don't know. We all have to grow up at some point."

The hour was up. Allen re-crossed his legs, nodded at the clock. "I'm going to ask you one last question. Your answer will be confidential but it will help me if you and Ethan are going to both keep your next session."

Meryl stood, put on her coat, stuffing the Lancôme smock into her purse, eager to take a bath and get ready for her date. "What?"

"Do you love Ethan?"

It wasn't what she was expecting. Her brow furrowed. The answer had always been automatic, like when someone asked how she was doing, she always replied "fine," regardless of how she was really feeling. "I don't know. I know him better than anyone on earth. And he knows me. I mean, I knew he'd forget his coat. I can look at a menu in restaurant and tell you exactly what he's going to order. He's afraid of spiders and lies about going to McDonald's. One time he carried me half a mile after I sprained my ankle. All these things add up, you know. But right now I am having a very hard time connecting with my feelings. I don't recognize our marriage anymore. You know someone for twenty years and suddenly you don't know them at all. Does that make sense?"

She could see Allen reaching for his standard, "there are no wrong answers here" statement but instead he surprised her. "Absolutely. I totally understand. Your husband failed you profoundly. What you do next is completely up to you."

Meryl felt grateful and understood. Remarkably, she felt better.

Allen stood, walking her to the door. "See you next week," he said.

"Maybe," was the best Meryl had to offer. She was already thinking about tonight.

24.

"When a man opens the car door for his wife, it's either a new car or a new wife."
-Prince Philip

Sam's house was in rural Munroe, down a winding series of ever-smaller lanes bordered by farms, middle class homes and huge estates surrounded by white-fenced horse property. The funny thing about this area, Meryl thought, was that a rundown trailer with its own personal junkyard could be next door to an elegant estate.

By the time her car bumped down the deeply rutted dirt lane, Meryl was second guessing herself. How well did she know this man? Wouldn't this be the perfect place for a serial killer to hide?

She'd left in such a rush of guilt and anxiety; she hadn't even left Sam's address with Faye. Nathalie was steaming over their argument about Zoe and subsequent grounding. Faye had radiated disapproval. She was in such a hurry to leave, she hadn't really thought about the location of Sam's house, way out in the boonies. Hadn't she read an article about men posing as police officers luring women out to the country?

A barking cocker spaniel rushed out of a single story grey shingled ranch house. Sam followed, yelling at the dog, Martha, to calm down. Meryl's anxiety melted at his welcoming grin. "Great, come on in, I've got a pot roast in the oven, so…" He waved her toward the house. "You have a hard time finding me way out here in the sticks?"

Small talk melted easily into a second glass of wine with dinner, eaten in the kitchen, overlooking a gnarled apple orchard. The yard was overgrown but pleasantly so, with long waving grass. Martha, a seasoned beggar, batted her long eyelashes; fervently praying for scraps until Sam pushed her away, calling her his "high maintenance blonde."

"I have to tell you, this might sound crazy but when I drove up here I thought, okay, I hardly know this guy. I'm way out here in the woods, what if he's some kind of murderer and I end up planted in his backyard and my kids are left to be raised by my wacky mother?"

Sam chewed a carrot. "How could you even think that about me? I took an oath of honor to uphold the law and protect people."

Meryl blanched. She'd gone too far. "I'm sorry; it wasn't as though I was being rational-"

Sam's stern face broke into laugh lines. He stomped his foot on the floor. "I'm sorry. I just, you know, I think it's so funny. That's exactly how a woman should think and they rarely, rarely do. Finally, I find a woman who is the right amount of paranoid and she's worried about me. I should have told you." He lowered his voice. "I have only killed six women."

She took another sip of her wine. "You're sick."

He fed the dog a scrap of meat. "What's so wrong with your mother raising the children? She seems like a nice gal. A little unconventional but sweet."

"Unconventional? Do you know what her idea is for digging me out of my financial pit? Opening a dance club to teach suburban women something called boudoir dancing: bumping and grinding in suburbia. I bet she doesn't even know what the word boudoir means."

"What does it mean?"

"French trash, as far as I'm concerned."

Sam thought about treading the delicate ground between mother and daughter. It was one thing for her to call her mother trashy. "I don't know. Her idea sounds reasonable to me. There's a new dog bakery in Kirkland that charges three bucks for a dog cookie for an animal that would be just as happy eating shit off a shoe, excuse my French."

They killed the bottle of red in the living room in front of the fire. Meryl sunk into a worn leather chair, thinking the couch was dangerous for two lonely souls. Sam settled on the other end, with the dog perched near his shoulder, dozing contentedly. Meryl's nerves unwound into a state of relaxation she hadn't felt since before That Terrible Night.

Admiring Sam's straight back and long-legged gait as he disappeared into the kitchen, she wondered when he'd last had sex. Surely there had been a few since his wife died. Someone had taken a great deal of care picking out perfectly worn chairs, mixing chintz fabrics with stripes.

"I love this room, and the kitchen. It's like an English country farmhouse."

Sam, returning with a plate of chocolates, pointed to a photo of a pretty redhead on the mantle. "Patty. She had a little antique shop down the road. It's a little girly for a bachelor but it's comfortable so... I just leave it." He looked into his wine glass, uncomfortable.

What a bone-headed move, thought Meryl. Of course the dead wife decorated. Martha conveniently distracted them both by stretching luxuriantly in her sleep, falling off the back of the couch with an undignified yelp. Meryl comforted the hound, scratching her ears. "You poor thing. How embarrassing."

"So are you going to do the dance studio? I think it's a great idea," Sam said, eager to get off the subject of his wife. It's not that he minded talking about her; it was just miles from first date territory.

The dog jumped into Meryl's lap. "I know I can't keep selling perfume at Macy's. I'll stab myself if I have to convince one more person that life is beautiful. Do you know how many bitter angry women have told me their life stories? The worst thing is that I'm using my sad story to sell perfume. I am shameless. I tell them that my husband spent our life's saving and slept with the younger woman next door and if I don't sell enough perfume I'm going to lose our house."

Sam winced. "That's terrible. Does it work?"

Meryl shrugged. "Yeah. It does. I've sold 30 gift sets that way. They're $430 dollars. These women feel so sorry for me, they hand me their credit cards. I couldn't even sell Girl Scout cookies and now look at me. It's scary."

He shook his head. "I don't see you sticking with it." He held up a bottle of cognac. She nodded. A moment later a snifter was in her hand.

She selected a dark, tiny chocolate, hoping it wasn't caramel. It was. "I'm already burning out. My manager, who is about twelve, thinks we shouldn't be able to go to the bathroom until we've sold twenty units. That kind of math just doesn't work for someone who's had two kids. A full bladder is not incentive. What I'm supposed to do, tell someone if they don't buy some perfume I'm going to pee on them?"

"Is it even legal to deny bathroom breaks? Wait, don't tell me. I have a better idea. Go into business with your mom."

"That idea only works if I can teach. And to teach I have to dance."

"You don't dance? I find that hard to believe. You move like a dancer."

Meryl hoped she didn't look like a cud chewing cow. Caramels always stuck to her crowns like glue. They weren't in the teeth picking stage of their relationship yet. "I used to dance."

"What kind of dancing?"

Washing a bit of the cognac through her teeth dissolved the caramel handily. "Not my mom's kind of dancing. Sometimes when the babysitter didn't show up, she'd park us in a club. I'd do my homework but I'd see her up there, bumping and grinding and working the pole. Men would stare at her like she was steak. I was disgusted."

Sam took a swallow of his wine, fascinated. "So you never danced like that for anyone?"

Meryl frowned. "No."

"Would you?"

She put down her empty snifter. "That is such a weird question."

Sam ran his fingers through his hair. "I'm sorry. My imagination is running wild. I'll shut up."

"I'm not the exotic dancer type. I'm the teacher type."

"So let your mom teach you. I know she's much more free spirited than you but I think you're underestimating your own ability. The first time I saw you, I could see from the way you moved, that you'd been a dancer at some point. What kind of dancing did you do?"

"Jazz and you know, some of the showgirl stuff my mom taught me. But I quit."

"Why?"

"It was a waste of time."

"I disagree."

She stared at him for a very long time. "I'm getting really uncomfortable."

Sam put his wine glass down, crossed the carpet, kneeled and took both her hands. "You have made me very uncomfortable since the moment I met you. You're much more like your mom than you'd like to admit. I'm sorry. I know women hate hearing that. I have the annoying habit of constantly saying what I think. Not when I am at work. Only when I'm with women I'm insanely attracted to. I'll shut up now."

She leaned down and kissed him on the cheek. "Don't shut up."

He lifted her up until they were facing each other, pulling her into an embrace, his arms low on her back. He smelled like wood smoke and wool. "You smell like Life is Beautiful. I like it."

"I'm never wearing perfume again."

"Fair enough. I got drunk on Peppermint Schnapps once. Now I can't even use minty toothpaste."

Every tipsy cell in her body was magnetically drawn to him. Fighting it was exhausting. "Thank you for a great dinner. I should go."

Hands on her shoulders, he held her in front of him, waving his index finger as if tracking her pupils. "Ah, you've had a wee too much to drink.. Time for a New Year's walk." At the word walk, Martha began turning in circles, barking hysterically. "Now we're committed."

"You're one of those crazy dog people, aren't you?" Meryl put on her coat.

Sam held up the plate of chocolates. "If by that you mean, did I get cable so she could watch the nature channel while I'm at work and do I plan on having her embalmed, yes, I am." He lifted the plate. "Have a chocolate."

Meryl took three for the road. "Embalming? Seriously?"

He winked as he pulled on a tweed cap that made him look like an Irish Spring commercial. "Stick around and find out." He held the door open. "Come on, my neighbor makes the best hard cider on the planet."

The cold took her breath away. The air smelled of fermenting apples, smoke and freshly turned earth. The dog raced ahead in the inky dark, chasing something into the bushes. She took his arm to steady herself; unaccustomed to the pervasive country darkness. It was calming and unsettling at the same time. "Cider? I thought this was a sobering walk."

"Point taken. We might have to spend some more time together. Don't worry. I'll get you home before midnight so we don't have that awkward; it's midnight on New Year's Eve moment. See? I did it again. Said what I was thinking."

Arm in arm, they meandered slowly down the unpaved lane, following the dog's tail as it flitted ahead.

"I don't think it would be awkward at all," she said, squeezing his arm. The truly awkward thing for Meryl was choosing the right time to tell him who baked pot into the brownies.

***

Ethan spent New Year's Eve driving around in Margherita's old rust bucket, looking for house rentals; foreclosed houses that the bank would be happy to have occupied at a reduced rate. The pick-up burned a furious amount of gas, which was problematic. Buying gas on a credit card was temporarily a thing of the past. Ethan had snipped up all his credit cards rather than accrue one more cent of debt.

It had been twenty years since he'd had to choose between fuel for the car and fuel for his body while standing in line at a convenience store. Since it was New Year's Eve, he treated himself to a pricey seasonal lager and, for sheer value, a burrito. He hoped his wife's asshole boyfriend wasn't doing DUI duty tonight. With his luck, he'd get pulled over with an open beer by the guy dating his wife.

After finishing his beer, he drove to the third listing he'd found online. Although no one would meet him tonight he'd managed to speak to the current renters or glimpse in the windows. The first place was painted deep purple with faded black sheets hanging in the windows, an ideal haven for a meth lab. The last place reeked of cat urine.

His parents were having their traditional New Year's Eve casino night, with rented tables, professional dealers and caterers.

"Darling of course you're invited but if you don't want to rent a tuxedo don't worry about making yourself scarce," his mother said in their longest exchange yet. Blowing on her wet nails, she managed to avoid his eyes.

He could take a hint. The only thing more embarrassing than being a forty-three year old failure living at home was being that failure's mother. He had seen his father once in the driveway, twice at the front door and once at breakfast. They had spoken exactly nine words: Hi, son. Excuse me. Have you seen your mother? Ethan counted.

The third rental house was on a busy road near Interstate 405. Broken fences dotted the street. The white noise of the freeway hissed beyond a thin stand of

cottonwood trees. An angry dog patrolled the chain link
fence next door. Not very inviting but he'd been adjusting
as the night progressed. Seeing promise in the wreckage
was Ethan's new attitude. He realized that his biggest
problem wasn't going to be finding a place to start over; it
was talking his new landlord, and his family, into trusting
him.

***

Faye scraped the Velveeta topped casserole from the dishes
into the sink. Henry had eaten like a champ but she'd barely
touched her food. She went into the living room to look
out the windows again. Nathalie had flown the coop 20
minutes after her mother left, even though she'd confided
earlier that she and Denny were fighting. No surprise there.
Nothing, Faye knew, was easier than a fresh start.
Maintaining it was the problem.

Henry and Faye had been racing Henry's
cockroaches. Their home turf was normally a box under his
bed. Tonight they'd been liberated for sport, scuttling
around a track constructed of shoe boxes, duct tape and
empty paper towel rolls. At first Faye had to be coaxed into
participating in the construction but once she started, she
was very enthusiastic. For a while Henry was deeply
engrossed, forgetting, temporarily, about all his problems.

At 11:30, Nathalie returned home. Her vacant stare
could have been the result of the pot she'd smoked but
there was more. With Nathalie, Faye thought when she saw
the girl drag in, there was always more. She was a girl with a
story she didn't want told. Faye knew all about that kind of
life.

"Check it out," Nathalie said, peering down
forlornly at La Cucaracha Downs. Cold wafted from her

body but her face remained pale. Her mascara was blurred as if she'd been crying. Faye wasn't sure if her backwards t-shirt was intentional or not.

Faye dragged her upstairs, telling her that if she ever, ever appeared stoned in front of her brother again she'd kick her ass from here to Tennessee. "I promise you that. Your brother deserves better. If you want to trash your body and your life, that's your own dumb ass problem but don't you let that boy down. He don't need to see you looking like a coked out zombie," she said before violently slamming Nathalie's door. A second later she opened the door again. "And if you ever want to go to an AA meeting, just let me know. It's very peaceful."

Faye stopped in her bedroom to get some change from her purse. If they were going to race cockroaches, they might as well place a few bets. She wanted Henry to have a memorable New Year's Eve. He'd been disappointed enough.

***

Walking back from his neighbor's house, Sam told funny stories about his neighbor Mac's cider bottling adventures. "The first batch was over-carbonated so the lids shot off like pistols. Bam, bam, bam. About one every thirty seconds. I thought it was gunfire. So I show up with my Glock, locked and loaded, expecting a home invasion. No one is home and I'm just about ready to call for back up when I look in the kitchen window and see these bottles sitting on the kitchen table oozing foam." He squeezed her hand. "This is the part where you should laugh or call me a moron or something."

"I'm not listening. I'm working up the guts to tell you about my daughter's drug habit. It was her boyfriend trying to sneak pot in our house when she was grounded that led to a horrible chain of events whereby you and I both got high. I'm not sure how to tell you that."

Sam turned toward Meryl, holding both her hands. The air smelled heavily of winter apples fermenting in the orchard. "Fair enough. Since we're both being brutally honest, I'm not sure how to tell you that I'm falling in love with you and I'm scared to death. So why don't we both stop talking?" He bent down to kiss her, tasting of hard apple cider and chocolate.

***

Two hours later, Nathalie shocked Faye, appearing downstairs, wet haired and sober. She peeked into the living room before disappearing into the kitchen. Henry had popped microwave popcorn. Faye had finally talked him into dancing a little by promising to play his favorite music.

"I can't tell you my favorite music," he had said.

"Why not?" Fay asked.

"Because my friends would tease me."

"Okay. I promise not to tell."

"Pinky swear?" He held out his pinky. She linked fingers with him, delighted with the ritual, thinking this grandparent thing might work out after all.

"Honey it can't be that bad."

Henry shut his eyes, nodding and cringing. "It's Justin Bieber."

"Who's that?" Faye glanced at her watch, thinking Meryl's rules about bedtime were too strict for New Year's Eve.

"Only girls like him," Henry said, turning his Iphone on to speaker. "Listen to this one. He was just fourteen when he wrote it. He's a really good dancer too."

They were grooving to Justin Bieber when Nathalie surfaced, eating a bowl of casserole, picking at the potato chip crust with her fingers. Faye was showing Henry a few knee dips and spins. Sweaty and relaxed, he further confessed that not only was he a fan, he was a Belieber, which was, he explained, something technically reserved for girls.

"I'm pretty sure that means you're gay," Nathalie said, popping a Velveeta soaked hot dog slice into her mouth.

Henry stopped dancing. "Why?"

Faye was apoplectic. "That is just a load of hooey. You can like whatever kind of music you want." She pointed at Nathalie. "I been real patient with you tonight kid, so zip it." She turned to her grandson. "If you know to dance, you'll meet a lot more girls," she reassured Henry. "Most boys don't know how to dance."

She turned up the music, motioning to Nathalie to join them. It took a while. Nathalie remained stubbornly planted on the couch, scraping the Velveeta out of her bowl. Henry refused to keep dancing, objecting to his sister "judging him."

"This is not *Dancing with the Stars* darling boy. This is dancing with Grandma Faye. Anything goes. Shake it or break it."

After digesting the casserole, pronouncing it one of the best things she'd ever eaten, Nathalie joined them. She whipped her hair with such abandon that she hit Henry in the face. A fight was averted by Faye remembering that she'd purchased a telescoping pole from Home Depot, originally intended for irrigation purposes. After gouging the ceiling a few times, they properly installed it, using tension to keep it in place.

Although pole dancing was a relatively new form of dance, Faye, with her naturally strong upper body, had taken to it quickly, eventually helping the newer girls perfect their technique before she retired. She became something of a legend, which suited her fine.

After a few stretches, deep breathing and one silent prayer, asking Jesus to please put some fire into her limbs, Faye asked Nathalie to find "Pour Some Sugar On Me" by Def Leppard. After a quick search on YouTube the live version was located.

"Turn the volume up on that sucker as high as it will go," instructed Faye, giving her grandchildren the shock of their short lives.

Not only could their grandmother "shake it like a Polaroid picture," as Nathalie said, she could hoist herself upside down on the pole, scissoring her legs, twirling her body like a snake, defying gravity in a sensual and frightening way. Although several attempts to hold herself sideways resulted in failure, Faye gamely showed them the moves her 62 year old body still allowed, which were plentiful, impressive and provocative in a way that wasn't lost on either child. It was uncomfortable, alarming and appealing all at the same time.

After her routine, her stunned grandchildren gave her a spontaneous standing ovation, partially because they didn't know what else to do. How did one respond to a grandmother who did these kinds of things? Clapping a hand over her heart, Faye managed a gracious curtsy on shaking legs. Sweaty and tired, she went to the kitchen for a glass of water and a towel, returning a moment later.

"Your turn," she offered Nathalie.

Nathalie picked a song called "Titanium," by a fellow named David Guetta, although, as Faye pointed out, it was a girl doing all the singing. Faye loved the song because it was about surviving. But what she enjoyed even more was the strength, power and freedom Nathalie exhibited on the pole. She took what she'd seen Faye do three steps further, rising and falling with bicep and abdominal strength seemingly impossible for such a skinny girl. Some of her volleyball muscles had survived the months of dissipation. Her eyes were closed, hair whipping sensually, lost in the rhythm and emotion of the song. Instead of the vacant look that Faye had adopted after years of professional dancing, Nathalie looked at them, her eyes snapping and alive.

Even Henry, who'd been feeding his leftover casserole to the cockroaches, noticed something different about his sister. She was happy.

The music was so loud that no one heard the sound of the garage door closing. Nor did they notice the laundry room door opening or Meryl's heels on the hardwood floors. What they could not miss over the music were Meryl's furious screams.

25.

*"A wedding is like a funeral,
but with musicians."
-Mobsters, 1991, Patrick Dempsey*

When Meryl drove past the living room and noticed lights left on downstairs and movement in the living room, it didn't really register that something was terribly off. It was after midnight, the kids should have been asleep. Faye was a night owl, she expected her to be up, blowing smoke out a window or drinking one of her Snapples. She even secretly hoped, in her lowest moments, that her mother would drink, so she could kick her out.

What she didn't expect when she opened the laundry room door was a twelve foot tall stripper's pole installed at the edge of her cathedral ceiling. Nor did she expect her 16 year old daughter to be whipping her long legs around the pole, her head flung back in abandon, her hair streaming behind like ribbons. The last thing she noticed was her own mother, clapping and cheering to the rhythm of the empowering song as if this were cheerleading tryouts.

"Stop this. Stop! Stop!" Meryl entered screaming and after that she wasn't really sure what came out of her mouth. At one point she shouted, "What kind of a woman teaches her own granddaughter to strip?"

Nathalie struck a pose, fluttering her hands up and down her torso. "Fully clothed; garments intact."

"Mom, you should see Grandma dance!" Henry said. "She can hold herself upside down."

Meryl stood with her hands on her hips, glaring upwards. "Look at my ceiling. How can I sell this house with big black marks?"

"No one looks at the ceiling," Henry shrugged.

"Upstairs!" Meryl growled at both kids.

Nathalie looked regretfully at the pole, at her mother's pale, taut face. Of course, now that she'd found something she really enjoyed, besides getting stoned with Denny, her mother would hate it. "Happy New Year to you too," she sniped before following Henry upstairs.

Meryl waited until both kids had gone into their rooms before launching a fresh assault on Faye, who sat, calmly sipping water. "What is wrong with you? What the hell kind of woman thinks it's okay to install a stripper pole in her daughter's living room?"

Faye saluted with her water. "Me."

Meryl collapsed on the couch. "I want you out of here."

"Fine. Gimme back my $38,000 and I'll hit the road."

Meryl rested her head in her hands. "I don't have it and you know it. I paid the bills with it."

"Then you're stuck with me."

Meryl looked up, vehemently shaking her head. "No, I'm not. I will not have you around my children."

Faye set the water glass on the table. "Honey, I don't know the fancy therapeutic way to say this so I'm just gonna say it the way we do back home: you're a bitch. The harder I try to make amends to you, the more you hate me. You're a hard woman Trixie Louise. It makes me sad."

Meryl started to cry. "Thanks Mom. That's really helpful. Now I can add you to the list of people who hate me."

"I don't hate you and you know it." Faye took another sip of water. "You used to love to dance. I felt like we shared something, me and you. And now you see your own daughter enjoying something, just because she saw me do it and you shoot off like a ten dollar rocket. Would it be the end of the world if she was like her grandma just a little bit?"

"She is like you. She dates losers and gets high. Isn't that enough? Oh no wait, maybe she'll get pregnant with two different men and married four times. And lie about being married to the nice one because it was just too much work to go off and make it official."

Faye lifted her hands in defeat, standing up. "I'm going to bed. I'll leave in the morning."

The muscles in Meryl's neck stood out with tension. "No wait. Do you really want to know why I quit dancing? Why I still, to this day, remain afraid of the one thing that made me feel free?"

Faye crossed her arms, sat back down. "Yes, I do."

"Fine, you want the truth, you got it." Meryl went to the liquor cabinet in the kitchen, poured herself three fingers of whiskey and swallowed it, neat. Returning to the living room, she sat down, placed both hands on her knees and sighed. "I was fourteen. One morning while you were passed out, Kyle, remember Kyle? The croupier from the Venetian? Well Kyle decided that he was going to teach me the tango. I thought it was strange because we kept bumping into things. I was worried we were going to wake you up but we didn't. Jackie was at a friend's house. Kyle started running his hand down my back. He said 'let's go get donuts.' I didn't worry when he pulled into an alley behind Red's donuts instead of the main parking lot."

Faye jumped up, pacing the room nervously. "Stop. Please stop," she pleaded, fumbling in her purse for a cigarette with shaky hands. "I know where this is headed." She'd known it was something bad when Kyle's name came up. Faye kept backing up until she was near the Christmas tree, in the corner.

Meryl rubbed her temples. "No. You listen. He choked me. He told me that if I ever told you or Jackie or the police that he'd kill me. He said no one would believe me." Meryl wasn't crying. Her eyes were flat, hard and angry.

Faye shook like a leaf, smoking her cigarette as though it were a lifeline.

Meryl looked at her watch, realizing that the calendar year had turned. "I decided to be perfect. My whole goal in life was to not be you."

Faye stared into the center of the tree at the tiny knobs of sap on the trunk. "That was a good goal," she said vacantly.

Meryl sniffed the air, catching a whiff of smoke. "Where's your cigarette?"

Faye lifted her right hand, staring at her empty fingers as they weren't part of her body. She scanned the red velvet tree skirt for the dropped butt. Both women saw the smoke rising from the base of the Christmas tree before it ignited. Flames shot up the dry tree with surprising speed, igniting the wooden blinds on the French doors like tinder. Faye hopped back without thinking, holding onto the piano.

The fire grew rapidly. In seconds the tree was a raging six foot inferno, orange flames licking the ceiling, filling the room with smoke. After a few moments of numb disbelief, their brains caught up with their senses.

"Get the kids out!" Faye screamed at Meryl, scrambling to find her phone.

Meryl raced upstairs, yelling at Faye to call 9-1-1. Faye found her phone, dialed and ran out the front door, racing down the front porch. Jumping off into the boggy grass, she kicked open the side gate to the house. The freezing mud sucked Faye's slippers off as she lurched toward the garden hose, neatly coiled on a stand.

When the emergency operator asked the nature of the emergency, Faye screamed, "Christmas tree fire!"

"Ma'am, what is your address?" asked the operator with professional calm.

"I don't know. It's in Kirkland." Faye had the phone wedged on her shoulder while she reconnected the outdoor hose to the spigot, a task impeded by her long acrylic nails. "Damn, I broke a nail," she muttered into the phone.

"Ma'am, we need the address. Is there someone at the location who knows the address?"

Faye knew she had to decide quickly: run inside, get the address and let the fire rage or battle the fire herself with the garden hose. Too many decisions in her life had been based on fear. This one was easy. "We'll call you back."

Tucking the phone into her waistband, Faye turned the spigot to full blast. Water spit ahead of her as she dragged the hose the length of the house. It took all her might, her feet battling the pitted lawn. She reached the French doors. Fire licked at the windows. They were locked. Faye scanned the garden and porch for something to break the glass. The wrought iron patio set was too heavy. Ditto the planter.

Henry's new skateboard was propped next to the front door. Dropping the hose, Faye grabbed the back wheels, closed her eyes and swung hard. Glass shattered just as her grandchildren shuffled out the front door. Flames eager for oxygen shot out into the night air, some of them very close to Faye, who jumped back.

"Grandma!" screamed Henry, who'd seen his favorite Christmas toy sacrificed to the fire. But that was nothing compared to seeing his grandma. She edged close to the flames, spraying water; steady, as though staring down a cobra.

Meryl and Nathalie held Henry back from rescuing his skateboard.

Finally the water made some headway into the flames, allowing Faye to creep one step closer. The flames inched toward the wooden mantel. Once she'd doused the front half of the tree, she reached in, unlocking and opening both doors. Grabbing the tree, she used all her strength to pull the burning tree half way across the threshold. A shower of sparks escaped into the air

Meryl left the children with instructions not to move. She ran to the porch, toward her mother. Nathalie wrapped her arms around her shivering brother. He looked up at her worriedly. "Are they going to be okay?"

"Shut up. Of course they are," she snapped but her brow was furrowed. She rested her chin on his head, feeling the heat from the fire. She couldn't imagine how hot it was near her grandmother.

"Are you crazy? You're gonna kill yourself!" Meryl screamed as she reached her mother, trying unsuccessfully to pull her away.

"I am not going to let your house burn down waiting for a fire truck."

"If I can let my own house burn, so can you!" Meryl screamed above the smoke alarms.

Faye shook her head defiantly. "You're not the one who set it on fire!"

Meryl threw her arms in the air, throat hoarse with smoke. "Who cares? I won't blame you. No one has to know."

"I'll know." Faye wiped her sweaty forehead.

Meryl screamed, "Oh my God, you are so stubborn!"

Faye smiled, her face smeared with ash. "And you're a chip off the old block!"

"You're going to get us both killed!" Meryl bumped her mother aside, finding a safe spot to grab the tree.

"Or die trying!" Faye grinned.

Groaning with effort, both women managed to tug the tree, with several great heaves, onto the porch. Once they had it outside, Faye ran back into the living room, pushing the tree stand until it was on the dirt, leaning against a frozen hedge. She staggered onto the front lawn, coughing horribly.

Meryl hit her on the back. "You really should quit smoking."

Faye shook her head, coughing harder.

Distant sirens sounded in the night as Faye continued to cough. Meryl noticed that Faye's wig was smoldering, seconds from bursting into flames. Meryl snatched it from her head, throwing it into the damp bushes.

"That was a two hundred dollar wig!" Faye wailed between coughs.

"It was on fire!"

Still coughing, Faye marched back onto the porch, grabbing the streaming hose. "You gotta lift that hose off the ground or it's going to melt," she said to Meryl who followed.

Meryl looked into the living room where her watered silk curtains were being eaten by flames. "Are you kidding me?"

Faye tugged firmly at the hose, caught on one of the Adirondack chairs. "Are you going to help here or not?"

"You just don't know when to quit, do you?"

"Actually it's one of my better qualities." Faye coughed a few more times, looking like a baby duck without her wig.

"You're right," Meryl said. A surge of adrenalin shot through her body as she bent to un-snag the hose.

"That's my girl!" yelled Faye.

Faye entered the smoke-filled living room, spraying ahead of her. Meryl was right behind, holding up the weight, making it easier for Faye. Both women acted instinctively, moving away from the smokier areas, concentrating the water on the worst spots. Luckily, it wasn't a windy night.

***

It wasn't until the Fire Chief asked Meryl to produce her mother that they realized Faye was missing. In the flurry of firemen, who quickly took over the fire fighting, she had disappeared. They called her phone but there was no answer. Henry, when questioned, said he saw her drive off.

Her car was gone.

After promising the Fire Chief that she would a) take her mom in for a proper examination and b) give her the same lecture about the dangers of playing fire woman, including several references to how much luck had been on their side tonight, Meryl signed the necessary paperwork to be filed for the insurance claim. Their policy, Meryl thought as she walked over to talk to the concerned neighbors, was probably lapsed.

As an after-thought, she returned to the Fire Chief, who was on his computer in his truck. "So did we at least slow down the fire?"

He looked up, taking a long look at the house. "I don't want to encourage this kind of behavior."

Meryl put her hands together. "I promise, I won't tell a soul, just my mother."

He took off his glasses. "Did she have something to do with the fire?"

Meryl cocked her head. "Well, she smokes."

"You tell her that yes; she probably did save the house. If it had gotten to the stairwell, that fire would have taken over. But please, I don't need any articles about grandmas with garden hoses saving the day, alright?"

Meryl zipped her lip and threw away the key.

"She got lucky and so did you."

Meryl's eyes misted over. "I guess I did."

After the firemen packed up their gear, laboriously turning their huge rig around in the cul-de-sac, Meryl went inside. She put the kids to bed and surveyed the damaged downstairs. Her luck would probably run out when it came to finding her mother. She wouldn't be at a church this time. She went upstairs to change her clothes, talk to Nathalie and call her sister.

Jackie promised that she would catch the next flight from Boise.

***

Of course there was a bar across from Jackie's condo. There was always a bar, Faye thought ruefully. This one was a step up, several in fact, from her previous haunts. Even the New Year's Eve decorations were tasteful. By now the place was nearly empty, most people had moved on. It was nearly closing time.

She'd driven across the 520 bridge, wondering how in the Sam Hill she'd ever pay the toll that was electronically recorded via her license plate. They'd probably mail the damn thing to Vegas. One more thing she'd have to take care when she slinked back to desert with her tail between her legs. She imagined the conversation she'd have with her therapist. As usual, Lee Ann would have a lot of questions.

As she drove, she enjoyed what people in AA annoyingly called a Pity Party, although enjoying was hardly the word, Faye thought. More like enduring. She always endured. She was, she thought, the Grand Canyon of endurance. Men, kids, jobs, hell, if she was perfectly honest, club managers she dated to get a better shift. She endured them all.

Jesus rode across the bridge with her, saying nothing. He finally made an appearance and was silent. His lemon yellow shirt had a smiley face on it. Underneath: Have A Nice Day. That was ironic. If having a nice day meant hearing that your boyfriend had raped your young daughter and then setting that daughter's house on fire; then yes, she was having one hell of a nice day.

By the time she'd entered the bar, Jesus had disappeared. She didn't care. She wasn't in the mood to hear whatever it was he was thinking in the car. He'd probably just dredge up some speech he'd given thousands of years ago to Mary Magdalene. He knew she'd end up on another bar stool staring at the drink in front of her just like he knew every other eternal thing. What a boring life, always knowing what was coming next.

And here she was, as if this was a movie and she was some sad broad telling her life story to the bartender, currently keeping an eye on the football game. He had a nasty scar running from one corner of his eye to his jaw.

"You gonna drink that?" the bartender asked, surprising Faye, who thought he was kindly ignoring her. A good bartender, Faye thought, knew when people wanted to quietly drink themselves to death, or at least to numbness. Wasn't that the point of alcohol?

She stirred the drink with the little plastic straw, trying to imagine what it tasted like and more importantly what it would feel like to just detach, to float a little bit above her body, a boozy buffer. "Yeah. No." She eyed him, her smile crooked. "Honestly, I don't know."

His scar lifted as he smiled back. It was pale red, probably from a knife. "You live around here?"

A bartender who liked to chat. Perfect. Faye cocked her head toward the door. "My kid lives in those fancy condos across the street."

"Nice. He or she must be doing okay. Pioneer Square is quite the happening place these days, if you don't mind the drunks."

She grinned, stirring her drink again. No, she didn't mind the drunks. "She's doing real good. She's even on a TV show. She wrote this book called Marriage Maintenance and after that things really took off for her."

He laughed, moved a little closer. "Jackie. Totally. I tried to hit on her when she first moved in. She was really nice about it. I don't know how she could resist all this and a job as a bartender too? Anyway, she's seeing someone now."

He flexed his muscles, making fun of himself but Faye hardly noticed. "She is?"

"Yeah, tall dude. I think they went skiing or something. Or they were talking about it the last time they came in. I don't know. Seems kind of serious which is nice, you know. She seems like the type who works too much, right?"

Faye nodded noncommittally, reaching for the drink. Jackie lied to her about dating? For how long? It was embarrassing that some kid in a bar knew more about her daughter's life than she did. And this was the daughter who spoke to her. How much did she know about her kids? They didn't tell her anything. Why should they?

Finally she threw together some kind of answer. "Yeah, I came down here to see her. I forgot that she was out of town." What with all Christmas tree torching and bad news. Her head throbbed.

"Wasn't it Sun Valley?" The bartender noticed that something was wrong. Faye seemed dazed. She lifted the drink toward her mouth with a shaking hand.

He frowned, suddenly recalling Jackie saying, when she first came in, that it was nice to have a neighborhood bar. That she could finally enjoy a drink now that her mother was sober. "Hey!" he nearly shouted, grabbing the drink before it reached Faye's lips, apologizing profusely

The drink spilled all over Faye's hands and lap. She swabbed with the napkins that the bartender kept thrusting in her hands.

"What was that about?" Now she smelled like a booze hound.

The bartender frowned. "You don't really want that drink, do you?"

Faye frowned back. "Yes."

He ran his finger down the length of his scar, thinking. "Okay, let me say that a different way. You don't really need that drink, do you?"

Faye pursed her dry lips. She gazed at all the liquor bottles neatly lined up above the bar; thousands of dollars worth of liquor; enough to ruin a few lives. "I need it and I want it and I know it can kill me." She met his gaze directly. "There you have it: the story of my life."

He took a phone out of his back pocket and handed it over to her. "Call your sponsor."

Faye studied the phone as if it were a snake.

26.

"If we take matrimony at its lowest, we regard it as sort of friendship recognized by the police."
–Robert Louis Stevenson

After she hung up the phone, buoyed by the promise of Jackie's imminent arrival, Meryl did damage control in the living room, duct-taping cardboard over the French doors, rolling back the soggy carpet. While she worked, she tried desperately to put herself into her mother's mind, wondering where she'd go on New Year's Eve at an hour no longer safe to be out. She had no idea what she'd say to her, other than thanking her for saving the house.

Something had shifted. What if everything wasn't her mother's fault? What if alcoholism had been foisted upon Faye by the same unseen forces that led Kyle into their lives? What if nobody had control, ever? No wonder Faye had found Jesus. It would be wonderful to think that someone was at the wheel.

Meryl stripped off her cleaning gloves. The soot stains on the wall could wait. Her mother couldn't. As she left the ruined room, the place she'd dreamed of living her picture perfect life, Meryl thought that maybe grace isn't attaining anything at all. Maybe it's as simple as forgiving.

She put on her coat. It wouldn't hurt to stop by the church. Strangely enough she found herself yearning for the same peace she'd sought Christmas Eve. What if she was becoming one of those catastrophe converts? Bounce low, find Jesus.

She left a note for Nathalie, taping it to the banister where she'd be sure to see it. Exiting the house through the laundry room she smiled at herself, running to church again, her mind freighted with worry. She was the worst kind of Catholic. She should stop doing this. If she didn't stop now it might become a habit.

***

Meryl spotted him as soon as she entered the church. At least she thought it was him. What was this place, a magnet for lost souls, or perhaps, in their case, sinners? She stood rooted at the back of the cool, silent church watching him pray, wondering if she should just cross herself and leave, maybe dab a bit of holy water on her forehead for good luck. She should just get on with the job of finding her mother.

But still, she remained.

She was probably wrong, anyway. It was foolish to think that at this distance, in this dim light she could recognize her husband. There was something about his shoulders and the shape of his head that had tipped her off initially, although now that she was over-thinking it, perhaps she was wrong. Her first instincts, normally, were dead on. But lately everything had been so off kilter, he could be anyone. She had to know.

"Ethan?" Her voice echoed across the still, open space.

He turned around immediately, his tired face lit by a broad smile. "Hey stranger."

"Happy New Year."

His lips twisted into a rueful smile. "No place but up, right?"

"What are you doing here? You're not even Catholic."

He left the aisle and they walked side-by-side toward the church doors, an irony that was not lost on either of them. "No, I come from hearty repressed WASP stock, something that has become abundantly clear to me. My family worships at the altar of commerce. It's something I'm trying to get away from."

"Here?"

They stopped in the lobby, both of them wondering why two people who had been to church less than a handful of times in their 16 year marriage should run into each other here, of all places, when their union was looking anything but blessed.

Ethan shoved his hands into his leather coat. He was cold. "Among other places. It's kind of stupid really but I wanted to come here tonight. Even though we never came inside I used to stop with Henry when he was little. We collected acorns from those oaks out front and watch the squirrels. And if I'm going to be really honest, I used to come here when things were going to hell. Just to think. I knew I was tanking my life and out of control so I came here to clear my head. It's odd, I know."

She shook her head. "No, it's not. I came here tonight to think."

He sighed. "Yeah. It's like neutral ground. No one's trying to sell you anything."

She grinned. "Oh I don't know about that."

"You know what I mean."

"Yeah, I do." They settled back into silence. Ethan tried not to get excited that they were having a civil conversation. She didn't tell him about the fire. She didn't want to worry him any further. Also, she was protecting Faye.

Meryl shifted uneasily, not sure what to say. Her cell phone rang. She excused herself, moving away from Ethan, who pretended not to listen.

It was Faye. "Honey, I'm over at Victor's house."

A man, of course it was a man. At least she sounded sober but the words came out sharp. "Who is Victor?"

"My sponsor."

Meryl was contrite, relieved that there was a real live sponsor. "Oh." Where's his house?"

"Not too far. It's so late. I'm going to stay here. He's upstairs making up the guest bedroom."

"You sure you don't want me to come pick you up?" Meryl offered, even though she wanted nothing more than a night without Faye in the house and some sleep.

"Yeah, I'm sure. I think we both need a little breathing room."

"Maybe." Meryl wanted tread gingerly, unsure of where they stood.

"Listen, I want to talk in the morning. I think that you should tell Ethan everything you told me."

Meryl gazed across the gray carpeted lobby hung with New Year's wishes and bulletin boards offering classes, support groups, various meetings. "I don't think I can."

"I don't think you can end your marriage without telling him. It wouldn't be fair," Faye said.

"Do you think what he did was fair?" She hated the whininess in her voice.

"No. Not at all. But we're all damaged goods. It's how we play the hand we're dealt that determines our worth."

Meryl was silent for a while, thinking about what her mother had just said. It sounded like something she'd heard in AA. "Okay, I'll think about it."

"Good night sweetie."

"Good night Mom. I love you."

"I love you more than you could possibly imagine," Faye said. "You're going to be just fine. No matter what you choose."

Meryl wasn't sure if Faye was referring to her marriage or the business. "Thanks Mom."

It was only after she hung up the phone that Faye realized her daughter had called her mom for the first time in seventeen years. She broke down in tears and cried.

***

She blew in late to therapy wearing her Lancôme smock and started talking, interrupting whatever they'd been discussing. She told them about the rape as quickly as she could. It spilled out like water from a cracking damn. Her mother had been right. Chalk up another point for Faye. It was the last piece. Of what she didn't know.

She remembered Jackie talking about adult children of alcoholics who thought, as children, that they had something to do with their parent's drinking. If they had been better children, their parents wouldn't drink.

It was the same with rape, thought Meryl. She'd carried this belief that if she ran harder, worked faster, learned quicker, dressed better…the list was endless; that somehow she could outrun the rape.. In the process she'd allowed the rapist power over her. Her marriage had been built on a paradigm that had just shifted.

At some point, she'd run out of energy. Allen had taken over, explaining why she'd become a perfectionist.

"It's called neural association." Allen was saying. "A very intense experience is mapped into your brain with certain associations. You couldn't help it. It's normal." Allen cleaned his glasses as he talked, clearly trying to gain control.

"After it happened, I felt like if I let anything slip I would fall to pieces. I couldn't sleep unless my room was perfectly clean. Every hanger in my closet had to be exactly one half inch apart or I couldn't function. Looking back, it was weird but it made total sense to me back then."

"You were creating order from chaos," Allen said, nodding. "It's an emotionally healthy response, given the circumstances."

"But maybe not so great to be married to," Meryl blurted out, surprising herself. She turned to Ethan, her voice softening. "I was a bit of a control freak, wasn't I?"

Ethan got up from the couch, pulling Meryl up by her hands, wrapping his arms around her. "You could have told me." His voice was rough with emotion.

"I wanted to be p-perfect." She paused, trying to control herself. She hiccuped the last word. "I wanted our marriage to be perfect; untouched by all that."

"You're perfect to me." Ethan fought a primal urge to jump on a plane, find the man who did this horrible thing to a girl younger than his own daughter. He'd bash his skull in with a rock. He knew he wasn't capable of such violence and furthermore, the rapist was probably an old man. But it made him feel better to imagine it, briefly, while he stroked Meryl's hair.

"Just perfect," he repeated.

"No, I'm not. And neither were we." She pulled away from him, unable to meet his eyes. "I can see why you didn't want to tell me that Inspire was going under. I can see how you kept thinking that it would get better even when the numbers said otherwise. Yes, I did like things in tidy little packages and neat little rows. I hated any kind of mess." Here is where it got harder. "But what I cannot see is how you ended up in bed with Leslie. It all comes down to that because no matter how much we talk in here I can never, ever erase that imagine from my mind."

Ethan felt a surge of anger. "So you can forgive your mother for ruining your childhood but you'll never forgive me for my mistakes?"

Allen stood up, clasping his hands together. "Okay, Meryl, don't answer that. There have been too many emotional highs and lows in here today so I'm going to stop you right here. We need to take a break and regroup. What time do you want to meet next week?" he asked them both.

Ethan said, "The same time," but Meryl remained stubbornly silent. Ethan gave her a questioning look. She avoided him by putting on her coat.

"I'm sorry. I can't do this anymore." She hoisted her purse over her shoulder, offering Allan her hand. "Thank you for all your help."

She left.

Both men stared at the closing door, shocked. Allan had seen this many times before but never felt easy or acceptable. Ethan felt punched in the gut. He gathered his coat and perfunctorily shook Allen's hand.

"I don't know what to say," admitted Allen. "I'm sorry."

Ethan shook his head. "Thank you. I guess it's not over until the fat lady sings."

Allen blinked, bewildered. "I don't know what that means."

"It means I'm not giving up."

Allen shook his head. "She might need some space Ethan."

Ethan shook his head. Clearly this man wasn't in business. "I gave her seventeen years of space. Look what that got me."

***

"Do you want me to close the blinds?" Sam asked Nathalie. It was her lunch hour. She was supposed to meet Denny behind the track.

She shook her head, eyes darting nervously out into the hallway. Kids looked into Sam's office, staring at her and talking excitedly. Annoyed, Sam shut the blinds.

"Here's the deal kiddo. I know that it was Zoe who baked the pot into those brownies but I also know that it was intended for you and your boyfriend, Denny Newton, who was the one who gave Zoe the pot. I also know that Zoe has been your best friend since kindergarten. From what I've been told, she's an ambitious kid whose life goal is to get into an Ivy League school. That is not going to happen if she gets busted for giving an officer an illegal substance, which is a felony."

He paused, waiting to see if his words were having any effect on Nathalie's smug posturing. Years seemed to melt off the kid as his words sunk in. One moment she was a hard-eyed teen and the next a scared little girl. He could practically see the thought bubble over her head: This is some serious shit.

"You have gotten your friend into water that is way, way, way above her head and the sharks are circling, Nathalie. You cannot drug a law officer and walk away, whether you meant to or not." He let that settle. "So what

I'm going to do is offer you a deal." He reached behind him, offering the contents of a nearly empty box. "Donut?"

Nathalie shook her head, gulping as he returned the box to the top of the file cabinet. "I'm the one with the crap grades and no future. Charge me."

Sam shook his head, swallowing the one bite of donut he'd allowed himself. "I'm not interested in you."

"Yeah, you're interested in my mother."

Sam cocked his head, thinking smart cookie, bringing up his Achilles Heel. "If you think your mother is the reason I'm helping you, you're wrong. I've seen kids like you, hanging in the balance. Thinking you're too cool for school, starting down a road that leads to dead end jobs and men with heavy fists. You think Denny gives a shit about anyone but himself? He's using you to get to your rich friends who will buy his product. Or in clubs because a couple doesn't attract as much attention as one underage guy nursing a drink between bathroom deals. Does he keep his stash in your purse?" She blanched and he knew he'd hit pay dirt.

"I've been trying to bust your sweetheart for two years and you just might be the girl to help me. So even if you don't give a rat's ass about your future, what about your friend? What about her chance at a big time East Coast college?"

Nathalie stared at Sam, scared out of her mind. Betray her best friend or betray her boyfriend? What kind of choice was that?

27.

"Marriages don't last. When I meet a guy, the first question I ask myself is: is this the man I want my children to spend their weekends with?"
–Rita Rudner

Meryl, sitting at her kitchen table, dialed the number and hung up. Again. Her heart beat like a frantic animal. "Come on, come on, come on," she said by way of a pep talk. It didn't help that she could envision Susie Alverson in her immaculately remodeled Mercer Island ranch, answering the phone sporting a ring once owned by Grace Kelly. Susie was the entertainment chairman for the Winter Tea, who, Meryl had read in an e-mail, was failing miserably at finding entertainment for the Guilds second biggest annual fundraiser.

Convincing herself that Susie probably wasn't even home, Meryl dialed again. A cranky familiar voice answered. "What is it now, mother? I'm late for my colonic."

"Susie, it's Meryl Howe."

There was an awkward silence. "Oh goodness, Meryl. How nice. You've been such a stranger."

This was, Meryl knew, an invitation to share all the juicy details of Ethan's infidelity and Inspires deliciously tragic demise. If Meryl confided in her, Susie would probably skip her colonic appointment and rush over to the Bellevue Athletic Club to spread the dirt. Meryl could see her now, flitting from table to table, which was fortunate, because it supplanted the image of Susie with a rubber tube stuck up her butt.

"Yes, I've been busy. Christmas and all. Have you found anyone yet to entertain at the Winter Tea?"

Annoyance crept into Susie's voice as it all came gushing out. "I can't believe Geneva put that item in the newsletter. I have been doing all I can. Most members want a fashion show again and the ones that don't say it's boring watching a bunch of half naked anorexics prance around. They say they'll boycott us if we do another one. Have you ever tried to find a model with thighs that isn't plus sized? They don't exist. I booked an Andean flute group but everyone just hated that idea. They said Andean natives look morose. So I cancelled them. At least I think I did. They don't really speak English so they might just show up anyway."

Meryl screwed her eyes shut, jumping into her pitch. "I have the perfect group. They're a dance group out of New York. If they performed you wouldn't even have to worry about installing a runway. They could use the existing stage at the Meydenbauer Center."

"You have to *install* the runway?" Susie squealed.

"Oh yes. It's such a headache and you have to hire their technicians for sixty dollars an hour each. This dance group is spectacular." The runway at the convention center came out with a push of a button but Susie didn't know that. Meryl knew that and a lot more. Susie was desperate.

"I don't know. What are they called?"

"Divine Moves." Her mother came up with the name. She'd said something about Jesus choosing it but Meryl had learned to ignore these types of comments. They led to very odd conversations.

"Never heard of them."

"Melinda Gates used them for a private charity event and everyone loved them." It was frightening how naturally lying came to her. Maybe she did have a future in sales.

"Really? What kind of dancing?"

Meryl crossed her fingers. "I'm not sure what you call it. Modern, I guess. Anyway, they got a standing ovation at Melinda Gates' event." Repeating Melinda's name couldn't hurt.

"Okay, well let me run this past the other members of the committee and I'll get back to you."

Meryl felt a catch in her throat. Someone was bound to Google Divine Moves and the jig would be up. "The only reason they're available is that a paying gig cancelled. If we wait any longer, they'll get snatched up. They're probably already booked anyway. Of course, you can just go with the fashion show. That would be the much safer choice."

The chairwoman fell silent. Meryl kept her fingers crossed. This better work. The Winter Tea would be an audience of well over 750 women, depending upon who bought tables, all of whom could afford exotic dance lessons. They were like sheep. All it would take is one and many would follow. At the very least they'd be so scandalized that they would tell their friends. Meryl held her breath while she waited for Susie's answer.

28.

"Marriage is neither heaven nor hell, it is simply purgatory."
-Abraham Lincoln

"Let me get this straight. You want us to do a strip tease in front of a bunch of rich white women at your freakin' Guild Winter Tea?" Sandy Chen asked.

Meryl and Faye faced the book club in the freshly painted living room. It bore few scars from the fire. The stones on the fireplace, if one paid attention, had smoke stains. The carpet near the mantel was mottled. Faye had cheerily suggested dim lights and candles, insisting that no one would notice. Meryl had agreed, for once not worried what other people might think.

She was more interested in getting this business off the ground. The success of their marketing campaign rested on recruiting enough dancers to perform at the winter tea. Although they hadn't yet found a studio, they needed bodies in the door before they signed a lease or they'd run out of money in three months. They'd promised the bank a full enrollment in at least 3 weekly classes. That was the predicted number they needed to make their first loan payment.

"They're not all white," said Meryl.

Sandy rolled her eyes. "They are fifty shades of white with a couple of East Indians from Microsoft thrown in. Come on honey, this is the Eastside."

"What difference does it make?"

Sandy shook her head. "You ever see a bunch of women at a strip club? No, you don't. Because women don't like it."

"This is totally a different dynamic. It's all women. Women who are dancing and having fun. And these are women who have money to spend on dance classes. I'm hoping enough of them are willing to try something new."

Faye stepped forward, resplendent in a filmy silk wrap and high heeled dance shoes. Every woman in the room noted, again, that dance had kept her figure amazingly youthful and trim, which is precisely why she chose the outfit. These ladies could use some trimming. "You'll get ten free dance lessons at a value of seventeen dollars each. I used to barter for free therapy in Vegas and my therapist cost a hundred and eighty bucks an hour so you're getting real good value here. Unfortunately we're going to have to jam them all in every night after work 'cause the performance is in two weeks. I know that is not ideal but I can whip you ladies into shape. I've helped showgirls with two left feet become pretty decent dancers. I can do the same for you."

Diane shook her head. "You really think those rich skinny women want to see me shake my cellulite?"

Lorraine shook her head. "Excuse me? I've got more junk in the trunk than all of you combined."

Sandy laughed. "And I've got the body of a twelve year old boy. Not exactly stripper material."

"This isn't about titillating men. It's about having fun. We don't have to be Beyonce or Madonna," Meryl said.

"That's a relief," said Diane. The other women laughed although Carol remained silent, clutching her wine glass uneasily.

Faye clapped her hands, dimmed the lights and pressed down on the IPod stationed on a dock on the mantel. "Here we go. I'm going to show you what kind of moves you're going to be able to do when I'm done with you. Are you ready?"

"Cream" by Prince filled the air as the women watched, goggle-eyed as Faye transformed into a high-stepping, butt-shaking, leg-whipping dancer who exuded confidence as she looked down at the women with heavy lids. She moved with the authority of a woman supremely confident in herself, dropping down vertiginously, balancing herself with a throw of her arms. Bouncing up again, she moved to the pole in the corner of the living room, whipping herself around it with one arm while removing her robe sash.

"Come on ladies, let's hear some clapping," Faye yelled, throwing herself around the pole. She was wearing a t-shirt and short skirt. The t-shirt stuck to her belly when she lifted herself up with her arms, scissoring her legs in the air delicately, doing a flip on the side of the pole, landing soundlessly as a cat. The room erupted in cheers.

Spurred on by the audience, Faye left the pole, gyrating her hips, holding out the elastic of her skirt until she'd pulled it down to her ankles, stepping out of it delicately, throwing it into the corner with abandon. Although she wasn't wearing any, she did an elaborate mime of removing gloves, finger by finger, winking at each member of the audience after each finger. Only Carol remained still. The rest of the women were clapping and hollering with delight.

"I can't fucking believe that she's sixty!" Sandy Chen yelled over the music.

"Sixty-two!" yelled Meryl.

"We should all be stripping!" said Lorraine as Faye shimmied out of her t-shirt revealing a lacy bra.

As a finale, Faye turned her back, unsnapping her bra in the front, running it up and down her back in time to the music. At the exact moment the song ended, she spun around to reveal two sparkling silver pasties on her nipples. Glistening with a fine coat of sweat, she gulped lungfuls of air with a huge, happy grin. The women clapped and yelled bravo.

"That was amazing Faye!" said Lorraine. "Sign me up. I'm all for learning how to do that. My cats might be my only audience but if I could shake my cellulite like that it might be willing to let go."

Carol was the last to leave, clasping Meryl's hand at the door. "I think it's a wonderful thing that you're doing and I wholeheartedly support you but I don't think this kind of thing is for me."

"You never know until you try," said Faye, still glowing.

Carol could finally look in her direction now that Faye had pulled on a wrap. Watching Faye strip was possibly the most stressful thing she'd endured in her entire adult life. Those hip gyrations and the way Faye ran her hands up and down her body. It was definitely not living room appropriate. During the dance, she had prayed, fervently, trying not to move her lips or spontaneously combust from humiliation. She didn't even want to think about how those pasties were glued onto Faye's nipples.

Also there was the unnatural shape and firmness of Faye's breasts. Clearly those breasts were not sixty-two. It just wasn't right. Meryl had said that her mother had found Jesus but Carol couldn't imagine what church she attended. She certainly was not a Lutheran.

Meryl, seeing her distress, hugged her. "I understand Carol. Please don't worry about it. Thank you for coming. I appreciate it."

After Meryl shut the door, Faye clucked her tongue. "Shame we couldn't get her to sign up. Those church ladies really know how to rip it up."

Meryl rolled her eyes. "I don't think Carol takes her clothes off to sleep."

Faye collected wine glasses off the coffee table. "I could turn that mouse into a tiger."

"I think you've got your work cut out for you, turning a bunch of middle aged women into exotic dancers in less than two weeks."

Faye winked at her daughter, talking over her shoulder as she walked into the kitchen. Her heels clicked on the tile. "Honey you would be surprised at what lies inside the body and soul of a middle aged woman. Besides, I'm not doing it. We are."

Meryl felt a frisson of fear race down her spine quickly followed by something else: a tiny bubble of hope.

***

Ethan was exhausted. He had spent all day ripping up carpets in the rental home, hauling them out to the rent-a-wreck truck. After sanding the doll-sized dining room, he was sweeping up the sawdust off the parquet. He'd reached an agreement with the landlord. If he fixed up the place, he could move in with no down payment and a reduced rent. As they negotiated, Ethan had told his whole story, which was weird but in the end, the guy was surprisingly sympathetic. Everyone, Ethan was learning, had a story.

The house was a long way from perfect but it would be a hell of lot better than living with his parents. His mother had begun talking to him but solely, it seemed, to rub salt in his wounds. She kept telling him about her friends' children and their success. She'd end her monologues with, "You should call him. Take him out to lunch. See if there's anything available at his company." Like Ethan was going to call up his old high school buddies and ask for a job, especially after the way he'd bragged at their 20th reunion.

He was listening to a podcast on reinventing your life so he didn't hear the knock at the door as he swept. Nor did he see Nathalie until she was already in the room. Sensing someone, he turned quickly, knocking his head on the low hanging dining room chandelier.

"Hey, how'd you find me?" His face split into a grin as he took out his ear buds.

Her face was drawn and tired. She leaned gratefully into his embrace. "Grandma."

He nodded. So his mother did hear some of what he said. "I've got some Coke in the fridge. Want one?"

They went into the shotgun kitchen. There was no place to sit so they leaned up against the counters. He'd sprayed the tile counters with bleach, trying to restore the grout, so he laid down a towel to protect her coat. The place smelled like a swimming pool.

"Don't tell your mom about this place yet. I want her to see it when it's all fixed up. There's room enough for all of us here."

She took a long sip of her Coke. "Uh-huh."

She was a blunt kid, never very good at hiding her feelings. "What's up?" Ethan asked.

She played with the soft drink bottle running her finger down the glass grooves. "Have you ever had to make a choice between friends?"

He cocked his head thinking she'd gotten even prettier and taller since the last time he saw her. "What do you mean?"

"Like what if your one friend had gotten your other friend in trouble and you had to be the one to turn the first friend over to the authorities or your innocent friend could get in a whole lot of trouble."

Ethan's brow pressed into a deep frown. He crosses his arms. "Authorities? I don't like the sound of this."

"The cops."

"You'd better start from the beginning."

"Daddy, I can't. I can't tell you the whole thing because it's really complicated and I'm right in the middle of it. I just need your advice on it without you knowing the specifics. I can't figure out what to do."

"Have you talked to your mom about this?"

Nathalie shook her head. "No. I can't. I know what she'll say. The problem is that the one friend who got my other friend in trouble, if I turn him in, he'll probably go to jail."

"I can't answer you without knowing exactly what he did."

"I can't tell you what he did. I just need to know what to do."

Ethan moved to the other side of the counter so he was beside Nathalie. This was the kind of moment he'd always prepared for, as a parent. Now he was separated from Meryl and everything had gone to shit. But still, the moment had arrived. He put his arm around her. "I cannot tell you how much it means to me that you sought me out. I think you already know what to do. You called your one friend innocent, right?" Nathalie nodded. "So why would you let that friend get in trouble for something your other friend did? Just standing by and letting that happen would be wrong."

A tear leaked out of her eye. "You're right. I'm just so scared. I'm afraid everyone's going to find out what I did and they'll hate me."

"Isn't it better to be honest than popular?"

Nathalie laughed through her tears. "No!"

He smiled at her reaction. "You had me scared for a minute there. I thought maybe you were all grown up."

***

In theory, they were supposed to writhe and wriggle as fluidly as Beyonce. Or at least give it their best shot. That's what Faye said. Lorraine felt more like a slug who'd digested another, larger slug. Instead of pushing herself up from the floor, she gave in to her mounting exhaustion, frustration and despair. She should have never, ever, in a million years signed up for this. She was going to be humiliated.

With a great moan, she fell flat on her face on Meryl's living room carpet. Adding to her dismay was the strong odor of mildew invading her blocked sinuses. The carpet hadn't dried properly in the damp Northwest winter and needed replacing. "Just like my knees," thought Lorraine.

For the past eight nights they'd worked hard, moving their middle aged bodies in unnatural ways that occasionally made them feel sexy and sometimes, most of the time, just plain ridiculous. Except for Sandy Chen. She hopped around like a "midget on cocaine," said a slightly annoyed Faye, who worked tirelessly to instill some grace and sensuality into Sandy's frenetic efforts. If she had some

boobs, thought Faye, she'd have to slow down and deal
with gravity. But she didn't.

"Who says Asians can't dance?" Sandy quipped as
she karate chopped and ninja kicked her way through the
routines, apologizing profusely when she kicked Diane.

"You're very… aggressive," said Diane through the
blue ice pack and swollen upper lip.

Sandy couldn't help but shake it a little bit. "Like I
am in court honey. I've got the moves."

"Oh my God," whispered Meryl to Lorraine.
"We've created a monster."

Lorraine laughed but she was worried. Could she do
this? Faye was a great cheerleader but Lorraine was a
spiritual woman, an old soul. She could look into the
mascara'd depths of Faye's baby blues and see the doubt
hiding behind all the you-ladies-can-do-this confidence. She
was a whale in a pod of dolphins.

Faye had worked out a chorus style routine with a
lot of high kicks combined with sexy shoulder dips,
shimmies, fancy foot work and one segment that involved
lying flat on the floor, pushing themselves up by their arms
and jumping up, in one swift movement. It was at this
crucial point in the rehearsal that Lorraine's arms gave out.
She flopped down on Meryl's living room floor, screaming
into the carpet, "I can't do this! I'm too fat! I'm too old and
I'm too damn fat."

Faye stopped the music.

"You said fat twice," Sandy pointed out, wiping her
face with a small towel.

"That's because I'm twice as fat as I ought to be.
When I get out there on the stage everyone's going to
wonder who the dancing whale is and how did she stuff her
fat feet into those high heels?"

"People aren't going to say that," Diane said, uncapping her water bottle.

"They're going to be thinking it," countered Lorraine.

"That is the most lame-assed excuse I have ever heard in my entire life. I'm too fat. And I'm too Asian. I'm a freaking divorce attorney. How many attorneys do you know who get up in front of an audience and strip? We've all got excuses you know. Believe me I know what it's like to have an inner critic giving me shit all day long. Maybe yours says that you're too fat. Mine says I'm Asian and good Asians don't swear, work much harder than I do and God knows they dress better. I got my mother in my head telling me a good Asian girl does not get up on a stage and shake her butt in front of other people. That is called your inner critic and you need to go into your head and murder that little ass-wipe."

Diane, resting on the floor, clapped while Sandy took a bow. Diane turned to her friend. "Lorraine, you're going to do fine. You're not the only one nervous about this."

Faye offered Lorraine a water bottle. She gratefully took a sip. "None of you know what it's like to be fat. I feel like a sausage in this leotard."

Faye squatted down until she was eye level with Lorraine. "There isn't a woman alive who hasn't looked in the mirror and hated what she saw. It's a disease peculiar to our sex that men just don't have. But the nice thing about dance is that if you work hard at it, you can feel free and beautiful and sexy and all those other feminine things that we all deserve to feel. Those things aren't just for the young and skinny you know. But you do have to look for them."

She pointed at her head. "Sex appeal is all in your brain. If you truly feel sexy and confident and powerful then that's what the world is going to see."

"And if they don't. Fuck them!" said Sandy cheerfully.

"Well said as always!" added Diane, crawling to a standing position. "Now let's nail this number, okay? I have to go home and make tacos."

Faye checked with Lorraine. "Give it another shot?"

Lorraine stood, positioning her chin up, her shoulders back and her aching feet in their high heels at an angle. "Okay."

Faye patted her on the back before assuming her position in the front of the room. "From the top then!" She pressed the remote on the IPod and music flooded the room.

Every night when she dragged her tired legs upstairs, Meryl wondered if she was asking her friends for too much. They all had families and jobs and obligations. Besides, getting on a stage in front of all of those people, let alone stripping down to their unmentionables, was asking a lot of anyone. She didn't bother to discuss this with Faye. She knew her mother well enough to know that she thought they were doing them all a huge favor. And who knows, Meryl thought, as she collapsed on the bed, maybe she was right.

***

Friday night, Henry was in his room on his computer when his mother knocked. She was dressed up, smelled nice and had that same gunk around her eyes that Grandma wore. But on Mom, it looked normal. She kissed him on the cheek, told him that she was going out with a friend. Henry knew it was Sam. The more his mom went out with Sam, the surer he was that his parents were going to get a divorce.

"I thought tonight was your last dance class?" Henry asked. It was all Grandma could talk about. Tomorrow was the performance in front of 750 people, she kept saying. Henry could tell that Grandma was nervous and excited at the same time. She kept saying that once you were a performer, you couldn't get it out of your blood.

Henry knew that lighting the car on fire had made matters worse between his parents. Maybe his dad even thought that his mom did it. He felt like he'd pushed the button that led to his parents living apart and possibly divorcing. It was an awful feeling, knowing that you had started it all.

Henry kissed his mom on the cheek and told her to have a good time. For a moment, he thought about telling her about Mark, aka Fuzzy Boy but then realized that would be stupid. His mom would ask all kinds of questions. Besides, she was stressed out enough without worrying about him. Maybe he did have lying in his system. It was getting harder and harder to stop.

There was only one person who could possibly understand everything. It was time to meet Mark in person.

29.

"It is a curious thought, but it is only when you see people looking ridiculous that you realize just how much you love them."
– Agatha Christie

Half way through the dance class at Meryl's house, there was a knock at the door. Faye, sweaty and impatient, irritated that Meryl was out gallivanting with a boyfriend, flung open the door, prepared to be furious with whomever had the temerity to interrupt her class. Carol stood, red-faced and flustered, averting her eyes from Faye's ensemble. If she looked too closely at the coordinating hot purple leopard print leotard and matching headband, she'd change her mind.

"I am so s-s-sorry to come in at the eleventh hour like this but I have been p-praying and it came to me that the good lord wouldn't mind if I h-h-helped Meryl out." She smiled nervously, leaning in to whisper. "My husband thought so too."

Faye gathered her in, crushing her into her spandex covered breasts, which, Carol noted, were awfully firm. "That is fabulous. Just terrific. I always think the good Lord doesn't mind if you shake it a bit for Jesus." She didn't notice Carol blanching. "You might need to stay a bit afterwards and get some extra help but I am sure you can catch right up."

Carol allowed herself to be pulled into the living room. She took off her coat revealing a pair of middle school gym shorts borrowed from her son and a loose t-shirt. "I did gymnastics in high school."

"I'm sure it'll help," said Faye.

Carol hesitated before joining the other women. "There aren't going to be any men there, right?"

"My husband will be there," said Sandy.

"I invited a guy I have a crush on," said Lorraine. "I told him it was a holistic fair."

Faye moved Carol until she was in the right position, between Lorraine and Sandy. She glanced around at her friends, who all encouraged her. "I have always been shy about my body. I changed in a bathroom stall during PE. Even with Richard, I'm modest." She took a deep breath. "I think this will be good for me."

"Once you show your tits to a total stranger everything is much easier," said Sandy, slapping Carol on the back a little too hard.

"What are you talking about?" Diane asked Sandy.

"Spring break, 1996," said Sandy with a wink.

"Maybe this was a bad idea," said Carol, backing up toward the door.

Diane grabbed her shirt, holding her in place. "This was an excellent idea. Faye, let's get going."

Nathalie waved at Faye from the hallway. "Grandma, I'm going to a study group at Nina's house."

"Be back by 10," Faye said, barely paying attention. She needed to keep Carol engaged. "Alright, let's run through the whole thing slowly for Carol. Remember, I want some major attitude. Sexy, sexy, sexy."

Carol's face flushed six shades of peony as she started to follow Faye's movements.

***

Sam walked Meryl to the door after their date. It was the rare kind of Northwest winter night when the stars shone, the clouds went elsewhere and the rain mercifully let up. Sam felt ridiculously "high school," thanking her for the nice night, saying their goodbyes. He was thoroughly enjoying kissing when they both heard a man nearby clear his throat. It was Ethan, sitting on the other end of the dark front porch.

He waved at them from the shadows. "Don't let me interrupt."

Meryl rapidly disentangled herself. "Ethan what are you doing here?"

Ethan stood up but remained on the other end of the porch. "Just thought I'd drop by. Say hi."

Sam patted Meryl on the back. "I'll call you later."

"Did you enjoy my wife?" Ethan called out.

Without turning around, Sam gave Ethan the finger as he walked off.

Furious, Meryl strode over to Ethan, who smiled impishly. "Sorry to scare off your date like that."

"I don't think you scared him." She couldn't resist adding, "He's a cop."

Ethan held his tongue. Instead of blurting, "Big fucking deal," he calmly said, "I came here to give you this." He handed her a slip of paper. She unfolded it. Written down was an address in Kirkland. She looked up, puzzled. "It's a good place for your dance studio."

Although she was surprised, even pleased that he'd changed his mind about her business plans, she was furious. How dare he embarrass her in front of Sam after what he himself had done? "That's it?"

"That's it." He pulled his bike, which he'd just liberated from the garage, from the bushes at the side of the house. Getting in shape was part of his larger plan. Throwing his leg across the seat, he said, "I love you," with a grin. "And I hope you had a lousy time on your date."

***

Faye was on the couch, still in her purple leotard, damp with sweat. She'd removed her leg warmers and heels. Before Meryl could get her coat off, she asked, "Did you commit any sins?"

"Subtle Faye, very subtle," Meryl said. "Goodnight."

"You did, didn't you?" Faye asked but Meryl was already upstairs.

Meryl opened the door to Henry's bedroom quietly, although he was probably already asleep. It took a moment for her eyes to adjust to the dark. When she finally did, she sat down on the bed, resting her hand on Henry's back. It was surprisingly soft. She pressed harder. It was a pillow.

Faye was picking up water glasses from the living room when Meryl thundered down the stairs. "Is Henry over at the Max's house?"

Faye shook her head. "No, I tucked him in at 9:30."

"He's not in his bed."

"Are you sure?"

"Of course I'm sure. I've checked the whole upstairs."

"You'd better call the neighbors."

But Meryl was already on the phone, dialing Carol's number. A few seconds later, she hung up. "He's not there."

"Where's Nathalie?" Panic crept into Meryl's voice. She dialed Nathalie's cell phone number.

"Studying at a friend's house. She'll be back by ten."

Meryl shook her head, while listening to Nathalie's phone go to message. "It's Friday night. She's not studying."

Faye's voice betrayed her growing doubt. "She said she'd be back by ten."

"She's probably getting high with that creep Denny. I knew this would happen. I leave you for one night to look after my children and you blow it." She pointed an accusing finger. "If anything happens to Henry, I'm blaming you."

Faye's first reaction was to scream, remind her that she was setting Meryl up in business, training her fat, crazy friends, while her she chased after a man while still married. But she kept her mouth shut.

Lord she wanted a drink. Four years sober and she still felt the crushing thirst for booze at the slightest sign of anxiety. Her body was a record that got stuck in the same groove. "I'm doing the best I can." She shut her eyes and was relieved to see Jesus right there, smiling his beneficent smile, immediately calming.

Suddenly, she knew what her daughter was looking for: guidance. She was scared and looking for direction. Rather than responding to Meryl's anxiety, she'd rise to the occasion. Now, finally, was her golden opportunity to mother. She was not going to blow it.

The plan came to her as she talked. "I'll go get Nathalie. She knows more about her little brother than either one of us think. She'll know where he is. You call Sam and ask him to put out a bulletin. I don't think they do it unless they're missing for longer but ask him to do it anyway. You call Ethan and tell him what's going on. Tell him that I'm getting Nathalie and not to worry. Don't call

Jackie yet. We'll find him soon. I know it. You start looking around the neighborhood in your car."

Meryl's eyes flooded with tears. "This is not like him. Not like him at all."

Faye gave her a quick hug, flooded with relief that Meryl wasn't going to get mired in accusations, was going to let her lead. She straightened her already ramrod posture. "Everything is going to be okay. I got Jesus riding shotgun."

Meryl nodded, wiped the tears out of her eyes, grateful for Faye's confidence and even her weirdly reassuring faith.

"Are you okay to drive?"

Meryl nodded yes but Faye disagreed. "I'm going to call Diane. You need a driver and a looker."

***

The Shark Club was crowded for a weeknight. The dance floor was packed to capacity, the bar three deep. It was a young crowd, which suited Denny. They had cash to burn and knew where to find him. The older ones asked too many questions and the high school crowd always felt entitled to a deal because they knew him from summer or carpool or even Camp Orkila. He stood along the wall with Nathalie. She was driving him crazy.

He tried to ignore her but she just wouldn't shut up. She was killing his buzz and scaring away the customers with her doomsday garbage, which is exactly what he was telling her when a drunk girl in a silver shirt approached.

"My friend said you had some X," the drunk girl said, swaying to the music. Her face looked pale behind her red lipstick.

"I might," Denny said with a sly smile. "For the right person."

The drunk girl waved a wad of cash. "Oh I'm Ms. Right alright!" she giggled.

Danny quickly shoved her hand down, slid the cash out, pocketing it quickly. "Hey, be cool." He slid something into her hand.

The girl tilted her head, sweeping her long damp hair out of her face. "Don'tcha wanna count it?"

Denny winked at her. "I trust you. Is there any reason I shouldn't?"

"You're cute!" said the drunk girl.

"Thank you. I'd totally flirt with you but my girlfriend here might not like it."

The drunk girl swiveled her head towards Nathalie as if just realizing she existed. "He's cute," she slurred before dancing her way back into the crowd.

"That's what I mean. You whole future is in the hands of people like her," Nathalie said.

Denny took a sip of beer. "She's sweet."

"She's drunk," Nathalie said.

He winked at her. "A good combination, I might add."

All night, in between transactions, she'd been trying to talk him out of selling. Taking drugs was one thing but selling them was going to land him in jail. He'd laughed, saying that the cops weren't interested in him.

"I fly below their radar. That bozo Officer Friendly at school brings his drug dogs in every couple of months trying to pin something on me. Never works. He's freakin' inept. I'll make my wad and get out. In the meantime, I'm making people very, very happy. Look around you. Do these people look unhappy?"

Nathalie gazed around the bar and had to admit that there wasn't an unhappy face in the bar. She also agreed that if people wanted drugs, they would find them somewhere. She also knew that he wouldn't get out. The money was too easy. He wouldn't last one week on a roof or in an office.

She faced Denny and he kissed her, shoving a pill in her mouth from his own. Instinctively, she inhaled, causing the pill to stick halfway down her throat. She began coughing violently. Denny quickly handed her a beer. She gulped it down, sputtering, "What was that?!"

He gave her another kiss. "Relax dude, it's X! You're going to totally love it!" He kissed her harder, even though she resisted. "And so am I, dude. So am I."

***

Panic had Faye by the throat, threatening to strangle her as she drove around downtown Kirkland, wondering where the hell she was going to find her granddaughter. Why hadn't she just stopped dance class and confronted the kid? She knew Nathalie wasn't going to a study group. She was more worried about Carol catching up than the whereabouts of her own granddaughter. Maybe she wasn't fit to be in charge of children. She'd lost two of them in one night. What kind of a track record was that?

She drove past a bar with a group of twenty somethings milling around the front door and decided to investigate. Going in, she attracted a few stares but made her way easily to the bar. It was a small place and the bartender wasn't busy. He wiped the bar, raising a brow.

"What can I get you?"

"Water."

It was easy. She was in a bar and ordered water. Simple. She found a picture of Nathalie on her phone. When the waiter returned with her water, she showed the smiling beauty on her phone. "Have you seen this girl tonight?"

He shook his head. "She doesn't look familiar."

Faye scratched her number on a cocktail napkin. "If she comes in, will you call me?" As an afterthought, realizing she'd just given a man in a bar her number for the first time in decades, she added, "I'm her grandmother."

"Sure thing," he said, pocketing the napkin. Faye thanked him and rose from the bar, leaving quickly. Across the street was a car she recognized parked in front of Hector's. It was Sam's squad car. He was on the radio. Faye waved to him as he pulled out of his parking spot. He didn't see her so she grabbed a yellow crossing flag from the signal post on the sidewalk, waving it frantically, hoping to get his attention as he drove past.

***

Diane drove Meryl's car past the dark, empty elementary school. The playground was forlorn and soggy, the fence strung with limp forgotten jackets.

"How about the skate park?" Diane asked.

Meryl looked up from her phone, busy scrolling through her contacts looking for friends who wouldn't mind missing a few hours of sleep to search for a missing child. "Do you think he'd go that far?" The skate park was several miles away.

Diane shrugged. "It's worth a shot. Didn't Jackie just take him there?"

Sam had been perfect: reassuring, sympathetic and confident that this problem could be solved. He didn't tell her not to panic, or offer statistics about the first few hours being crucial. He didn't say, "This doesn't sound like Henry," as if he knew anything about the boy just because he'd met him a few times.

What he did say was that he'd get a description out to all the squad cars in Kirkland and get officers to check the major bus stops, parks and convenience stores. He asked for a description, what he might be wearing. He didn't ask for identifying birthmarks because that would lead Meryl's mind into dark places better passed over. They'd need that for the Amber Alert but it would wait. It had been his idea to call friends, get people out there looking for him, pointing out that the more eyes they had on the street, the better.

Right now there were twelve different people driving around, looking for Henry. Before he started searching himself he had to stay in downtown Kirkland, until the next shift came on duty.

Ethan had been half way back to Bellevue when he got the call from Meryl, cursing his luck to be on a bike. "I'm going to get my mom's car," he said.

After he hung up, he intended to ride the last five miles as hard as he could but after the first mile, thinking about all of Henry's favorite places, he had a very strong hunch that he knew where to find his son. He turned the bike around and peddled with all his might towards Juanita Village.

***

The yellow pedestrian flag caught Sam's eye as he drove down Lake Street. Circling around through a parking lot, he wasn't surprised to see Faye, waving him down on the corner with a panicked look on her face. Nothing about

Meryl or her mother shocked him. Police work was the
ideal training in dealing with this family. He pulled up,
rolling down the window.

"You know about Henry?"

He nodded. "Yeah. I'm going over in a little while.
I'm still on duty."

"I think Nathalie's down here somewhere with that
kid Denny. She might know where Henry is. I have to find
her." She caught her breath, leaning her hands on her
knees. "She's not answering her cell."

Sam nodded, getting out of the car and opening up
the back seat. "I bet I know where they are." She climbed
into the backseat before he could apologize. "I can't let you
in the front because-"

Looking up at him from the backseat she winked.
"Darling, I've been in the backseat of a police officer's car
before. I know the drill."

He shut the door with a wry smile, thinking he
could get used to this old bird. Checking his rearview
mirror, he pulled into traffic smoothly. "This isn't the
regular drill, ma'am. This time you're here for a good
reason."

30.

"A successful marriage requires falling in love many times, always with the same person."
-Mignon McLaughlin

Other than a distant glow of streetlights from nearby Juanita Drive, Juanita Beach was empty and dark. The wind-whipped stretch of beach wasn't meant to be inhabited at this hour. A lawn with benches bordered the parking lot. It ended in a lonely playground. In the distance the sign for Spuds, a fish and chip shop, glowed blue. As Ethan rode his bike into the parking lot, he saw a car pulling in and someone getting out. He also saw the shadow of a kid, walking in the parking lot. He couldn't tell if it was Henry.

"Henry!" The wind whipped away the word.

Ethan thought he saw the kid's head turn but he couldn't be sure. The man, limping, tall and overweight, dragged the boy toward the car, shoving him into the passenger side. The kid struggled but got into the car. Glancing in Ethan's direction briefly; the driver slammed his door. The car pulled out of the parking spot. Ethan rode his bike toward the car at full speed but he couldn't catch it. The car was gaining speed, heading for the park exit.

Ethan pumped his legs with all his might, jumping the curb onto the mangy winter grass, pockmarked with gopher holes. He prayed that the old bike tires would hold.

Prayed that his heart would rise to the occasion and not burst from his chest.

Everything burned: his legs, his mind, his instinctual protective drive that screamed: someone is taking your child. If that car, which Ethan was ninety percent sure contained his son, reached Juanita Drive, the driver could head straight, turn left or right. Each choice led to escape. To the right was Interstate 405. Ethan's mind wasn't going there. Every cell powered his legs across the bumpy stretch, around darks pines and towards that street

He was going to stop that creep, even if it killed him.

***

Sam was on the radio, explaining to dispatch that he was entering The Shark Club in search of another missing minor. When he came off duty he would remain in his car, searching for the other missing minor but this one was probably inside the club with illegal ID, he said. He didn't bother explaining that both missing minors were related.

Faye's phone rang while she waited in the backseat. The caller ID said Nathalie. The background music was so loud Faye could barely make out her words.

Nathalie was crying, hysterical. "I'm at a club, in the bathroom. Denny gave me something and I think I'm having a bad reaction. I'm sweating and shaking and my heart is racing. I'm really scared. I feel awful."

"Give me a name. What's the name of the place? Is it called the Shark Club?"

"Yes. It's down by the Marina. It's called the Shark something," Nathalie repeated, obviously unable to follow Faye, possibly losing consciousness from the sound of it.

Sam dropped the radio, waving his hands to get Faye's attention. "Ask where Denny is. Where's Denny?"

Faye nodded at him. "Honey, stay with me okay. I'm right outside the club. Office Richer is here."

Sam shook his head violently as he heard Nathalie saying, "No, don't let him come in here. Denny is really sweet. His parents are so fucked up. He really…" Nathalie lost the bead on the conversation, talking to someone who had just entered the bathroom, telling them she was fine.

Faye wrinkled her nose at Sam, who was getting out of the car, changing out of his uniform into a denim shirt with a gun holster. From the trunk he took a tweed blazer. "Hang on there!" she said to him as he put on the blazer, covering the phone with her hand. "Just a minute."

Into the phone she said, "Sweetheart, I'm going to get you to the hospital. You gotta tell me where Denny is. You're in over your head honey. Take it from someone who's spent most of her life there, it's time to call in the cavalry."

Nathalie moaned. "I love you."

"I love you too baby girl. Where is he?"

Nathalie slurred her words. "In the back at the second bar. He's wearing a leather jacket." Faye held the cell phone out so Sam could hear it as they walked toward the club.

A moment later, Sam nodded at Faye. "She hung up."

Faye stepped up the pace.

When they reached the club's door, Sam grabbed Faye's arm. The neon Shark Club sign flooded the empty patio with an electric blue light. Music throbbed into the frigid air. The dark lake soaked up the sound in the black distance. "You have to wait here until I bring her out. It won't take long."

Faye shook her head. "I'm going in there right now and getting my grandbaby." She lowered her chin, giving him the full benefit of her baby blues on high beam. "Try and stop me."

Sam knew that look and stepped aside, ushering her up the steps. "Ladies first."

***

Sam drove to the hospital, keeping his speed steady on I-405. He was trying to decide the best time to inform Meryl that her daughter was en route, via ambulance, to Evergreen Hospital to have her stomach pumped.

There was no good time, he thought. It was like police work, you just kept moving. A Caucasian male in his forties on a bike had been knocked down by a hit and run on Juanita Drive. Sam turned down the radio, trying to concentrate on his keeping his speed down. Staying steady, Sam learned years ago, was half the battle.

Faye had been surprisingly calm during the entire ordeal, scraping her grandbaby off the filthy bathroom floor, carrying her like a trophy outside to the waiting Medics. She even cracked jokes about loving a man in a uniform in an effort to keep Nathalie conscious while they loaded her into the ambulance. As they took her vitals, Sam overheard Faye talking about Hot Jesus to Nathalie, whose pinpoint pupils faded in and out above an oxygen mask.

Sam's replacement had taken Denny to the precinct, confiscating his wad of cash, the X, cocaine and God knows what else the little pisser was peddling. Luckily, he'd just turned 18, so they could sentence him as an adult. Sam thought it would feel much better finally nabbing the little SOB. But he was too worried about Meryl and her children.

***

Evergreen Hospital was where it all started, Sam thought as he pulled the cruiser into the parking spot for police vehicles. What seemed like months ago the charge nurse had heard Leslie complaining that Ethan's wife had cut his arm and Sam got the domestic abuse call. And his life changed.

Getting out of his car he recalled how disappointed he'd been to learn that the cute ER nurse was engaged. Now he could care less. He paused while a flashing ambulance pulled into the ER bay. The glass doors of the hospital slid open and emergency personnel flooded the drive. When the EMS van doors cracked open, Sam was stunned. It was Meryl. She emerged from the dimly lit van in a halo of hazy light, following a gurney into the open maw of the hospital ER.

Instinctively Sam stepped forward to comfort Meryl but her eyes, red and raw, couldn't or wouldn't focus. She didn't stop.

"It's Ethan," she said roughly, following the gurney into the hospital without another word.

After a long moment, during which Sam reminded himself that he was a cop and crisis was his job, he went into the hospital. He wanted, now more than ever, to check in on Nathalie, who he'd already been informed by radio, would be fine. Needing time to think, he waited in line at the triage desk. Normally he would have flashed his badge and gone upstairs.

A Jamaican nurse, a musical lilt in her voice, leaned in, whispering to the receptionist. "That guy they just brought in? He rode his bike right into a car trying to stop some creep from kidnapping his son. That car hit him so hard he went flying into the bushes. The son, he jumps out

of the car and he runs into Spuds, you know? He screams
for help, says his Daddy's been hit."

"You mean Spuds right down on Juanita Beach?"
The receptionist asked, twirling a finger in her blond hair.

The Jamaican nurse took a report from the
receptionist's desk, her excuse for emerging from the ER to
gossip. "Yeah. Megan says the kid met the creep online.
That kid is totally fine and with the neighbors right now.
It's his poor daddy that might die."

The Jamaican nurse recognized him. "Hey Officer
Sammy, do you know if they've caught that hit and run
with the cyclist yet?"

Sam's throat constricted. Their usual routine was
that he told her to quit calling him Officer Sammy and
she'd laugh, showing her stunningly white teeth. Sam shook
his head, inhaling deeply. "No. I'm here about the
accidental overdose. Nathalie Howe."

The blonde receptionist looked over the admitting
chart. "That's like, so weird. That's the same last name as
the guy on the bike."

Sam nodded. "Yeah. Weird. What room?"

"Seven twenty-two." The receptionist frowned
when she looked up at Sam. Although they all worked the
night shift, he was a deeper shade of exhausted. "You
okay?"

He nodded. "Yeah, fine. Seven twenty-two, right?"

He was half way down the hall when he pivoted,
returning to the reception area. Taking the Jamaican nurse
aside he asked, "Hey, you don't happen to know if that guy
on the bike was wearing a helmet, do you?"

Looking at her pink Swatch, she shook her head.
"No, sorry I don't. You know him?"

Sam met her eyes, nodding. "Yeah."

"I'm sorry," she said.

"Me too," Sam said, not really sure what he was sorry for.

***

Nathalie had a private room. Faye had learned in rehab that if you told the admitting nurse that you had a cold, they'd quarantine you, which was nice because this wasn't jail. It was a lot nicer, Faye noted, as she sat in a gray leather chair staring at her sleeping granddaughter. Although the cold had been a fib, Faye felt okay with Jesus, given that Nathalie's daddy was fighting for his life in the ER. Hopefully all this peace and quiet would be unnecessary.

The intubation of Nathalie's stomach had been avoided. Nathalie upchucked all over Faye in the ambulance, which was par for the course, since she'd missed Nathalie's toddler years. Trixie, back when she was Trixie, had barfed on Faye twice.

Faye herself had developed a tolerance to alcohol that had precluded barfing. "I was more the blackout type," she thought to herself, taking out her lipstick. She could also hide her hangovers. She then admitted to herself that this was lie. You can fool adults but you can't fool kids. Tonight had been a lesson from that chapter. All Henry had wanted, he had tearfully said, was someone to talk to.

She felt a hand on her shoulder, thinking it was Jesus, offering hope, but it was a nurse. "You're the grandmother, aren't you?"

Faye nodded, waiting for the other shoe to drop. Could this night possibly get any worse? "Yes."

"I've heard her mother is in the ER with her father. I checked on him." She cleared her throat.

Faye nodded. "Good news? I could use some of that right now."

The nurse smiled. "He's stable. Would you like to get a cup of coffee? I can stay here with your granddaughter if you'd like."

Faye knitted her brows, wishing she had on make-up. "No, thank you. I'm fine."

The nurse pulled up a chair, placed the chart in her lap. "How are you doing?"

Faye held the lipstick in her hand. "Okay, considering." She sighed. "This is Coty Tangerine. They quit making it twenty years ago so I ordered fifty tubes. This is my last one."

"It's pretty," said the nurse.

"Yeah, guess it's time to find a new color."

"I'm sure you can find the same one online." She looked at her watch. That was the worst part of her job, walking out when she was needed.

Faye shook her head. "Nope. I'm ready for something new."

The nurse leaned over, patting Faye's knee. "My grandma died before I was born. I don't know if it matters to you at this point but I think your daughter and your granddaughter are very, very lucky to have you."

***

A hand slipped into Meryl's so softly, she barely felt it. She turned her heavy head. It was Jackie, who had somehow moved a chair next to her without Meryl noticing. "Hey."

"Hey. How's he doing?"

It took her a while to think of the answer. She'd lost track of time, unsure of how long she'd been at the hospital. "They opened up his skull to relieve the pressure. After the swelling goes down they can determine…" She nearly started crying. "…if there's any brain damage."

They held hands, watching the prone figure in the bed, hooked up to so many tubes snaking under and over the covers, it was impossible to count. An oxygen mask covered Ethan's mouth. His breathing was steady but slightly labored.

"I think he'll make it."

Meryl shook her head. "He could have been killed."

"He saved his boy. He did it."

Tears squeezed out of Meryl's eyes. "He did."

"It was incredibly brave."

The corner of Meryl's mouth went up in a crooked smile. "Always the show-off."

Jackie wrapped her arm around her sister. "I'm so sorry I haven't been around."

"Stop apologizing."

"No, just listen. I've been trying to keep Rob from seeing everything about me, including my family. I thought he would only love me if I was this super competent professional with no complications."

"There are always complications," Meryl said, not sure whose relationship she was talking about.

"Sometimes I feel like if people find out where I came from, my whole career will be taken away from me; like I'm this white trash kid who somehow pulled the wool over everyone's eyes."

Meryl sighed. "Exactly."

Jackie leaned her head on her sister's shoulder. "What do you think would happen if we both stopped living in fear?"

Meryl kissed her sister's head. "We'd explode." They both laughed. Meryl sighed. "I guess we'd be more like Mom."

"Oh God. You're right," said Jackie. "Without the tats."

"Do you want to say a prayer with me?"

Jackie cocked her head, not sure if her sister was serious. "Really? Uh, sure, I guess. I don't even know where to begin."

Meryl scooted off her chair, getting down her knees by Ethan's bed, clasping her hands together. "Like this."

31.

"Lots of people want to ride with you in the limo,
but what you want is someone who will take the
bus with you when the limo breaks down."
– Oprah Winfrey

"Oh my God, oh my God, oh my God!" Lorraine said, turning an alarming shade of parchment.

Fifteen minutes ago Lorraine made the mistake of peering out from behind the curtains into the vast sea of faces. "There are hundreds of people out there. Women in suits and dresses. I can't do this. I cannot get up on stage and dance in front of them, let alone take off my clothes."

"She's freaking out, what do we do?" Diane asked as Lorraine started breathing in rapid, throaty gasp.

"Slap her!" said Sandy, looking both domineering and adorable in her tuxedo with tails and fishnet stockings.

Carol rushed up, intercepting Sandy by grabbing her wrist before she could administer a blow.

Sandy jerked her arm away, annoyed. "What? It works in the movies."

"This isn't the movies," Diane snapped. She rubbed Lorraine's back, trying to soothe her. "Look, we're only out there for nine minutes and then we're done. Nine minutes."

Lorraine went from parchment to winter white. "Oh my God! That's forever. I had to give a speech when I was ten that lasted three minutes. It seemed like weeks. I ended up farting and the whole class laughed for the last minute. It was awful. I will literally die out there. I'm going to faint or throw up or fall or have a heart attack. Oh my God, maybe I'm having a heart attack right now!"

Faye marched into the backstage area, saw what was happening with Lorraine, briskly approached her and slapped her face. "Get a hold of yourself!"

"Damn! My one chance to slap someone and you go and wreck it for me!" Sandy snapped at Carol, whose eyes were closed in prayer, asking for strength.

Diane patted Sandy on her back. "You're young, you'll get another chance."

"We're onstage in four minutes. Is everyone all stretched out and done panicking? Once that music starts we're out and shakin' it, right?" Faye asked.

"Why do I feel like we're about to be publicly executed?" asked Sandy.

"Way to calm everyone down Sandy," snapped Diane.

"That's exactly what it feels like!" squealed Lorraine. "We're lambs to the slaughter!"

"You are going to go out there and show those women how much fun it is to shake your rear end and what wicked dance moves I have taught you. This is about fun, this is about being sexy, this is about showing those ladies out there that you can kick it with the best of them," Faye said.

All four women stared at her, looking frightened and nervous, shivering in their lacy tap pants, tux tails and top hats. A make-up artist had done dramatic make up with false eyelashes and dragon red lipstick. Instead of making them feel powerful and sexy, they felt like they'd stumbled into a dream where their neighbors were there but all strangely dressed and nearly unrecognizable.

"I don't think I can remember one dance move," whispered Carol. "My mind is utterly blank."

Meryl, previously missing, climbed up the back steps, joining the group backstage. "Two minutes ladies. How's everyone doing?"

"Freaking out," Sandy said.

"Oh no!" Lorraine covered her mouth, bolting for the stairs, trying not to throw up backstage.

Meryl watched her go. "Is she doing what I think she's doing?"

Sandy nodded. "Yep. She's stress puking. We had to stop three times on the way here. I can tell you everything she's eaten in the last eight hours, in reverse order."

Meryl gave her mother a panicked look. Faye rubbed her hands together before motioning to the other women to join her. "In times like this there is only one thing to do."

"Can I slap someone?" asked Sandy.

"No you can't," said Faye. "Gather round me and hold hands. We're gonna pray."

"To the great God of stripping?" asked Sandy.

"Shut up and listen Sandy," Faye said. "I know you think that aggression and smart-assed comments are the answer to everything but in times like this you have to call on your higher power." The women made a small circle in the backstage area, huddling like penguins.

They lowered their heads and tried to concentrate, ignoring the swelling noise from the auditorium. "Dear Jesus, in the last few days we have gone through, well, a lot. But Ethan is alive. Thank you. I'm asking you Dear Lord to stay with us today as we celebrate what you've given us: our health and our bodies and our courage to get out there and shake our groove things. In Jesus' name amen."

Halfway through the prayer, Lorraine, who had assumed a spring green tinge, joined the circle, holding hands with Carol and Diane.

"That was a very unique prayer," said Carol.

"Thank you. I'm going to take that as a compliment," said Faye.

From onstage the women could hear themselves being announced as Divine Moves. The announcer read from a card, saying they were ready to energize the stage with their fresh new moves.

Carol raised her eyebrows at Faye. "Do they know what kind of dancing we're doing?"

Meryl winced. "Sort of."

Their musical cue: Vogue by Madonna blasted into the auditorium. "They have no idea," Faye said gleefully.

Suddenly overwhelmed with emotion at what her friends were about to do, Meryl tried not to cry. "Whatever happens, I love you all to death!"

Sandy Chen tripped in her heels. "Good because it might come to that."

As the music filled the auditorium and the women strutted out onto the stage, Sam looked around in the back of the auditorium for a good place to stand. He was only going to be there for a moment but he wanted a clear view of the stage. He moved through the last minute stragglers rushing to their tables, their eyes trained on the stage. He didn't realize until it was too late that the small person in a sweatshirt he bumped into was Nathalie.

"Excuse me, oh, hey…" he said awkwardly.

Nathalie grinned up at him in the dark. She whispered over the booming music, "It's okay. I saw you and I wanted to say thank you."

Sam could barely hear her and was honestly puzzled. "For what?"

Her face was pale and small. "For everything."

"Okay, I guess. You're welcome." Whatever she was talking about, this wasn't the time to discuss it.

This was supposed to be a quick, anonymous, admittedly stalker-ish goodbye to the first woman he'd fallen for since his wife died. "Well, I'm gonna keep moving," said Sam.

A pretty brunette moved quickly toward Nathalie, grabbing her. Rob stood by her side.

"Sam this is my Aunt Jack-" Nathalie turned around but Sam had vanished.

Jackie put her arm around Nathalie. "Come on, Victor got us all a table at the front. You're missing it."

Nathalie shook her head. "I want to stay back here."

Jackie exhaled, looking to Rob for support. Rob reassured Nathalie. "It won't be that bad."

"That's easy for you to say, it's not your mother up there, getting naked," Nathalie replied.

Rob blanched. "Okay, thanks for that visual. Not."

Jackie frowned at Rob. "You're not helping."

"Yeah, did you hear what she said? Admittedly, you haven't met my mother yet but picture Eleanor Roosevelt nude and you'll get the general idea."

"Getting a little off task here," Jackie said, thinking that meeting Rob's mother would be terrifying.

Nathalie stepped forward. Aunt Jackie's boyfriend was okay. "It's okay, I'll sit with you."

Rob poked Jackie's side. "See, honesty works."

Nathalie shook her head. "If I can have both your desserts."

Up on stage the women moved in perfect unison, twirling and kicking with force and power, dipping down and jumping up. The women in the audience were open-jawed with shock. Wasn't that Meryl Howe? Good Lord. Then the first glove came off. Each dancer lined up behind one another, side-kicking until the woman ahead of them peeled off, tossing their glove into the audience, giving the next dancer a turn.

As Meryl stood in line, waiting to toss her glove, she grew increasingly nervous. Up until this moment she could fool herself that she was dancing in her own living room. But when Sandy peeled off to the right, she was faced with a bright glare of stage lights. She froze, feet rooted to the ground. The other women kept on with the routine but Meryl didn't budge. She remained utterly motionless, a deer pinned in a flashlights beam. There wasn't a thought in her brain other than the high pitched hysteria of panic.

In the audience Jackie and Nathalie reached out for one another, clasping sweaty hands under the white tablecloth.

"Come on Mom. Come on…" Nathalie whispered under her breath, exchanging an anxious look with her aunt.

Rob rubbed Jackie's back. "It's okay. She's doing great," he said.

Victor crossed his fingers. "Come on kid. You got this."

Onstage, Faye motioned for the rest of the dancers to keep moving while she grape-vined her way to Meryl. Faye was nothing if not the consummate professional. Dancing her way around the stock-still Meryl, she whispered in her ear, spinning circles, using her daughter as a stationary prop as if it were all part of the act.

"Baby girl, I'll tell you what you're going to do. You are going to finish this dance not for you and not for me but for every girl who has ever had a man take away her shining light and made her feel less than beautiful. So I want you to come back inside yourself and find the power that God gave you." She kissed her cheek, firmly squeezing Meryl's shoulders. "You are not going to let any man take away your God given grace. You got that?"

Meryl's nodded dumbly at her mother.

"Then let's dance our asses off!" Faye said, giving her daughter's arm a squeeze for good measure.

Like a robot coming to life, Meryl dramatically and with great flair removed both her gloves and tossed them into the audience with a twirl. Blowing a kiss, she strutted back into her place in line as the women made their second pass at the audience.

The audience went wild. Women in the audience started to clap and scream.

"Go Mom!" screamed Nathalie, who felt a sudden, deep pride in her mother. She thought about what Aunt Jackie told her, that she was part of a long line of survivors.

Faye felt the audience reaction infuse her and the other dancers with a burst of energy. Lorraine embellished her hip bumps with a little slap to her ample, jiggling rear. The audience grew louder. One by one, women of every age and size stood and screamed their approval. A few women remained unimpressed, planted stoically while their tablemates reacted. By the time the dancers had torn off their tap pants to reveal black lace underwear, the siren song "You Can Leave Your Hat On" blasted over the clapping, mimosa-fueled crowd.

The dancers moved seamlessly into a smooth routine with canes and top hats they picked up at the side of the stage. Using the canes as pivot points, they spun around, picking them up to do a grapevine across the stage. Near the end of the song, they removed their bow ties, twirling them into the air before simultaneously tossing them, fluttering, into the perfumed air.

Black silk ties flew like leaves in the air. There was so much noise that Faye had to scream, "Jackets!" signaling their last strip. Playing with the lapels of their tux's they eased out of them one shoulder at a time. Everyone except for Carol, who opted for a bra, was wearing pasties.

As the music stopped, the women stood in their fishnets, underwear and bras, panting heavily, tilting their hats. They accepted the crashing applause from the audience like flowers. Lorraine sobbed with relief, accidentally crushing her hat.

Meryl stepped forward, addressing the audience with a microphone set up onstage. "My name is Meryl Howe and if you'd like to learn some fun, sexy dance moves, join us at Divine Moves Dance Studio in Kirkland. There are cards on your table. Please take them all and give them to your friends. We're offering special grand opening rates. I hope to see you there. Thank you ladies!"

Waving to the continuing cheers, the dancers filed offstage, welling with euphoria and relief, collapsing into a group hug as soon as they reached backstage. It was over. They'd killed it.

On her way out of the auditorium, Jackie sought out a visibly agitated Betsy Howe, clearly trying to avoid any family. "Hey there Betsy! Long time no see." Jackie pulled a reluctant Rob forward. "This is my boyfriend, Rob. He's a liberal Democrat."

Betsy blanched, sniffing indignantly. "I cannot believe that Meryl is opening up a dance studio to teach women how to strip. In Kirkland." Her eyes narrowed. "I knew she was just like her mother!"

"I know. It's great isn't it?" Jackie said.

Nathalie stepped forward, a wicked grin on her face. "Grandma Faye got me my first tattoo, isn't that cool?"

Betsy's jaw dropped as Jackie dragged Nathalie away.

Jackie punched Nathalie's arm. "You're horrible."

Nathalie laughed. "Did you see the look on her face?"

Jackie slung her arm around her niece as the three made their way backstage to congratulate the dancers. "I know right? We're terrible!"

She turned back to Rob, trailing behind. "Welcome to the family!"

About the Author

Ellyn Oaksmith is a native Seattleite, a graduate of Smith College and The American Film Institute. She worked as a screenwriter for several years before Adventures with Max and Louise was published by Harper Collins. She lives with her family and a shelter dog in the suburbs of Seattle.

Divine Moves is her second book.

For a sneak peak at her next book, Fifty Acts of Kindness, visit her at www.Facebook.com/EllynOaksmith or www.EllynOaksmith.Tumblr.com

Book Club Questions

1) What enabled Jackie to forgive her mother when Meryl couldn't?

2) Do you think there is significance to the fact that Jackie chose to move to Seattle, where her sister was, or was it a career move?

3) Do you feel sympathy for Ethan or does he deserve everything he gets?

4) Is Meryl justified in dating someone while she is still married?

5) Do you like the character of Faye or do you find that her lack of parenting and drinking made her ultimately unsympathetic?

6) How do you feel about the appearance of Jesus? Does it work for you to have him appear as a character? Why do you think he disappears in the end?

7) How does the idea of faith play out in the story? Does the author have something to say about God's love?

8) Would Meryl have forgiven Ethan without the bike accident?

9) What do you think is going to happen with Nathalie? Did you like her?

10) Would you ever get up on stage like the women in the book?

Made in the USA
Charleston, SC
11 March 2015